For my family

MY BROTHER'S NAME

by

LAURA KRUGHOFF

SCARLETTA PRESS

MINNEAPOLIS, MINNESOTA

Copyright © 2013 Laura Krughoff

Published by Scarletta Press, an imprint of Scarletta

This book is a work of fiction. Names, characters, places, events, and incidents are either a product of the author's imagination or are used fictitiously. Any resemblance to reality is entirely coincidental.

Library of Congress Cataloging-in-Publication Data

Krughoff, Laura.

My brother's name / by Laura Krughoff. — First edition.

    pages   cm

ISBN 978-0-9830219-4-0 (pbk. : alk. paper) — ISBN 978-0-9830219-5-7 (electronic)

1. Brothers and sisters—Fiction. 2. Identity (Psychology)—Fiction. 3. Mental illness—Fiction. I. Title.

PS3611.R847M9 2013

813'.6—dc23

                                                        2013009113

Book Design by Mighty Media, Inc., Minneapolis, Minnesota
Interior: Chris Long   ·   Cover: Anders Hanson

Printed and manufactured in the United States
Distributed by Publishers Group West

First edition

10 9 8 7 6 5 4 3 2 1

Prologue

I DID NOT GROW UP IN MY BROTHER'S SHADOW. I GREW up in his light. I have been John's sister since the very beginning. He was not yet four when I was born, but he claims to remember the event. He remembers naming me. He tells the story of my naming as if that morning still shimmers, a perfect mirage, in his memory. Our father dropped John off at an elderly neighbor's house on the afternoon before I was born. John says it was terrible to have been left behind, that the woman was strange and her house dusty, that he feared our parents would not return for him. He says he thought about me a great deal, that he imagined me just as I turned out to be.

Everyone agrees that on the morning my parents brought me home from the hospital and my father crossed the street to collect John, he found John waiting with his face pressed against the bay window of the neighbor lady's living room. Our father carried John home. Once Dad set him down in the living room, John didn't run to our mother who was reclining on the couch. He ran to the bassinette where I lay sleeping through the massive trauma of having arrived so recently in the world. He reached out with his chubby hand and touched me.

"Finally," John said. "Finally, finally, finally."

"What do you think, Johnny?" our mother asked. "What do you think of your little sister?"

"I've been lonely for her for so long," John said.

There is little to do when you come into a family like that other than to cleave to the brother who claims you.

"What should we call her?" Dad asked. My birth certificate read only Baby Girl Fields. Our parents, for all the lack of imagination our names seem to reveal, waited days to name us.

"We didn't know you yet," our mother used to say. "How could we name someone we'd never met?"

"I think she's Jane," John said, looking down at the sleeping me. He has spoken of that moment so often, and with such mystical wonder, that I feel as if I have my own memory of that bright winter morning, the sun sparkling off the snow on the spruce tree, the heat in the house turned up too warm for everyone but me.

John has been telling the story of me ever since. And because we have been bound to each other by sibling love rather than by sibling rivalry, John's stories of me are always stories about John. In high school, for the sheer pleasure of watching me go crimson, John told his friends about how I wore his hand-me-down underwear.

"Fucking hippies for parents, right?" he said. We were in the parking lot behind the high school, and all the guys from John's drum line were hanging out after practice, kicking skateboards, talking loudly. I had been hanging out with John's drummer friends for years. I was everyone's little sister. I was public property. But that was the summer I finally joined John's drum line. He was a senior and I was a freshman. If naming me is John's magical memory, that year we spent together in the drum line is mine. "You don't mind, do you, Janie?" John asked.

"Come on, John," I said. I could feel a rash of hot blood spreading up from my throat, bright and blotchy under my skin.

"John, her head's going to explode," Drew, John's second snare, said.

"No, she's fine. She doesn't mind. This is funny shit. Listen."

John winked at me from where he sat on the hood of a rusted-out Camaro. I looked away, watching the heat ripple off the blacktop. The color guard was still practicing out on the football field, which was half the reason the drum line hadn't left yet. The girls were stripped down to sports bras and running shorts, their long hair pulled back in ponytails, their flags snapping in the hot breeze above their heads. The section leader of the color guard was John's girlfriend that year. She was the blondest thing I'd ever seen.

"So we've got hippie parents, right? And Janie's whatever age kids are when they potty train. Two? Three? Something like that. She's this fat little toddler. You guys should have seen her. She's my fucking shadow. She's my little-sister-side-kick. Our mom calls Janie a John-boy, instead of a Tomboy, right? She thinks it's hilarious. So now Janie is potty training and needs underwear instead of diapers, and this super-duper problem solver of a mother of ours sticks Janie in my hand-me-down underwear. Janie runs around shouting about how she's a big boy now and won't wear pants over her underwear."

The boys were all grinning, sunlight glancing off braces. One of the quads lit a cigarette. Everybody's bright eyes cut between my brother and me. I worried a blister on the inside of my right thumb, tried to act like John was boring me.

"It gets better," John said. And this part of the story I remember. I really think I do. I remember the way the sun fell through the splayed branches and green leaves of the sugar maple in the backyard. I remember looking up through the leaves and branches at nicks of blue sky amongst all that green. "So Janie and me are romping around in the backyard. Just running wild, doing kid shit. Janie's wearing her favorite *My Little Pony* t-shirt and my underwear and no shorts. She's turning circles like dizzy is a drug. And then our mom comes home from shopping. 'Janie,' she goes. 'Janie, honey, I bought something for you.' Janie goes staggering over toward our mother, and Mom pulls this package of girls' panties out of her shopping bag. She tears open the plastic and unfolds a pair of polka dot, pink panties, and the next thing you know, Janie's out of my underpants and in a pair of her very own girl knickers. She's standing there with her legs spread-eagle. She looks down at herself, and then kind of pulls around on the ruffles. 'There's no pocket,' Janie says."

John paused for effect.

"Screw you, John," I said. The boys roared.

"'There's no pocket,' Janie wails. 'I don't like them! I want John's! I want a pocket for my hand!'"

The boys were laughing so hard I thought they might choke. John was laughing and looking at me. I narrowed my eyes at him, but a smile flickered at my lips. I couldn't help it. He mouthed, *I love you, Janie.* He lit a cigarette.

Years later, after his first break, after dropping out of college and being locked down in a psychiatric hospital, after one terrible round of medications after another, after stabilizing briefly and then secretly flushing his meds, after our mother and father started saying things like, "Well, what do we do? I'm honestly asking, what are our options here? For God's sake, what do *you* think we should do?" at night, when they thought they were alone, when they thought I was in bed, I thought about how John used to spread his wings for me. I was out of high school, taking classes at a community college, working at a coffee shop, waiting for John to get well so I could figure out what to do with myself, when John started talking about the two of us making a break for it.

He'd been off his medications again, this time for months. He refused to see every doctor except for his psychiatrist, who eventually refused to see him since he wouldn't take what she prescribed for him. John was more or less living in the basement. He refused to set foot in his old bedroom, claiming it was wired funny, that our parents had installed magnetic fields to record his every move. He thought our mother was trying to poison him, refusing for what seemed like weeks on end to eat anything but pack after pack of cheese crackers with peanut butter. He'd begun setting little traps around the house, complicated rubber band slingshots hooked up to the bathroom doors and spring-loaded mousetraps in our father's shoes. He dumped a jar of rubber cement in the flour canister and drowned goldfish in a tub of yogurt. I think our father and I would have gone on forever like that—it's amazing what you can get used to—but our mother was being driven to her own breaking point. When I tried to talk John out of his mind games and convince him to give our poor mother a rest, he looked me in the eye and swore he had no idea what I was talking about.

"It's like living with a monster in the basement," she said one night. She and our father had been fighting. She was livid. She was crying. "It's insane, Richard. Literally. I'm frightened to even be in the kitchen with him down there. I really am. I'm terrified of my own son."

"I can hear you," John called from the bottom of the basement steps.

"John," our father said sternly, as if John were a boy he could discipline.

"Fucking hamster-face," John said.

Our mother stormed out the back door, and our father followed her. I crept down the basement stairs to see about John. When it was just the two of us, he was rarely angry. He would grow meek with contrition and anxiety. His eyes would dart, wounded and frightened, refusing to light on anything. I found him at the bottom of the basement steps, chewing on a lock of his hair, reading a biography of Syd Barrett, his foot twitching to "The Scarecrow," as if he hadn't just been shouting at our father.

"John," I said.

"What are we going to do, Janie?" he asked. His eyes were red-rimmed. "Don't let them throw me out. Don't let them get rid of me."

"No one's trying to get rid of you," I said. I sat on the steps. He leaned his unwell, unwashed head against my knee. I stroked his hair and he banged his temple gently and rhythmically against me.

"She's making things up, Janie," he whispered. I tried to still his head. "She imagines things. She has these wild ideas and then she blames them on me."

"John," I said softly. "I saw the goldfish in the yogurt."

"I won't blame you, Janie, if you stop loving me."

"Shut up, John," I said. "Don't be stupid. I'm not going to stop loving you."

John stopped banging his head against my knee and began to hum.

"Do you have a comb?" I asked. "I could work on these rat nests."

John found a comb on our dad's workbench and then sat again at my feet. I worked the comb through tiny sections of snarled curls.

"Could you talk to Dr. Margolis?" John asked. "Could you get her to talk to me? I feel like she might be able to get through to Mom and Dad. She sees everything. She's the kind of person who can look straight into your head."

"She's your psychiatrist," I said. "She prescribes meds. She said she isn't going to see you until you agree to start taking them again."

"You're the only one who hasn't abandoned me in my hour of need," John said. "If it were just the two of us, Janie. Don't you think? Don't you think, maybe, I just need time to breathe?"

I didn't answer him.

"Tip your head down," I said. "Your hair is one huge tangle here at the base of your neck."

Within a week, John and I had rented a van. We told the U-Haul people that John would be the only one driving it, but John hadn't driven in months. He gripped the steering wheel, and the color drained from his face. He couldn't seem to focus his eyes on the road. We made it two blocks before John slammed the van into park and we changed spots. John kept turning around to see if we were being followed, but I drove calmly toward our parents' house where we would pack up our few things and leave. I discovered then that the more John's paranoia overwhelms him, the more centered and rational I become. It's as if our hold on ourselves is inverse and proportional. So much of who I am is out of sheer necessity.

I parked the van at the foot of the hill in front of our house. I killed the engine, and John and I sat quietly. I don't know what he was thinking about, but I was thinking about the slope of our front yard, the way our parents' house sits atop a hill, its siding painted blue to match the towering Colorado blue spruce whose boughs shade the French windows in the living room. I was thinking about how John and I used to play in the front yard on summer evenings, tumbling down the hill in a game we called "log roll," our small, tough bodies thumping hard against the concrete sidewalk. Sometimes our mother would open the windows and play the piano while we chased fireflies at dusk.

"Have you ever thought about how streetlamps show people where to find us?" John asked.

My eyes fell on my brother, his puffy, sweaty face and tangled hair, his roaming, nervous hands pawing at his ears. His lean beauty obliterated by mania and years of psychotropic meds.

"Like from way up, not space or anything, just way up in an airplane. If you fly at night you can see where everyone's at. We put up lights, lights, lights, like all this light is going to keep us safe, but it's really just a pattern, all these tiny pinpoints revealing where we huddle at night."

I couldn't fathom how to answer him.

"We're so vulnerable, Jane. That's the thing I like about you. You never seem to think about it. You're belly-up all the time. That's why I like you."

He began to drum his fingers against the dashboard. He hummed something from *Piper at the Gates of Dawn*.

"Let's get this over with, John," I said.

"Ay-ay, captain," he said. "T-minus forever and counting."

We climbed the flagstone steps up the hill to our front porch. John gave me a hand gesture I didn't understand, and then led the way up the porch steps to the front door. We'd said nothing to our parents ahead of time. When we got inside, John went straight to the basement to break down the drum kit, and I tried to say reasonable things to our parents. The afternoon devolved into a parade of panic and fear and accusation. John hollered from the basement. I talked calmly about how John needed space, how I knew him better than anyone, how much sense our moving should make. Our mother stopped addressing me and began begging our father. "Richard, do something. Put a stop to this." But, of course, he couldn't.

"Don't worry," I kept saying. "Don't be afraid. I'm going to help John get well. I'll take care of everything."

We loaded our clothes and the drum kit into the back of the van. Our father left briefly, and when he returned he gave me a thousand dollars in cash, the bills rolled and wrapped with a rubber band. He gave me the money once John was already buckled into the van.

"Tell us what we can do to help, Janie," Dad said, taking my head in his hands. "Don't be afraid to call us. Your mother and me—whatever you need. Whatever we can do for John, okay?"

"We'll be fine, Dad," I said. "Give us six months. I know that seems awful, but just give us six months to get organized. We'll get on our feet. Once we're set I'll let you know how to get a hold of us, but give us six months, at least. John just needs a little space to breathe."

"Okay," Dad said. Our mother had long since left the house, claiming she refused to be party to such madness.

It was evening before John and I were speeding north on the

interstate. As the sun bled into the horizon to the west, John grew anxious about the promise we'd made to the U-Haul people. He adjusted the rearview mirror so he could watch fretfully for a police car lighting up behind us.

"Drive slower, Janie," he instructed, and then, with the traffic whizzing past us on the left, "Faster, faster! Keep up with everyone. You just have to blend in."

His fear mounted until he decided we should pull off at a rest stop. I parked the van under the yellow glare of a sodium security light and killed the engine.

"Okay, John," I said. I was tired and hungry, and we were in the middle of nowhere. "You win. What now?"

I wasn't looking at my brother. I watched half a dozen kids and a fat couple pile out of a Suburban parked two spaces down from ours. One of the smallest children, a girl, stopped in the middle of the parking lot for some reason and burst into tears. Her father hoisted her into his arms, and the girl draped like a rag doll over his shoulder. One pink arm swung loosely against his back. She cried bitterly, her wet eyes closed and her wet mouth open wide.

"I'm going to have to drive," John said.

I looked at him. John had one leg wedged between his chest and the glove compartment so he could retie his sneaker.

"That's nuts," I said. "You can't drive, John. You nearly blew a gasket after two blocks of a side street. You're going to drive on the interstate?"

"Wouldn't you agree it's preferable to all this sneaking around? What if they catch us? What if this is all a set up to send you to jail? Isn't me driving preferable to us trying to pull one over on our fellow citizens?"

"No!" I said. "It's not. It's lunacy."

John whacked a meaty palm against his forehead. He closed his eyes and massaged his temples and then stuck his fingers in his ears. I watched the mother of all the children feeding quarters into a vending machine for Cokes.

"Janie-Jane," he said after a moment, "I have an idea."

"Does it get us out of here?"

"Yes, indeed. You could be me."

I glanced over at my brother. He looked yellow in the glow of the security lights.

"We said John Fields would drive," John said. "That doesn't mean John Fields has to be me."

"What are you talking about?"

John scrambled in his pockets for his driver's license. The picture on his valid license—taken when he was twenty-one, during a two-month stretch of relative sanity—didn't look at all like me, but John had managed to hold onto his expired license from high school. He switched on the interior lights and held the expired license up to his face.

"You could use this license, Janie," he said. "I don't even look like this, but it's got my name. This isn't me. Who is that guy?" he asked, considering the reflection of himself and his old license in the rear-view mirror. "It might as well be you, Janie-John." A smile crept across his face. "This is wrong," he said, tugging at my t-shirt. "And this is wrong. All of this is wrong." He waved a hand indicating my clothes in general. "And your stupid, puffy girl-lips, but other than that, I think it could work."

John held his driver's license out to me. I took it from him, turning the plastic card over in my fingers, trying to figure out if it was just exhaustion that had me thinking my brother was making sense. I'd kept my hair short and boyish since my freshman year of high school. John and I had always looked remarkably alike. Half the clothes in the duffel I'd brought from home were his clothes from high school—concert t-shirts, hooded sweatshirts, and a pair of jeans that almost fit me if I cinched them with a belt. When John started to swell on psychotropic medications, he said I could have any of his old clothes that I wanted. I kept most of them.

"Do you have John clothes in your bag?" he asked.

"Yeah."

"What should we do about your breasts?"

"I know you're my brother and everything," I said, "and I'm glad you haven't noticed, I guess, but if I put on a sports bra, the question's more like, what breasts?"

"Perfect," John said. He waved toward the bathrooms. "Do your best."

I rummaged in my bag for a Nine Inch Nails t-shirt and John's old jeans. I left the keys in the ignition, and the van dinged when I opened my door. I paused to watch the family loading back into the Suburban on my way to the women's room. The father still had the little girl slung over his shoulder, his thick left arm bulging under her weight. When he turned his back to me, I could see she'd fallen dead asleep. Her long blond hair stuck to one sweaty cheek. When I emerged from the restroom properly dressed, I could see that John was pleased.

"Not bad, little sister," he said. "Not bad. It's a good thing it's dark, but still, you look a hell of a lot like me."

"Back in high school, people used to mistake me for a boy all the time," I said. I buckled my seatbelt and started the van.

"When?"

"You know, at band contests. Drum line events. That sort of thing."

"Well, yeah, sure," John said. "That was the point. You played in a drum line. What were people supposed to think?"

"Are we ready?" I asked.

I stepped on the brake and put the van into reverse. John handed me his wallet, and I twisted in my seat to stuff it in my back pocket. Soon we were back out on the highway speeding north, and there was no one to even know or care to be deceived. John leaned his head against the dark window and slept. A river of headlights swept past us on the other side of the meridian. I clicked off the Black Sabbath album John had loaded into the CD player and drove in peace. I sped us through the night. I drove without music and more or less without thinking. I didn't know how our lives would unfold once we reached the city. It was enough just to drive, just to let my brother sleep.

Our first weeks on our own terrified the both of us. We slept in the van for two nights until we could find an apartment that would take our dad's cash as a deposit and let us sign a lease. We had no jobs, no credit. We couldn't figure out what to do about John's disability checks, how to get his payments transferred and change his address. I sat on hold on payphones in front of grocery stores and gas stations for what felt like hours without getting any answers. I looked online and in the papers for jobs, but couldn't find anything. I walked block after block around our apartment, stopping in at coffee shops and restaurants and shoe stores and bookstores and finally a fancy shop that sold nothing but handmade wrapping papers. John couldn't sleep for the first week. He spent the nights roaming our apartment, rattling doors, running the taps in the bathroom and kitchen, turning on and off the burners on our gas stove to watch the flame flare orange and then burn blue. We were blowing through the few hundred dollars I had in savings fast. John grew despondent and fearful in the mornings when I'd leave to look for work and accusatory and angry when I'd come home at night. He thought our parents had set us—or maybe our parents and I had set him—up.

I came home on our sixth day in the city, after filling out applications at a CVS, a yarn and knitting store, and a Subway. We didn't have a phone yet, so the managers who accepted my applications glanced them over, glanced me over, and suggested I stop back by in a week to see if something was going to work out for me. It was all I could do to step up to one stupid counter after another and say, "Are you hiring?" I couldn't force myself to speak up. The person behind the counter would say, "What? What?" and people would turn to look at me if there were anyone else in the store. "Are you hiring?" I'd say again. I had bought bread and peanut butter and milk and cereal and a bag of carrots on my way home that sixth evening. I lugged it all the six blocks between us and the grocery store, and I'd cried, briefly, in our stairwell. I was twenty, and it was beginning to dawn on me that I didn't know anything.

"I was just about to give up," John said, when I let myself into the apartment.

I ignored him and headed straight for the kitchen.

"I thought maybe today was the day, Janie," he called from the living room. "I thought, yes sir-ee, today is the day Jane jumps ship. She's a swimmer, that one. My little Janie-Jane. Today she swims for her life and leaves me to rot on an island all by myself."

"Shut the fuck up, John," I said. I put the milk and carrots in the fridge and set the bread, cereal, and peanut butter on the counter.

"That's in keeping with your character," John said. We had no furniture, nothing on the walls. Our voices echoed. "Where have you been?" John demanded. "Can you tell me? Can you share that bit of information with your own flesh and blood?"

"Where do you think I've been?" I hollered. I stomped into the living room. John was standing at the front windows, peering around the blinds, chewing on one of the cords. "Where the hell do you think I've been? I've been looking for a goddamn job."

"It's funny how keenly you seem to believe that," John said. He was still looking out the window. I turned around. "Where to now, Janie?"

"I'm going to bed," I said. "No. I'm not going to bed. I'm going to floor because that's where I sleep, in a sleeping bag on the fucking floor. Or at least that's where I would sleep if I could sleep, but I can't sleep because you're prowling all over the place until the sun comes up. I haven't slept in days. I've walked a hundred miles and done everything I know to find a job to keep your sorry ass fed because you had this brilliant idea that you'd get less fucking crazy if we moved out of our parents' house. Except you're here climbing the walls and accusing me of treason every goddamn time I come home!"

John turned his face on me, as cool and blank as a stone. "Every time you step out that door, you have everything you need to walk away from me completely. You could vanish, Jane. You are your own walking rapture. When you're gone, I start thinking up things, but I don't think up anything that couldn't be true. Try living with that. Try living my goddamn way."

I stood in the threshold of the living room, my arms slack and suddenly numb at my sides. John crossed the room. He turned sideways but still brushed my shoulder as he squeezed past me.

"Where are you going?" I asked. I started to cry. Hot, angry tears burned my cheeks, but John didn't seem to notice.

"I'm going to lie down," he said. "I think we both could use some sleep."

He turned out the light in the hall and disappeared into his bedroom. The late summer sun was still casting enough light to see by. I listened for a long time, but after some rustling of his sleeping bag, I didn't hear anything from my brother.

In the morning, John was gone. When I emerged from my bedroom, the front door stood gaping open. I closed the door but didn't lock it. In an icy calm, I walked from empty room to empty room, looking for John. In the kitchen, I discovered an empty cereal bowl in the sink. The milk sat sweating on the counter. I was glad to see the carton was still cold enough to sweat. I put the milk back in the fridge and decided to change out of the clothes I'd slept in before trying to figure out what to do next. I was not yet to my bedroom door when I heard the security door open and bang shut downstairs. Heavy feet pounded the stairs, and then John came crashing through the front door.

He was sweat-drenched and red-faced, his massive chest heaving, stretching the seams of his enormous *Ride the Lightning* t-shirt. When he grinned at me, relief flooded my blood with a chemical that made all of my joints weak.

"Problem solved," John said when he could talk.

"Where have you been?"

"I thought I'd be back before you woke up—you were gone, Janie. Sleep-drugged. But it doesn't hurt to see for a second how the shoe fits on the other foot."

John took me by the hand and led me into the living room. He had the morning paper stuffed under one arm. It looked like it had been opened and windblown and folded and crumpled into a jumbled mess. John and I sat on the floor, and he spread the classifieds out between us.

"Here," he said, stabbing a forefinger at a tiny notice in the Help Wanted section. "I found a job that's perfect for me."

"John, you can't—"

"Not me, me. I know that. I'm not ready for a job yet. Can you imagine? I'd crack like a walnut and everyone would think I was crazy, which I am but only for a little bit longer, I think. I've got to get these drugs out of me. I can still feel them fizzing in my bloodstream. Once they've all bubbled through my brain and seeped out of my skin I'll be back to being how I used to be, back when everybody loved me, but this job's for you. Just for now. Read it. Right here."

John turned the paper toward me, and I smoothed a hand over the damp newsprint. The notice read: *Stew's Music. Seeking clerk/*

sales associate. Know your sh*t. Be cool. The ad listed an address in a far north neighborhood. I looked up at John, who licked his chapped lips.

"What are you thinking?" I asked.

"No offense, Janie, but you couldn't get that job. I'm the one who's qualified."

"I know as much about music as you do," I said.

"In your head, yeah," John said. "I know that. But other people don't see it that way. I'm the dude this Stew guy is looking for. I've got the history and the know-how, but you've got the brain that works. You could get that job for me."

"How?"

"How? How? What's your problem, Janie-Jane? It's like you're trying not to understand. I'm telling you. Like in the van. You be me. You remember, that guy I used to be. He's perfect for this job. You'll be this John kid who has a job and makes things happen, and I won't have to be so afraid that Jane is going to leave. You see? Problem solved. Two birds, one big, fat fucking stone."

We looked at each other across the rumpled newspaper. John blinked. He chewed his bottom lip.

"There are so many things..." I said.

"I know," John said. "I've thought about it. I can help you. We just have to pull this off long enough for me to get well, and then I can take over for you. We'll turn you into me for just a little bit, and then we'll pull off some other switch-a-roo. Don't worry. Not yet. I've already solved half of everything."

That afternoon we went to the DMV. I'd bound my breasts and was wearing John's old clothes. I was waiting to see who was willing to be fooled. I stood in line, my brother's Social Security card, his birth certificate, his expired driver's license, and our lease in my damp hands. John sat in a row of orange plastic chairs, his legs splayed out, his arms crossed over his chest, his dark eyes never leaving me. I inched along, dreading the moment when I'd have to lay my papers on a counter and ask for a new driver's license. Surely, I thought, this is the moment where someone intervenes. But the man behind the counter hardly looked at me. I signed a form, took a multiple-choice test, paid in cash, and he stamped my application and sent me to stand in a new line to have my picture taken. In under an hour I had a legal driver's license with my own photograph and my brother's name: John R. Fields.

We spent the afternoon at the library, searching the Internet for tips about how to pass. We read one blog after another posted by female-to-male transsexuals. John took notes furiously in a spiral-bound notebook, his eyes flickering between the screen and the page. We followed links from site to site, from blogs to medical websites to commercial homepages for chest binders and fake penises.

"Could we get you on hormones, do you think?" John asked at one point.

"John," I sad. "Be serious. I'm not actually a transsexual. I'm not trying to become a man."

"I was just asking," he said. He bit his nails defensively.

It took us two hours to get me ready the next morning. John filled a condom with hair gel. He'd found that trick in a discussion forum for drag kings, but even when it was secured between my legs with a jockstrap, I found I couldn't stop walking funny. We fell apart with laughter, and John had to give up his goal of sending me out into the world with a fake penis. "I'll buy you a real fake penis for later," he promised. "We'll need one."

I bound my breasts with an Ace bandage again even though most of our information cautioned against it. *An Ace bandage is designed to tighten with every move. They cut off circulation. They can be dangerous. Cut off the legs of a pair of support hose. Cut a hole in the crotch for your head*, one site said. *Or invest in a decent chest binder. An Ace bandage will make you flat as an ironing board, but it's way too risky, fellas.*

"Flat as an ironing board sounds good," John had said. "It's just for another day. For the interview. We'll get you something better soon."

I agreed. I slipped on a sleeveless undershirt and then a light brown t-shirt with Daytona Beach scrawled across the front in baby blue, one of John's favorites from high school. Once I was dressed, John stood in the doorway of the bathroom as I shaved, giving me all sorts of advice about how much lather to use and how to grip the razor. *Shave*, one of the websites has said. *Peach fuzz makes your skin look even softer than it is. Shaving won't make it grow back as whiskers, but shave anyway. Let your legs and pits grow, and shave your face.* Fear thrilled inside me as I drew the razor across my face. I didn't know if I believed the websites that said the hair wouldn't grow back in as whiskers. I didn't know how significant a step shaving might turn out to be.

When I was finally finished, John examined me from every angle. Sweat trickled between my shoulder blades and down my chest.

"Okay," John said. "Yes. Do you have the proper documents?"

I pulled his wallet from my back pocket.

"My John Fields driver's license, your Social Security card, an ATM card with my name on it. Six bucks."

"One more thing," John said. He scurried off to his bedroom and came back with a condom in its shiny, silver wrapper. He slid the condom into an empty pocket in my wallet. "It'll give you the right sort of feeling. You don't want to be caught unprepared."

I looked at my brother. He smiled encouragingly. I felt like I was watching myself in a movie, some strange girl and her strange brother trying to get away with such a strange thing. The whole plan only made sense when John was talking. I was almost certain that it would all fall in tatters around me as soon as I was out of our front door. John took my shoulders in his thick-fingered hands.

"Slay 'em, Johnny," he said. "Pretend like you're me. Don't be afraid. Just do everything you think I would do. You remember. Your eyes were open back when you were a kid."

"Right," I said, woozy with vertigo. And then I walked out of our apartment, down the dark stairs, and into the dazzling light of the afternoon. I took one bus and then transferred to another. No one said anything to me. The sky spun like a blue disk above me. Trees reeled along the sidewalk. I walked up an unfamiliar block, found Stew's Music, swung open the tinted glass door, and stepped into the store as if I knew what I was there for. I could see myself from a distance, the back of my close-cropped head and the thin edge of my shoulders. I tried to walk like my brother. The Stones were blasting on the store's sound system. John would have approved. A guy sat near the cash register, elbows propped on the counter, his long face resting on his fists, reading a magazine. He looked up and took a toothpick from between his teeth.

"Hey, dude," he said, and replaced the toothpick. He had wild, reddish hair pulled back in a ponytail and eyes so blue I didn't know how he could stand sunlight. In another universe, I would have thought he was cute.

I nodded. The room tipped. "Hey," I said.

"What can I do for you?"

"I saw your ad in the paper yesterday morning," I said, except it didn't feel like I said it. It felt like something being said by a laid-back kid I'd never met. I liked that kid. I had a glimmer of how it must have felt to be John. I felt braver than I'd felt in a long time. "Are you Stew?"

"Nope. But I'm his right-hand man. You ever work in an outfit like this?"

"No," I said. I surveyed the place. "But I've been playing music all my life. Piano. Percussion. The drums, mostly. I know the basics about guitars and the standard concert instruments."

Guitars hung from a rack bolted to the ceiling. Trumpets, trombones, French horns, and saxophones were displayed toward the back. There were three aisles of everything from capos and reeds to distortion pedals to recording equipment and software. The place had a little of everything. When I looked back at the guy behind the counter, he was smiling around his toothpick.

"You ready for the interview, man?" he asked.

"Sure," I said.

"Five questions."

"Shoot."

An hour later, I was bounding up our front stairs, trying to restrain my desire to shout. John flung open the door when I hit our landing, and I threw myself into his arms. He was laughing with glee before I even said anything. He dragged me into the apartment, swung me off my feet, and crushed me against his chest. I could smell the grime and sweat in his clothes, his hair, even in the folds of his neck, but we were both so happy I couldn't care.

"It worked, John," I finally said. "Can you fucking believe it?"

"Believe it? I invented it, Johnny-John. Right on. Didn't I tell you? Didn't I say so? Problem solved. Every problem. All of them!"

He set me on my feet. His eyes danced and flickered. His hands patted my head and my shoulders.

"Tell me," John said. "Tell me all about it. I want to hear the whole thing."

"Yeah," I said. I laughed. My heart kicked like a colt in my chest. "Absolutely. I will tell you everything."

I WILL TELL YOU TWO THINGS: FIRST, I AM NOT THE GIRL who tried to be her brother any more. The years have spun out between that person and me like sugar spun into cotton candy. I am someone else entirely. But I remember her. I remember that boy I got to be. Second, had someone told me years ago, before John's cataclysmic collapse, how easy it would be to become him, I would not have believed it. I would have said that's crazy. That's nuts. I would have said, "Have you met me? Have you met my brother?" But once upon a time we did look a lot alike, and I've come to know how essential the surface is. We believe so much of what we see. Even I learned to see what John and I asked the world to see—the lean, straight frame of the torso, shoulder to hip; the dark hair cropped close; the angle between dark eye and jaw line. Every now and again I would catch my own reflection in a darkened window or a security mirror, and my heart would catch. For a searing instant I would think, My god, John, before I realized whose face I was looking at.

I will tell you one more thing: when I think of that summer when I got to be John, when I remember, when I picture us, I begin by picturing our planet from outer space. I start way out. I start with one of those satellite or space probe photographs. I see our planet, suspended by nothing, glittering in unfiltered light. I watch it turn. And then I zoom in through the atmosphere. Continents rise out of oceans. I see my city rise up. I see block after familiar block. I see me. It is July 2001, and I am twenty, although I am supposed to be twenty-four.

I have just locked up at Stew's Music, and I'm waiting for the bus. It's eight o'clock, and the streets are starting to come alive with nightlife. I am hopped up on adrenaline because April has just given me her number. When she leaned across the glass counter to grab a pen from behind the cash register, something happened in my chest.

There's something about her that blurs the line between who I am and who I am pretending to be. I want to get home and talk to John about her. Across town, John is roaming our apartment. He is mad and no longer medicated. His vision sparkles and sings. He is flirting with his own divinity—exploring the outer limits of his ability to think the world into being.

Less than two hundred miles away, our parents are somewhere in our hometown, going about their lives in a suspension of hope, resignation, and ignorance. I know now, although I didn't know then, that our father, having recently telephoned our apartment and left a message on our answering machine, is pedaling his bicycle along the dark, tree-lined streets between the university where he teaches history and home. He wears a helmet and binds his pant leg with a Velcro strap to prevent entanglement with the bike chain. He has installed a flashing taillight and a headlight that casts out a bright, fixed, white beam. He glances over his shoulder before he veers around cars parked on the street.

Our mother, who has been at her studio giving piano lessons to mediocre students well into the evening, now sits at the baby grand in our living room to play for herself. I can picture her. She has turned on only one floor lamp in the living room, letting the rest of the house settle into the dark peacefulness of a summer night. She lets her fingers travel lightly over the piano's creamy keys. The windows are cranked open and a breeze lifts the sheers and the curtains. Our mother closes her eyes and lets her fingers find the familiar chords of a Chopin sonata she learned as a girl. She is so lost in the music that she does not hear when our father comes home. He hears her playing even before he emerges from the garage where he leaves his bicycle parked next to the station wagon. He stops to listen for several minutes out on the patio. He enters the kitchen quietly, leaving his helmet on the counter next to his wife's purse. She doesn't hear him until he's joined her in the living room, and then she smiles, stops playing, and rises from the bench. Though they will both want to many times before they go to bed tonight, they do not trouble each other by saying, Our son, John. Our daughter, Jane.

But I know none of this when I step down from the bus onto the sidewalk in front of our apartment. I wonder if John is watching me from our third floor window. He told me once that he sometimes spends entire afternoons on his knees, arms folded across the windowsill, chin resting on his wrists, waiting to see me. He said it's like waiting for the sun to rise. If you turn away for an instant, you'll miss it. I hurry toward our building. The street smells of fried food, diesel fumes, and starch from the plant that washes hospital sheets. Music and laughter float over the rooftops from the bars two blocks to the east. I slip my hands in my pockets and rattle the loose change and the drum key I carry with me. Our building is on the corner of a busy intersection—vacant retail space on the first floor, two floors of apartments above that. It's the kind of building you'd expect to find facing the dirty main thoroughfare in a neighborhood that's trying to gentrify.

Just as I reach our third floor landing, John flings open our door. Our apartment is black behind the shape of him. On nights when he's happy to see me, John greets me like a poorly behaved Saint Bernard. On other nights, he pats my pockets and the legs of my jeans. "Just checking, man," he says after frisking me.

Tonight, John glowers silently, one hand on the doorknob, one hand on the doorframe. His hair stands out wildly. As my eyes adjust to the shadows of our landing—the light above our door burnt out weeks ago and I've been meaning to replace it—I can see John's nostrils flare wide with each breath. *The Dark Side of the Moon* is playing on the stereo in John's room.

"Hello, Johnny," John says.

"Hey," I say. I stoop under John's arm and flip on the hall light. John blinks and squints. "Turn on the lights when the sun goes down. It creeps me out to come home to you sitting in the dark."

"I *have* been in the dark, haven't I, Johnny-John," John says. This is what I now answer to. The diminutive of my brother's name.

"Are you hungry?" I hang my keys on a hook by the door and head for the kitchen.

"Don't try to fuck with me," John says.

"Come on," I call from the kitchen. John is still standing by the front door, his feet planted wide, the living room dark behind him. I drop my jacket on a chair and pull open the fridge. It is more or less empty. "Let me make us some spaghetti. Does that sound good? Or what else do we have?" I check the freezer. "French fries? All we've got is spaghetti and French fries?"

On most nights, John sits at the table in the kitchen while I make us something to eat. I tell him about my day. He likes detail. I try to remember every item I stocked on every shelf, every customer who came in, what they bought and how they paid. John asks questions if I forget anything. Was his jacket red or blue? Was she white or black or Asian or what? He likes it when I have customers of mixed race, when I have to guess at two or three different ethnicities. On good nights, John tells me what he's done with his day: He's banged around on the drum kit in the living room. He's read *The New York Times* and a dozen blogs online at the library branch down the street. He's written letters to the president, our congresswoman, and the senators of two states we don't live in. I am always glad to hear that John has been out of the apartment, even if he's just gone down the block for a coffee, or for a chai if he's on a kick where he thinks coffee is toxic and to blame for his schizophrenia. When he sometimes thinks mental illness is the result of a sodium deficiency, he goes around the corner for a kosher hotdog.

"John?" I ask. "What's the deal here? Do you want something to eat or not?"

"I want you to get your ass back here so I can talk to you," John says.

I set the box of spaghetti and the can of pasta sauce on the counter. From the doorway, I look at my brother at the other end of the hall. Between us are fifteen feet of buckled wood flooring, the doors to our bedrooms, and an empty coat rack nailed to the wall. I feel as if I'm looking at John across the deck of a ship, as if a sea swell could come along and lift us up, knock us down.

"I'm listening," I say. "What's up? Talk to me."

"You just zip around like a goddamn bumblebee and you act like it doesn't matter if it all goes to shit around here," John says. "I've been fucking tearing my face off."

"Hey, slow down. Start over. What happened?" I ask.

John's eyes screw into me. They are red-rimmed and bloodshot.

He's chewed his lips bloody. He rams his hands into the tangled mess of his hair. The underarm seams of his t-shirt are split. My brother no longer looks like himself. I mean, he no longer looks like me. Or I no longer look like him. I don't know how to say it. There have been years of Zyprexa and Depakote. Prolix. Risperdal. There were panicked injections of Thorazine in emergency rooms during the early days of his diagnosis. He has not recovered from the endless rotations of doctors and their cocktails of drugs. I forget when and why he stopped getting haircuts. His skin is mottled, prone to rashes and eruptions of acne. His eyes are liquid and dangerous. When I catch my reflection in a mirror, I don't see John now. I see who John used to be.

"Dad called," he says, finally.

"Oh," I say.

"Yeah. Oh. He just talked, talked, talked, into the box. He said one word right after another. I thought about picking up the receiver and shouting 'Shut the fuck up, hamster-face!' but I didn't."

John's eyes flicker from me to the empty hall and then seem to focus on something off in the middle distance.

"Did you save the message?" I ask.

"Surely-burly, you bet I did. That one's hatching something. He's always had a tongue like fly paper. No wonder he can't hold it. It's covered with wriggling flies that are going to stay stuck there until they starve to death. Did you know that's why they die?"

"I'm going to listen to it," I say. I asked our father to give us six months. We've had less than half that.

"Of course you are," John says. "You do everything the hard way."

"I just want to hear what he has to say."

"It has nothing to do with what he says," John tells me. "If you were really listening, you'd know it's all in the stuff that happens in between. It's how he breathes. He's hatching something, Johnny-boy. Don't listen for what he says. Listen for what he means."

"Are you going to listen?" I ask.

"Not for a cup of my own blood," John says. "I'll be in the kitchen making spaghetti happen."

John knocks into me with his shoulder on his way toward the kitchen. I step into the dark living room. The phone sits on an end table next to the couch, the red message light blinking. I sit on the floor in front of the phone. Across the street, there is a theatre company that operates in the rooms above a funeral home. The theatre company's neon sign casts blue and yellow light into our apartment. I push the play button, and my father's halting, hesitant voice rises up out of the machine.

"Yes, Jane and John," my father says, and clears his throat. "This is your father, Richard, calling." As if we've forgotten his name. As if his name was ever what mattered to us. "We've missed your calls, Jane, these last couple of weeks. It's good to get your messages, but your mother and I were hoping to catch you at home tonight." I call my parents about once a week, from payphones, usually on my way to or from work. I try to call when I know they won't be home. I hope telephone messages will be enough to prevent our parents from coming up to the city and trying to find us, trying to drag John and me back home. So far, it has worked. "We just thought we'd touch base. We thought, well, it couldn't hurt to give you a ring. I suppose you must be out. But I was actually, or rather, we, your mother and I, were thinking it would be nice if we could have you to dinner. Both of you, of course. It's been such a long time, and I, we, we'd both like to see you. We could pay for your bus tickets, and if you came early in the day, you could catch the last bus back to the city at eight o'clock. We've looked at the schedule. You're welcome to stay, of course, I didn't mean you couldn't. But if you'd prefer just to come to dinner, your mother and I would understand. Either way. We love you."

There is a long pause, but then my father hangs up. I wonder what he chose not to say. I sit in the dark, on the floor, listening to the sounds of theatergoers lining up for tickets under the awning of a funeral home. I don't know how long I sit listening to John banging pots and pans together in the kitchen. Long enough for my legs to go numb. My bound chest aches.

When I join my brother in the kitchen, he is sitting at the table staring at a pot of water boiling over on the stove. The water splashing onto the burner makes the gas flames hiss and flare. John's fury is evident in his stillness. There's murder in the look he's giving the stove. I turn off the burner, grab potholders, and pour half the boiling water into the sink, turning my face away from the steam. Once the pot is back on the burner, I dump the box of spaghetti into the water. John shifts his huge, moody eyes from the stove to me. I pour the pasta sauce into a pan and place it on a back burner, the only other burner on the stove that works.

"If you tell me what I think you're going to tell me, I will not be able to tolerate it," John says. "I know you, Johnny. I know you want to go home. An idea like that blooms in you like a bruise."

John rocks in his chair, his rage melting, his eyes quick with worry. Emotions run like water around here.

"I didn't know Dad was going to call, okay? I'm sorry you were alone for that."

"It's not what you knew or didn't know. It's what you're going to do that worries me," John says.

"You don't want to go home, we don't go home. Simple as that."

"I don't trust you," John says.

"Of course you do. You're just saying that."

John drums his fingers on the tabletop.

"You're hungry," I say. "You probably haven't eaten all day."

"What do you talk about with them?"

"Nothing. I hardly ever call them when they're home. I just say hi and that we're fine. If one of them picks up, I tell them about what you're up to at Stew's. You know what I tell them. I tell you what I tell them. I told Dad last week that you were going to start sitting in with Sean's band. He was really glad to hear it."

"What about Jane? What do you tell them about Jane?"

John knows the life I've made up for me. He was the one who thought Jane should work at Starbucks, that our parents would buy it and that the green visors are nice. My life is boring enough that it's not hard for me to remember the details.

"That Starbucks is Starbucks. What do you think I say?"

"Jane should start doing something, don't you think? To throw them off the track. She should go to community college. She should take a history class. Wouldn't Dad love that?"

"Okay," I say. "Sure. I'll look into it. I'll see if there's a summer session or something. I'll tell Dad I'm thinking about it. I'll say that's why we can't come down right now."

"Jane," John says. "Jane's looking into it."

"That's who I am when I talk to them."

"Okay," John says. "I'm hungry. I haven't eaten all day."

I drain the spaghetti and mix it with the sauce. John takes down bowls and forks as a gesture of good will. He hands me a bowl, and I let him take what he wants from the pot. We sit across from each other at the table.

"I think you got asked out today," I say, and shove a forkful of spaghetti in my mouth.

"What?"

I shrug and chew and swallow. John's eyes narrow as he waits. "Or not asked out, exactly. More like this girl asked you to ask her out. I think that's what happened."

"There's a girl?"

"Yeah," I say. I can't help but grin. "I've mentioned her. She's a friend of Sean's."

"Is she an idiot like that wool-head?"

John is suspicious of my manager at Stew's. He thinks Sean smokes too much pot, which is probably true. It has taken weeks for John to decide that I should say yes to Sean's invitations to sit in with his band. Their drummer quit to have a baby right when I started working at Stew's. John said the band couldn't be any good with Sean on lead guitar and some chick at the kit. I've brought him around, provisionally. John says he'll decide for sure if we should take on this project once I sit in for the first time.

"She's not an idiot," I say. "She's cute as hell. She's kind of your type."

"Why haven't you told me about her before?"

"I've talked about her," I say. "I've mentioned her. April. She gives guitar lessons, so she's in and out of the store pretty regularly. She's got a flyer up in the window. Remember? I told you about this really cute girl with bleached blond streaks who came in to put a new flyer up at the store? Maybe a couple of weeks ago."

"I don't like people who are named after months," John says.

"Whatever."

"Do you have a crush on her?"

I can feel my throat and face and ears flush. "How am I supposed to have a crush on her?"

"It's easy," John says. "So she's interested? As in, in you?"

"It's got nothing to do with me," I say. "This is about how April feels about you."

"Tell me," John says. "Tell me what you guys said. What did you do?"

"It was at the end of the shift," I say. "We hadn't seen a customer in forever, and Sean was just about to switch off the signs in the window and lock up when April walks in."

"Describe her," John says.

"She's pretty in that way some girls stay pretty for a long time without being what you'd call beautiful, you know? A real round face. A great smile, great teeth. She's a dental assistant, so maybe she gets her teeth cleaned for free. Sometimes she comes in straight from work, still in her scrubs, but tonight she was in tight jeans. She looked great. She always looks great."

John's eyes glitter at me. The kitchen is hot, so I open the door to the back porch to let in a cross breeze. John waits.

"Her hair is parted down the middle, pulled back into two short, spiky ponytails behind her ears. Her hair is dark, really dark, except for where she bleaches it in streaks. I think I've told you about her tattoo before, a little blue star right on the back of her neck."

"Yes," John says. "I remember the tattoo. It's lame, but most girls are covered in lame tattoos these days. What does she say? What do I do?"

"She says, 'Hey, I know it's late, but do you mind if I just grab some strings and a new book?' And I say, 'Have at it.' She finds what she's looking for, and when I ring her up she digs in her pocket for cash, right? Which reveals this pink wedge of flesh between her t-shirt and her jeans."

"Oh, god," John says. "Girls do that! They do it on purpose. You're learning how to see things. Where's Sean at this point?"

"I don't know. The office, I guess. He's totally vanished. So April pays, right? But she doesn't leave. She kind of hangs around for a minute, leans on the counter, laces her fingers together. She's going nowhere. It's like she's going to stay right there, looking up at me through her bangs, for the rest of the freaking night."

I do not tell John that I could feel my heart pumping between my lungs.

"'You've got nice hands,' April says."

"You do," John says. "Your hands help."

I started playing the drums as soon as John did, so I've been playing since I was a kid. My forearms are muscled; my hands are calloused. John says my hands are the least girly thing about me.

"So she makes this astute observation and you do what, Johnny-John?" John asks.

"I say thanks."

"Of course you do," John says.

"So she says, 'Why don't I ever see you out? I never see you at shows or anything. You've never gone to see Sean's band play. You're never anywhere. Why is that?'"

"'I lead a pretty quiet life,' I say. I'm trying to play it cool, you know? At this point, I'm sure I'm blushing."

"You do turn pink," John says. "I've seen you do it. What's April's condition?"

"She's cool as a cucumber. She's just leaning there on the counter, looking up at me, and she kind of half-smiles and says, 'You wouldn't have to, you know.'"

"Oh, god," John says. "You're in way over your head."

"I know, right? She's some sort of professional. So I say, 'My life's quiet, but busy.'"

"Not what I would have said."

"Fine. But it's what I said. So she straightens up and takes one of the store's business cards from the box by the register. She leans across the counter and grabs the pen I keep by the credit card machine. She writes a cell phone number on the back of the card and holds it out to me. 'It's no big deal,' she says. 'Just a cup of coffee or something.' I take the card, and she looks at me with this expression I can't quite read."

"What do you say?"

"I say, 'I don't know. Maybe. We'll have to see.'"

"Maybe? We'll have to see? That's what you manage for me, Johnny? For the love of fucking Pete."

"What was I supposed to do, John? What the hell is supposed to happen now?"

"You go on a date with a hot chick, Johnny-John. Who in god's name are you pretending to be?"

"How am I supposed to go on a date?"

"It's not that hard," John says. "It's not algebra. It's not geothermal mechanics. It's not molecular megaton nuclear physics."

"Those aren't real things."

"Algebra is," John says. "I aced it in high school. I could do algebra with my eyes closed. You're going to go on a date."

"I don't know if I can make that happen," I say.

"I'll tell you how to do it," John says. He leans back in his chair and closes his eyes. "I'll tell you everything you'll need to know and then I'll watch the whole thing. I'll go with you. I'll sneak right in through the trapdoor in your brain."

"We'll see," I say, but I leave John to his imaginings. I take our bowls and put them in the sink. I put a lid on the pot and stick the whole thing in the refrigerator. By the time I'm running dishwater, John has slumped so far down in his chair that his head rests against the seatback. Sweat beads across his forehead and over his upper lip. He hasn't shaved in several days. His eyes flicker behind his lids. His lips move, but I don't know if he's dreaming or talking to himself. Minutes pass with nothing but the sound of water sloshing in the sink as I wash our few things. I wipe down the counters and the stovetop. John's breathing is even and regular.

I am standing in the line of life for my brother. I am holding his place. I am helping John remember who he was once, so that one day he'll get well and become that guy again. The hospitals and doctors and medications kept him unhinged for years, so here, on our own, we're trying a novel approach. I know that this is not normal. I know that John is not well. I'm not stupid. But what was supposed to heal him failed to. Being my brother's face to the world is such a minor sacrifice. I don't know what I'm still hoping for, for John, but I know that as long as we live this way, John and I both get to hope.

Back when we tried to believe in modern medicine, my parents sent me to group therapy with other siblings of crazy people. The participants moaned and lamented about a whole host of schizoid sub-diagnoses, manias, bi-polar conditions, and frightening personality disorders. My group was made up of the siblings of sociopaths. I would come home and reassure John. "Don't worry," I'd say. "Compared to these lunatics, you're only a little bit crazy." Shakespeare drove one kid's brother nuts. The brother had been into Shake-speare for years. He'd read all of the comedies before graduating from junior high. He was making his way steadily through the trag-edies and histories when his mom took him to London for his six-teenth birthday. The whole point was to see a production of *Othello*.

The kid had already read *Othello*, apparently a number of times. He knew every line of the play by heart, and somewhere in the first act, while watching Iago plant the initial seeds of doubt in the mind of the Moor, the kid began to believe that he was control-ling the action on stage with his hands. His hands were miracu-lous. By flexing and relaxing his fingers, he could send the actors dancing across the stage like marionettes. I can imagine the thrill of terror that must have run through him as he sat in the dark theatre, caught in the rapt silence of the audience, realizing that it was he who controlled the ebb and flow of the drama on the stage. Who wouldn't sit and sweat in his new navy suit and quietly go insane before intermission? The guy in my group said his brother was never the same after that. His psychotic break came on with the force and velocity of a freight train, and before the month was out, he'd tracked down the next-of-kin to the actress who played Desdemona. He sent her parents dozens of roses and a long letter explaining how and why he was responsible for the strangulation of their daughter. He promised to pay for it with his first thousand years in Hell. He sent a threatening letter to the actor who played Iago, and then he tried, unsuccessfully, to hang himself in the garage with a garden hose. I stopped going to group after that.

John didn't swan dive into schizophrenia the way that kid did. John went crazy little by little, all by himself. Except going crazy didn't look like going crazy in John's case. It looked like brilliance to me. It looked like beauty and rage.

"Hey, John," I say softly. "You ready for bed? It's been a long day, man. Let's hit the hay."

John wakes with a start.

"Bed?" I ask.

John looks around the kitchen, confused. His expression clouds, his face troubled by some emotion akin to fear.

"You promised," John says.

"What?"

"Not to go home. They'll brainwash you."

"No one's going home," I said. "It's okay."

"They could have you committed," John says. "They could have you hospitalized at the drop of a hat. And then it's all emergency rooms and restraints and needles and shrinks with mustard on their ties. They pump you full of so many chemicals you don't know what day of the week it is, and then they get you to agree to things."

"They can't have me committed," I say. "You're the crazy one. Not me. But I'll call Dad and tell him no."

"Tonight?" John asks. "Right now? Just to get it over with?"

"You usually don't want me to call them from our home phone."

"I'll hide in the hall," John says. "I'll just stay in the hallway where I don't have to see you but where I can hear everything."

"Okay," I say.

I hit the lights in the kitchen, and we walk through our dark apartment to the living room. The late show at the theatre across the street must be letting out. I can hear people laughing and telling each other goodbye. I can hear people hailing cabs and shrieking as they dart across the street against the light. They have no idea John and I are up here. I imagine for a moment that I am one of them. I have seen a silly comedy show and now I'll catch the bus or hop in a cab or just slip my hands into my pockets and walk several long blocks home to my apartment where I live alone.

"Johnny?" John asks.

"Yes?"

"You're good to me," my brother says.

"I know."

I pick up the phone and dial the familiar digits of our parents' home phone. John retreats to the hall but peers at me around the corner. I don't know how he knows when my father picks up, but he slinks further down the hall before I've said hello.

I WAKE IN THE MORNING TO JOHN ON THE DRUM KIT. He's working on a hard-driving rhythm, but I can tell from his touch that he's trying to keep it down. He's trying to be respectful of the hour. My watch, which I pick up from the floor, says it's eight o'clock. John sings as he plays. He's only recently started to do this. He doesn't sing a melody, or even notes, really. He howls, but the sound is so strange and sustained that I find it beautiful. I listen to my brother in the living room. I stretch. I rub my hands over my face and head, then over my breasts. My lungs feel so good in the morning, so expansive, that I sometimes just lie in bed enjoying the way my chest expands when I breathe. I used to only wear my chest binder when I went out in the world as John. I was Jane at home and my brother on the street. But now I pull it on first thing. I put on a sleeveless undershirt over my chest binder and jeans over my boxers. I've stopped shaving everything but my face. I'm hairier than I thought I'd be. I like my body more in this natural state than I thought I would. I am lean and muscled and scruffy, all of which feels good.

Sunlight is pouring through our living room windows when I join John. I flop on the couch, still yawning. John's eyes are closed, and he does not open them. When he's at the kit, my brother looks as much like his old self as he ever does. He hasn't lost a bit of his talent or his grace when he's got his hands on drumsticks. After a while, I realize John is working on a Bonham drum break.

On the day Sean hired me—the day I stood on the customer side of the counter, my newly shaved cheeks prickling with heat, my body slick with sweat under two t-shirts and an ace bandage—he fixed his cool eyes on me and said, "Five questions. You ready?"

"Shoot," I'd said.

"Why are you looking for a job?"

"I just moved to the city."

"Have you ever worked commercial retail?"

"No."

"Right answer. Do you lie, cheat, or steal? Be honest. I'm serious."

"No," I said. "Never."

"Really?" Sean asked. "No shoplifting? Nothing petty like that?"

"Nope," I said.

"Weird. What do you play and how long have you played it?"

"I learned the piano when I was a kid, but I'm a drummer. I've been playing the drums since I was six." This was true for me rather than for John. In my very first moments of being my brother, I was already getting us mixed up. John was nine when we started playing drums. We agreed that I'd use his history, and that I'd talk about leading the drum line all through high school. John auditioned for and got accepted into a drum and bugle corps after his senior year, but at the last minute he backed out and decided to go to college instead. I did neither. John hardly ever talks about that year away at college, that year he spent losing his grip. I imagine everything about that time must be tinged with the fright of nightmare for my brother.

"A drummer," Sean had said. He scratched his chin. "Favorite musician?"

"Art Blakey," I said without hesitation.

"A Jazz Messengers man," Sean said. "I like you. I don't quite trust a kid who's never stolen anything, so I'm going to keep an eye on you, but if you want the job it's yours. My last guy quit two days ago, and dicking around trying to find help is the last way I want to spend my weekend."

I stood there blinking at Sean, trying to follow.

"Monday?" he asked. "Is that cool? Are we on the same page?"

"Yeah, Monday," I said.

"What's your name?" Sean asked.

"John," I said. "John Fields."

"See you Monday, John," Sean said.

And just like that I had a job, and one person on the planet who looked straight at me and called me John. I wouldn't tell John about slipping up and answering for myself rather than for him. John loved Led Zeppelin's John Bonham. He used to threaten the drum line with physical violence if anyone said Bonham wasn't the best drummer ever. Art Blakey was actually the favorite musician of John's drum instructor, Eugene. He'd played us Blakey records when John and I were just kids.

I was the musical one back when John and I were little. Our mother, trained as a classical pianist, gave lessons at her studio downtown rather than at the baby grand in our living room. She tried to teach John to play, but he hated it. I took to the piano immediately. I used to like nothing better than sitting next to my mother on the piano bench when she played. She never gave me formal lessons, but she would play a simple line of melody a couple of times and then leave me to stumble around on the keys until I could repeat it.

"That's lovely, Jane," she'd call from the kitchen when I'd finally figure it out.

I learned to read music in a similar fashion. My mother would spread sheet music out on the kitchen table while she cooked dinner, and I'd kneel on a chair, elbows on the tabletop, and study the pages. When she wasn't stirring the ground beef that was browning on the stove, or chopping tomatoes and cucumbers to put into a salad, she'd lean over me, tuck her hair behind her ears, and sing the note names of the melody.

About the time I was learning to read music, our father bought John his first drum kit. It was nothing special, just a Yamaha starter kit with banged up heads, but the bodies of the drums flashed with red sparkles. Mom, John, and I stood in the backyard on a Sunday afternoon in late fall as Dad pulled the kit from the back of the station wagon. It was cold enough that we all should have been wearing coats, but when Dad honked the horn as he pulled into the garage, we all hurried out into the yard without them. We emerged from the house just in time to see Dad appear in the doorway of the garage with a high-hat in one hand a snare in the other.

"How could I not, Elaine?" our father asked. "There was a garage sale. It was just sitting there in a front yard over on Mechanic Street. It's perfect. Give me a hand here, John."

"Richard," Mom said, but we both helped Dad and John lug the kit down to the basement and set it up.

John loved that kit. He could thump away for hours, and though I could sit on the bottom step of the basement stairs and watch John for longer than I could do most other things, I would eventually get bored and wander upstairs. One evening, after I'd abandoned John in the basement, I found our father in the living room and asked him to read me a book. We had a spectacular collection of picture books about American history—tales of the Revolution, the Trail of Tears, the Underground Railroad, and the Civil War. I loved the Underground Railroad books best. I loved the night scenes, the way the dark colors bled into one another—blues, browns, purples, and blacks. Dark figures against black trees and a starry swirl of sky. My father did his best to explain that the railroad was a metaphor, but I could never quite rid myself of the image of miles and miles of tunnels and silent, stealthy trains. Our father was reading one of these books to me, his voice soft, his beard tickling my ear, when John stood in the doorway of the living room and announced, "I need lessons." He looked dark and serious, his drumsticks gripped in his fists.

"I want to learn how to play for real," he said.

Dad took off his reading glasses. "I'll call Frank," he said. "He might have students who give lessons. I'll see what I can do."

"Thanks," John said.

The following Wednesday evening, John and I watched Eugene—a tall, slender, young black man—climb the steps that curved up the slope of our front yard. He stood on our porch, his breath steaming in the cold, and rang the bell. John answered the door and held his hand out to Eugene.

"Hello, Eugene," he said.

"You must be John," Eugene said, and shook my brother's hand.

"Come in, come in," our father said. "I'm Richard. Thanks for coming."

"Dr. Hartman said it would be fun," Eugene said. John fidgeted at our father's side. Eugene stilled him with a serious gaze. "It looks like you'd like to get started, young man."

"Yeah," John said. He turned to lead Eugene toward the kitchen and the stairs to the basement, but then stopped. "Could Janie come, too?" he asked. "She could just watch."

Eugene looked at me for the first time since he'd stepped into our house. He shrugged. "It's your lesson," he said. "We can do whatever you want."

"Come on, Janie," John said, and my heart sang.

John led the way down to the basement. I sat on the bottom step where I felt most out of the way. Eugene walked around the drum kit, tapped a few heads, and nodded. Even under the fluorescent lights of the basement, I loved the way the red sparkles flashed.

"Not bad," Eugene said. "Not bad for a nine-year-old."

John held out his drumsticks. "Will you show me first? I want to see what it's supposed to look like."

Eugene smiled and took the proffered drumsticks. John had been holding them as if they might leap from his hands, but the sticks seemed to float in Eugene's fingers. He held them as if holding drumsticks took as little effort as wearing a shirt. Eugene spun the seat to the right height and then settled in behind the kit. I would have thought he'd look silly—long legs folded up like a grasshopper's—but he didn't. He looked beautiful. He held one stick overhand and one stick underhand and dropped into a drum roll on the snare.

"Good sound," he said. He tested each of the heads and thumped the bass twice. Then he sat silently for a moment, his head bobbing to an internal rhythm, as if music were something he leapt into instead of made. He lay down a beat with the bass drum and added each new drum on top of that. His whole body moved with the rhythm of the drums, but all motion was mediated through his wrists. I could see that John was thrilled. His dark eyes never left Eugene's hands. I don't know how long Eugene played, but I could have sat on the bottom step listening to him for years. The flight of the sticks across the drumheads narrowed until there was nothing but solid bass and a light rhythm repeating itself on the snare. Eugene raised an eyebrow at my brother.

"Yeah?" he asked.

"Yeah," John said.

"Okay," Eugene said, and when he held the drumsticks out to John, my ears rang in the sudden quiet. He stood and adjusted the seat for John. Once John was behind the kit, Eugene turned to me.

"You'll need to be up higher to see." He motioned me over to the freezer chest. "This is better." He swung me up onto the freezer, and I sat cross-legged with my hands in my lap.

John's first lesson consisted of nothing but learning how to hold the drumsticks and playing quarter notes on the snare. Eugene counted out the rhythm, his voice low and steady, keeping time with one slender hand thumping against his chest.

"Loose, two, three, four, loose," he repeated, reminding John once a measure to relax his grip on the sticks. When the sticks bounced freely off the drumhead, Eugene said, "That's right, Johnny. Now you've got it."

By the end of the hour, John was sweating. His dark curls stuck to his forehead and neck. Eugene put a hand on John's damp head. "You've got a nice touch," he said. "Teach your sister this week. It'll be good for the both of you."

Eugene headed up the basement steps. In the silence between us in the basement, John and I could hear Eugene emerge into the warmth of the kitchen. We could hear his voice shift into the kind of voice adults use with each other, a tone less full of mystery.

From that evening on, John and my world turned from Wednesday to Wednesday. We counted months in Eugenes. When John had fully mastered a new lesson, he'd turn the sticks over to me.

"Your turn, Janie."

I would screw the seat to my own height and settle in behind John's kit. He'd stand close over me. He'd show me the new rhythm or technique as if I hadn't been watching him practice it for days.

"Okay, John. I got it. Let me try already," I'd say. I loved the weight of the taped sticks in my hands. I could balance them perfectly on one finger. I loved the size of the drum kit and the beautiful, battered heads spanning out around me. I loved the reach for a cymbal and the thump of the bass drum, which sent vibrations up my shin and into my hip. When John finally finished showing me what to do, I would take a moment to hear the rhythm, as I'd seen Eugene do that first night, and then I'd start to play.

"That's good, Janie," John would say. "Now try it like this." He'd adjust my grip or pick up the tempo or change the rhythm and have me play it again. We practiced together at night after supper until our palms ached and our arms were sore and our ears rang. When we couldn't play any longer, we would lie on the concrete floor of the basement and listen to the records Eugene had left for us—everything from the blues to jazz to funk to the Rolling Stones.

One hot evening in August, a year and a half after John's first lesson, Eugene arrived with a folder of sheet music and a stand. John eyed him skeptically. Once we were all in our proper place in the basement, John behind the drums, me slung back in a canvas camp chair licking a popsicle, Eugene spread the sheet music on the stand.

"If you're serious about music," he said to John, "you're going to have to learn to read."

"John doesn't read music," I said, considering in which direction my popsicle was likely to drip. "I do."

"We'll teach him," Eugene said.

"I don't want to read music," John said. He was already thumping out a beat on the bass and tapping a syncopated rhythm on the high-hat. "I want to play the drums."

"Just here, by yourself?" Eugene asked. "Just you and Janie in the basement?"

John shrugged and kept whacking at the drums.

"A kid who bangs around on a kit in the basement could be a drummer, I guess," Eugene said, "but a percussionist reads music."

"I could be a percussionist," I said. "What is it?"

"A percussionist plays everything. Drums, yeah, but also the xylophone, marimba, bells, keyboard, tympani. You name it. Rock bands have drummers. Symphonies have percussionists."

"Which are you?" I asked.

"Both." Eugene grinned.

John continued playing. He was practicing a sixteen-bar break Eugene had taught him two weeks before. He was ignoring Eugene and me. I climbed out of my chair and set my popsicle down on my father's workbench. I stood beside Eugene, took a long look at his sheet music, and then sang the first few measures of the melody.

"You do read music," Eugene said.

"Yeah, I know," I said. "I said so."

"Are you going to give me a lesson or what?" John asked.

"The lesson is reading music," Eugene said.

"That's not what I want to learn," John said. His dark eyes flashed.

"Jane," Eugene said, his gaze fixed on my brother. "Do you think you could play this for me on the piano?"

I considered the sheet music, my pulse thumping in my throat. I hadn't practiced the piano in months. After the first few measures, the melody grew quite difficult. I couldn't think clearly with the crash of cymbals in my ears.

"I don't know," I said. Eugene tipped his head toward me in order to hear. "Maybe the left hand? The right looks too hard for me."

"Come on," Eugene said. He gathered his music and took me by the arm. "Let's go. You can come upstairs for the lesson if you want, John."

I felt stuck to the floor.

"Let's go, Jane," Eugene said, pushing me gently toward the stairs. "Here we go."

We surprised my parents in the living room. They were curled on the couch together, my mother's feet tucked under my father's thigh, working a crossword puzzle. Eugene had one hand placed firmly on the top of my head. I felt as if his palm closed a circuit that let a current run through me. It was the first time I felt that electric current of another person's touch.

"Jane's going to play the piano for me," Eugene explained. "We're working on reading music, but John would rather not this evening."

My mother patted my father on the knee. "Let's work on those dishes, Richard," she said.

"Yes, of course," my father said.

Eugene and I were, for the first time in all the months he'd been coming to our house, alone together in the living room. The French windows stood open, but the sheers hung slack in the still August night. John's drumming was a low thumping coming up at us through the floor. There seemed to be a great deal of air and space in the living room.

"Here," Eugene said. He spread the music out at the piano. "Let's see what we can do."

We sat side-by-side on my mother's piano bench, and I sight-read the music, moving from chord to chord in the bass clef. When I felt ready to play, I nodded up at Eugene. We each spread a hand across the keys. Eugene had an octave within easy reach.

"You've got the biggest hands I've ever seen," I said.

"Thank you," Eugene said. He stretched his fingers wide, thumb to pinky. "Yours are little still, but you've got nice fingers. You should keep up with the piano."

"Okay."

Eugene began to mark time with his left hand against his chest. He counted out two measures, and then we both began to play. When it came time, he deftly turned the page. The music was beautiful.

"Watch the key change," he said.

"I see it," I said, and we shifted into a diminished seventh.

We played together until there wasn't any more music, and then we sat quietly, our fingertips resting lightly on the keys.

"That was pretty," I said.

"Yes," Eugene said.

"Who wrote it?"

"Me," he replied. "It's part of my thesis."

"Can we play more of it sometime? If I practiced, I could get the right hand."

"I know you could," Eugene said. "Yes. Sure thing." But we never did.

After Eugene left, I went down to the basement to see what I could do about John. He was still playing, but more slowly and thoughtfully now. He was trying to work out a rhythm he couldn't quite get. I stood on the bottom step, my hands locked behind my back, until he looked up at me.

"How's your boyfriend?"

"He's not my boyfriend."

"You're so stupid, Jane," John said, shaking his head as if he really was sorry for me. "You don't know anything."

"Are you mad at me or just at Eugene?" I asked.

"How does this sound?" John asked. He launched into a rolling drum break, never once lifting his sticks to the cymbals. It sounded good, the kind of rhythm that you feel in your skeleton, and I said so.

"You're a total idiot, Jane," John said.

"Are you thinking about April?" John asks.

I am returned to my brother. Our living room. The morning sun falling through the windows.

"What? No. I was thinking about Sean's band. About practice tonight." I don't know why I lie.

"I've been thinking about April," John says. "But you're right. There's that, too."

"We've suddenly got a lot going on."

"That's how life is," John says. "One fucking thing right after another. Are you nervous?"

"About the band?"

John stops playing. He gives me a look of utter annoyance. "About April. What's wrong with you?"

"Oh, April," I say. "Yeah."

"How long has this been brewing, Johnny? She's been working up to this. I remember how girls operate."

"I don't know," I say. "She's been kind of around a lot. Sean says more than usual. He says she's had an eye on you for a couple of weeks."

John looks at me. He smiles and shakes his head. He climbs out from behind the drum kit and lies down on the floor. We are both beached on our backs, staring up at the ceiling.

"Johnny," he says, "you don't know the first thing about women."

"I know, right? I have no idea what's going on. What the hell do I know about all this?"

"This is a prickly peach," John says. "Girls are tricky six ways from Sunday. You didn't learn these lessons back in the olden days. You never were that kind of girl."

"You were going off the deep end when I was in high school. I had other things to think about than who was going to take me to the prom."

"Ah, the prom," John says. He drapes his hands over his face and peeks at me through his fingers. "I went to a prom once. What was that girl's name? Maggie or Molly, or something like that? Was she color guard?"

"Mindy," I say. "She was a flute."

"I got laid like you wouldn't believe."

"Spare me," I say. "What should we do? What do you want me to do about April?"

"You should do her," John says. He laughs, but the sound is forced, as if he's a bad actor whose director has just told him to laugh maniacally. He stops laughing and closes his eyes. "You should call her first, but then you should definitely do her."

"Fuck off, John," I say. I never swore before I started being my brother.

"I'm serious," John says. "We'll think of something, Johnny-John. I read about this medieval woman once who married a widow and raised her kids for six years before anyone found out she wasn't a man. Not even the widow. Apparently they were doing remarkable things with porcelain dildos in the Middle Ages."

"What happened to her?" I ask.

"She got burned at the stake as a witch. Up she went."

"Great," I say. "Thanks."

"I'm just saying that nothing is impossible, little brother. And you're not going to get burned at a stake. People don't even make stakes for witch burning anymore."

"You're supposed to be telling me trade secrets," I say.

"Sometimes a girl can rescue you. Sometimes, when you're out in the world, surrounded by people who are trying to see through you, sometimes a girl puts her hand on you. And the air that was too thin to breathe just a second ago is suddenly okay. And for a minute, as long as her body with all its electromagnetic energy is somewhere near to you, you don't have to be afraid. This soft, spiky-haired girl wearing a t-shirt that says *What Would Joan Jett Do?* puts her hand on you, and you're anchored. You're safe. She's not going to let you float away. Not yet, at least. Mostly, you don't have to do anything. If you're really lucky, she'll know what you need and come find you. Girls are all skin. That's better than fucking, almost. Getting to have your hands all over that skin."

We both breathe. A dog barks below our window. Two people greet each other in Spanish out on the street.

"Who was she?"

"Doesn't matter. Those days are over. See you later. *Hasta la vista,* baby."

I don't know what to say.

"We're not going to call her today," John says. "Tomorrow, okay? She'll wait."

"Okay," I say.

We do not talk any more about April. We plan for Sean's band's practice. John is nervous. He isn't certain I can pull off my version of him outside of Stew's Music. He decides, briefly, that he should come with me.

"I could follow you secretly," he says. I'm fresh from the shower, still in my boxers and undershirt, rooting through the pile of clothes on my bedroom floor for just the right t-shirt and jeans. John looms on the threshold. He never comes into my room. "No one would know I was with you, not even on the bus. I could walk around the neighborhood, just to keep an eye on things. I'd be there in case you needed me."

"Metallica or Pink Floyd?" I ask, holding each shirt up by a sleeve.

"What do you think?" John asks.

"I don't know. That's why I asked you."

"I'm not talking about t-shirts," John shouts. He slams a fist against the doorframe. "You're making me crazy."

"You following me to rehearsal is what's crazy," I say. "Rehearsal could take hours. We don't know the neighborhood. We don't know anything yet. Let me check it out, okay? Let me get the lay of the land." I pull on the Pink Floyd shirt, and now I have to find clean socks. "I'll tell you everything when I get home tonight. We'll figure out a way to get you there later, all right? We don't want to fuck things up here at the beginning."

John considers me skeptically. He chews his thumbnail. He doesn't like it when I'm right.

"This is just the beginning, yeah?" I say. "We've got all kinds of time."

"Right," John says. "You're right, Johnny-Jane. Maybe I'll go next time. This time I'll stick close to home. I'll be waiting for you. I'll just go with you in my brain."

I nod. "And maybe you could take a shower."

"As if showers would solve the world's problems," John says.

Sean's rehearsal space turns out to be the gutted second floor of a three-flat nestled in a hot, dirty strip of warehouses and body shops. He'd written the address and his cell phone number on a scrap of notebook paper. I turn down a side street that stinks of tarpaper and motor oil, and I come upon Sean and a couple of other guys standing out on the sidewalk smoking cigarettes.

"Johnny!" Sean cries, arms up as if signaling a touchdown.

"Sean, my man," I say, and we grip hands.

"Dude," he says. "You're here. This is awesome."

"Of course I'm here. I said I would be."

Sean whacks me on the back and takes a last drag on his cigarette, the butt held between his thumb and first finger. Night is falling, and the yellow sodium lights blink on above our heads. I inhale the sooty air and gaze down the empty street, trying to remember the look of brown paper and shopping bags scuttling in the gutter, the sound of Caribbean music leaking from behind the closed doors of a garage, the Mariachi trumpets blasting brightly from the white Nissan that rolls by.

"This is Roger," Sean says, pulling my attention from the street to one of his band mates. Roger is the kind of guy who wears thick, plastic-framed glasses and lots of polyester. He's tall and kind of paunchy, a thatch of blond hair slicked down over his forehead. "Bass guitar," Sean says. "Roger-dodger, this is John."

"Nice to meet you," Roger says, and we shake hands.

"And on keyboards, vocals, and now and again horns, our master of most things, Clint."

Clint presses his palms together and bows slightly. He seems older than the others, his long dark dreads shot through with strands of gray. We are the same height, his shoulders and chest even narrower than mine.

"Glad you could come, John," he says.

"Thanks," I say. We all stand around for a moment. John will find Roger absurd. He'll declare Roger's glasses and clothes a façade, a grotesque mask made of various plastics that absolves him of having an actual personality. He'll like Clint's pale skin and light eyes and dark dreadlocks.

Sean swings his arms in a wide arc, clapping his hands in front and then behind him. "Should we do this?" he asks, and Clint, the last man smoking, tosses his cigarette butt into the gutter. We troop up squeaky, twisting stairs in the dark. The light fixtures above seem to have been smashed, and only light spilling from the second floor illuminates the staircase. When we reach the landing, I see everyone's instruments and all the amps have been set up in the cavernous space. Instead of being lined with soundproofing, the walls have been stripped down to studs. A woman lounges on a couch. She's pouring Evian water from a large bottle into a paper cup when we walk in. She is stunning, her long, freckled legs bare to the knee, and her thighs encased in pencil-straight jean shorts. She wears a purple tank top that reveals most of her breasts. Her chest and arms and face are flecked with orange freckles, just like her legs. She stretches and stands. Her thick, red hair falls in a rope of a braid down her back. I think I look at women differently now than I used to.

"John," she says, offering me her slender hand. She's at least three inches taller than me. I take her palm in my sweaty grip. "I'm Leda."

"Lead vocals," Sean says. "Also Clint's wife."

I must look surprised and impressed, because Clint grins and Leda narrows her eyes. This is part of their routine.

"It's about time," Leda says, glancing at her watch. "I thought perhaps you guys were going to spend the whole rehearsal smoking cigarettes and drinking forties out in the street."

"No forties," Roger says.

"Alas," Leda says. She tosses me a quizzical look. "Are you old enough to drink forties, John?"

I flush and the guys laugh.

"Yeah, actually," I say, "if you'd like to check some I.D."

"I trust a baby face," Leda says. She pats my cheek, and says, "Oh, so soft."

A commotion ensues as people pick up instruments and test mics. Sean and Roger tune guitars. Clint seems in charge of testing levels. The drum kit is already set up. Sean had said their drummer left it in the rehearsal space for a while since what used to be her storage room was soon to be a nursery. The drumheads are scarred and some of the cymbals are dented, but it's a nice enough kit. I spin the seat to my height and take my sticks from my back pocket. I test the toms and the snare, take the drum key from my pocket, and tighten a few heads. As soon as I have my drumsticks between my fingers and my foot on the bass pedal, I am calm and certain. I can breathe.

"So let's start with a cover, something familiar for John," Sean says. "'Tell Me Something Good'?"

"Yeah," Leda agrees. She picks up a tambourine.

"Standard time, on the downbeat," Sean says. "Nothing funny or anything."

"I'll listen and take your lead," I say.

Sean counts off and the band begins. I do little more than mark time at first, letting my hands and wrists fall into the rhythm, closing my eyes for a while so that I can just hear, just feel, not even have to see. The band is rich and funky and tight. Leda's voice is smoky and bluesy, which I wouldn't have guessed just to look at her. Sometimes Clint joins her in a close harmony and for a moment I can't help but imagine what life must be like between them. I imagine they sing like this in the kitchen, Leda wielding a chef's knife. She's chopping vegetables, and Clint's holding her from behind, his dreaded head resting against her shoulder blade. I let the image materialize and then fade without losing my place in the music. My sticks venture out across the drumheads, rise to the cymbals, return. When the song is over, Sean smiles at me, clearly pleased. Leda raises her eyebrows, as content and distant as a cat.

"My man," Clint says.

Thick veins stand out under the skin of my forearms and hands. I'm sweating. Not the clammy sweat of anxiety, but the clean, wet sweat of work. I remember how much I liked the way sweat would run down me, rivers of it under my uniform when I played in John's drum line. We play another song, and another.

"Do you know Tom Scott, John?" Clint asks. "The LA Express?"

"Just *Tom Cat*," I say. I haven't thought about that band in years, but I can remember exactly what the cover of the album looked like as Eugene slipped the record out of its sleeve. "I haven't heard it in forever."

"Let's try the title track," Clint says.

As soon as Clint, Sean, and Roger lay into the opening bars, the whole album comes swimming back to me. Leda suggests I take a solo and everyone but Roger, who keeps on putting down the bass line, drops out to listen and nod and grin. "Ladies and gentlemen, John Fields on drums," Leda says into her microphone, and then mimics the roar of the crowd. We play until the metal band that rehearses on the third floor arrives and we can no longer hear ourselves above their din. Roger rolls a joint as we break down the equipment. He passes it to Clint who passes it to Sean. I shrug it off when Sean holds the joint out to me, so he hands it back to Roger. I want to feel exactly as I feel right now. Leda pats me on the back and then wipes my sweat off on her shorts. We laugh.

"Let me give you a lift," Sean shouts and I nod. Guitars scream above us. We carry all of the equipment down to the cars parked in the alley, and then Sean locks up the rehearsal space. He waves a brief blessing over the drum kit in the hopes that it won't get stolen before next week. We all troop back down to the alley and pile into cars. Doors slam and engines roar to life.

"You'll have to roll your window down," Sean says. "Sorry, man. No A.C."

I rest my arm on the edge of the window, my hand thumping happily against the door. Sean peels the tires and swings out of the alley without seeming to consider the possibility of traffic. We talk about music. Sean accuses me of holding out on him, threatens to fire me if I don't come back for rehearsal next Sunday.

"Does music run in your family?" Sean asks. "Does your sister play?"

I consider Sean's profile, his features limned in streetlight. I wonder if he would still like me if he'd met me as Jane. I wonder if I'd be in his car after band practice, or if he would have even hired me at Stew's. I try not to wonder if he would like me—really like me—if he knew. I showed Sean a picture of John and me once. We were dead at work, and out of nowhere I took this old photograph out of my wallet and showed it to Sean. It's from John's seventh birthday. We're sitting on the porch steps laughing up into the camera. John has an arm around me. We've both got pointy hats on, rubber band straps under our chins. I said my sister and I used to be close, but she went out east for school and we don't really talk that much anymore. We grew up and apart, the way people do.

"Yeah," I say. "She's a drummer, too. Or she was, back in high school. What makes you ask?"

"I don't know," Sean says. "You're good. Sometimes talent like that is a family thing. Sometimes it's in your genes."

I lean back into the fuzzy plush seats of Sean's car. I can feel the tires spinning against the asphalt, the earth spinning on its axis, our planet wheeling around the sun. I can hear the whole cosmos humming beneath the sound of the engine and the wind pummeling my head.

W HEN I LET MYSELF INTO THE APARTMENT, JOHN IS SIT-
ting on the floor in the darkened living room, his chin resting
on the windowsill. The lights from across the street frost his
matted curls blue. I close the door and hang up my keys. I
leave the lights off and lie down on the couch. John doesn't move.

"Sean drove you home," he says.

"Yeah. I'm more or less on his way."

"How did it go?" John asks. "I couldn't see it like I sometimes
can. I couldn't see through the camera in your brain."

"It was perfect. It was incredible."

John crawls across the living room floor and sits with his back
against the couch. I put a hand on his shoulder. His whole body
expands with each breath.

"Tell me," John says.

"Their rehearsal space is in this great immigrant part of town.
Caribbeans and Africans and Mexicans and all their music spilling
out of body shops and warehouses. The whole neighborhood smells
like tar and exhaust, and smack in the middle of it is the gutted
three-flat where all sorts of bands rehearse."

"Did you see the moon rise? Did the moon look different there?"

I try to think if I saw the moon or not. No image surfaces.

"I don't think I saw the moon. Maybe the sky was too bright. I
feel like the sky was neon, just a glowing haze."

"Because of the atmosphere?"

"Because of the streetlights."

"Right, streetlights," John says. "Tell me more. Tell me about the
people. Are they all space cadet aliens like Sean? Are they wool-
heads or do they have brains?"

"The bass player, Roger? You'd hate him. He's one of those guys
who wears plastic glasses."

"I hate those guys as much as I hate guys who iron their pants."

"Yeah, I know. But he's good. He doesn't talk too much, which is a plus."

"Silence is golden," John says.

"But the lead singer and the guy who plays keyboards are incredible. They're married, but you'd never know it to look at them. The guy is little and all dreadlocked. He's older. Older than Sean, even. You'd like him. He might be a Buddhist or something."

"I respect Buddhists," John says. "I'm willing to keep an open mind about Nirvana."

"That might be Hinduism."

"Don't lecture me on religion. Tell me about the woman."

"My god, John. She's unbelievable. She's got this alto voice and this red hair and these long legs. She's covered in freckles, head to toe, or at least all of the skin I saw was freckled. And I saw a lot of it."

John twists around to look at me. Only half his face is lit well enough to see. His one eye and half his face grin at me.

"How happy is their marriage?"

"Blissful. Nirvana."

"We'll see," John says. "Did they buy you? Do they believe? Are you Johnny-John, one hundred percent?"

"Absolutely," I say. "No one blinked."

"This is starting to get interesting," John says.

I tell him everything I can remember from the night, each song, each solo, each sound and smell and movement. I tell him how the air felt, how the bare studs vibrated with the metal music upstairs, how smoke curled from the joint Roger rolled, how Leda put her cool hand on my sweaty back. How we both laughed. I say, "They loved you, man. They loved you like people always do."

"People are sheep," John says. "People are sock puppets. That's the best thing about people."

John crawls across the floor again and returns to his former position—chin on windowsill, looking out the window.

"What do you see out there?" I ask.

"Wonders and miracles," John says. "Sometimes a fender-bender. Once I saw a car that was decorated with bedsprings. Huge bedsprings glued all over it. Sometimes you materialize."

Wind rattles the blinds. The light at the corner changes, and the river of traffic beneath our window comes to a halt. John's silhouette is utterly still.

"What did you do tonight?" I ask.

"My time is not your business, little brother," John says. "Tomorrow, before work, we're going to call April."

An electric charge hums over my skin.

"Okay," I say.

I learned from being my brother that nothing was impossible if I relied on the fiction of myself. The John that I was didn't really exist. Which made everything I did an act of imagination. If John and I could think it up, we could make it happen. I could watch from the outside, just like everybody else does. I knew I could never call April, but that didn't stop me from picking up the telephone. John is pacing in front of me, alive with excitement, when I pull my wallet from my back pocket and take out the card with April's number on it.

"Let me see," John says, holding out a hand. I give him the card, and John studies April's number. "She crosses her sevens. Huh."

"What does that mean?"

"Oh, any number of things," John says. He touches the ink. He looks at me. "Are you ready, Johnny?"

"Sure," I say.

My blood is delivering too much oxygen to my brain. Our apartment is stifling, and the ceiling fan oscillating above us is doing nothing. John laughs and hands me the card. I dial April's number before my hands quit working. I'm as nervous as any other kid who's never asked a pretty girl out on a date. April's cell phone rings and rings. Just when I'm sure I'm going to get her voicemail, April picks up.

"Hello?" she asks.

"Hey, April," I say, startled. "Hey. Hi. Hello."

I look to John for encouragement, but his eyes are wide with alarm. Maybe my voice is higher than it should be. I only ever call our parents. I'm Jane on the telephone. Maybe I'm Jane right now. There is a long pause as my brain spins for the next right move, but my brain is a bicycle with the chain off—the spinning pedals can't possibly catch the gears.

"John?" April asks.

"Oh, god, yeah. Sorry," I say. "Yeah, this is John."

John buries his face in his hands.

"Hi," April says. I can hear her smile. "What's going on?"

"Nothing," I say. "I was just, you know, I thought I'd call before leaving for work. I thought, maybe we could, um, get that cup of coffee we were talking about."

"Sure," she says. "I'd like that. When?"

She speaks as if she's got a script in front of her. It's like she's the only one who knows what's supposed to be happening in this conversation. John has abandoned me. He's pulled his shirt up over his head. I'm on the edge of hysterical laugher, so I have to stop looking at him.

"When? When. Well, I don't know. I hadn't really thought about it."

April laughs.

"Okay," she says. "How about something like, oh, Friday?"

"Friday's good," I say. "Friday would be okay."

"I've got this friend whose band is playing over at Phyllis's on Friday. They're kind of lame, unless you love a bunch of white guys in khaki pants doing Milli Vanilli covers, which I kind of do, but they're opening for this other band people have been talking about. They're supposed to be a sort of reggae-meets-Bollywood-meets-old-school-funk outfit."

"Phyllis's?" I ask.

"Unless you, like, have your heart set on this coffee thing."

"No, that'd be cool," I say. "I've got work, you know, but we could go after we close."

"I'll come by," April says. "I'll come grab you from Stew's."

"Okay."

We are both silent. I can't fathom what else I'm supposed to say, but I can hear April smiling. I can hear it in how she breathes.

"So, okay," she says. "I'll see you Friday."

"Perfect," I say. "Great."

"John?" she asks.

"Yeah?"

"You can chill out. It's going to be okay."

"Right," I say. She laughs again and we hang up. I hold the telephone in my hands as if it were a foreign object. As if I don't know what it is or how it came to be that I am holding it. John pulls his shirt back down. His face is red.

"Friday?" he asks.

"Apparently," I say.

"There have been worse disasters than what I just witnessed," John says. "I can't think of any at the moment, but I know there have been."

"Thanks."

"Back when I was the one the girls were after, I would have done that totally differently."

"I know," I say.

When I get to Stew's, Sean isn't perched on the stool behind the cash register as he usually is. Typically, when I arrive in the afternoon, he's leaning on the counter reading a paperback, his head bobbing to Al Green or James Brown or Stevie Wonder. He'll lift his eyebrows at the sound of the bell over the door, but keep his eyes fixed on his book until he's finished a paragraph or a page. Then he'll glance up and smile, pleased to see it's me and not a customer. This afternoon, though, the floor is empty when I step through the door.

"Hey," I call. "Hello?"

The office door at the back of the store swings open. Sean looks frazzled, his hair even wilder than usual, a cigarette pinned between his lips.

"Thank god," he says. "I've been waiting for your ass."

I check my watch.

"It's one," I say. "Same as usual."

"Yeah, well, I'm in a little bit of a situation here, dude." He takes the cigarette from his mouth and runs his free hand over his head. His lean biceps bulge. The insides of his upper arms look as if they've never seen the sun.

"What's the problem?"

"Nothing huge," Sean says. "I just haven't been exactly meticulous with the books. Stew's suddenly gone all anal on us. He wants a reckoning of the past quarter by tomorrow morning, which more or less sucks."

"On you, man," I say. "Stew's gone all anal on you. I just work here. I've never met the dude."

"Thank you, smart ass," Sean says. "I'm going to need you to hold down the fort today while I try to figure shit out, okay?"

"Sure," I say.

"And if it's dead, could you get everything shipshape on the shelves? Our inventory is a little out of order, it seems."

"No problem," I say.

"Perfect."

Sean swings the office door shut. I stroll down the electronics aisle. We have display models of twelve- and twenty-four-track digital workstations. A number of mini disc recorders sit on the shelves, some boxes open, some not. Three turntables are stacked on the floor, and one side of the aisle is a confusion of mikes and cables and shock mounts and clips and clamps and studio headphones and plugs and packages of remix, loop, and groove software. The guitar pedals are a mess. The office door bangs open.

"Do you want to get high?" Sean asks. He's standing at the end of the aisle, deftly rolling a joint. "If it won't slow you down or anything, it's the least I can do."

"No thanks," I say. I can't help but laugh.

"What?"

"Do you think that has anything to do with the fix you might be in?"

"Suddenly you're a hard-ass?" Sean asks. He licks the joint and lights it. He closes one eye against the smoke. "Suddenly you're a square?"

"I'm just saying."

"This, I'll have you know," Sean says, holding the joint between his thumb and first finger, "helps me think. I turn into an accounting genius."

We both laugh and get to work. Sean blasts Sun Ra until the first customer comes in and I rap on the door so he'll turn the music down to a reasonable decibel level.

The Saturday after the sheet music lesson, Eugene showed up at our house. Our mother had chased John and me from the basement into the front yard, but we had become unaccustomed to so much sun and pollen and grass. We were lounging in the shade of the porch, John on the porch swing, me stretched out flat against the cool concrete.

"Janie, come up here," John said.

I obeyed, scrambling up onto the swing beside John.

"It's your boyfriend," John said.

We watched Eugene approach from the end of the block. Still three houses down from ours, he raised a hand in greeting, and John and I waved.

"Mom," I called into the house, not knowing what else to do. "Eugene's coming."

Our mother came out on the porch just as Eugene began climbing the steps at the bottom of our yard. Her hair was pulled back under a bandanna, and she was sweating from cleaning the kitchen. She looked beautiful to me, smiling past us at Eugene. She dropped a hand on my shoulder.

"Hello, there," she said, when Eugene reached the porch.

"Hello, Elaine," he said.

"Get your shoes on, kids," our mother said, "and bring the sunscreen."

We stood warily, both of us barefoot, on the porch. Eugene had not yet spoken to us.

"I said go," Mom said. "Eugene has come to take you two somewhere."

"Where?" John asked.

"A drum and bugle corps show," Eugene said. "If you want. No one's making you go. I just thought you might like to see what a drum line can do."

"And Janie's going, too?"

I didn't know if he asked because he did or did not want me to go.

"Janie, too. Get your shoes," our mother said.

We caught a bus across town to the university football stadium. Eugene kept a hand on both John and me as he guided us through the crowded parking lot, through the turnstiles, and up into the stands. He bought a program, and once we found our seats high above the field, he sat between us and turned through the pages. He told us about each corps—where they were from, what they were known for, what to keep an eye on in each performance.

"Like a marching band, right?" John asked. "Like at a football game."

"Sort of," Eugene said. "Just wait."

The stands were jammed. The address system crackled, and the announcer boomed out that the first corps was about to take the field. The crowd leapt to its feet. John and I had to stand on the bleachers next to Eugene to see over the people in front of us. A hush rippled through the stands, and in that moment of quiet the drum major gave a short, clipped shout. The first snare counted out four perfect rim shots and the drum line broke into a marching cadence. The corps took the field. Tightly packed blocks of musicians opened up like a human accordion until the corps reached from one end of the field to the other in an elaborate pattern. The color guard—flags snapping above their heads—wove in and out of the clean, military lines of the drums and horns. The drum major climbed the tower at the fifty-yard line and brought the corps to attention. The drums fell silent, their last shots echoing off the cement walls of the stadium. The drum major saluted the judges' box above us. He raised both arms, gave a quick upbeat, and on the downbeat the musicians on the field burst into the biggest, richest, brightest chord I'd ever heard. The pattern on the field exploded into motion. The crowd roared. Beneath every note you could hear the complicated rhythm of the drum line, like a wild, intricate heartbeat. The patterns in front of us shifted like a kaleidoscope. Sunlight glinted off horns. Feet flashed. The drummers' hands blurred. The color guard dropped flags for rifles, which they hurled—spinning together in perfect sync—six feet into the air. I was mesmerized, but when I looked at my brother, he looked like someone who had just found religion, like someone who had just been saved. Eugene rested a hand on John's shoulder. That was the end of the rift between my brother and Eugene. I never stood between them again. I think about that sometimes, even now. That one evening of magic at the piano with Eugene, and that Saturday when Eugene won my brother back.

Maybe this is what is on my mind as the afternoon edges toward evening and the store gets quiet. If Eugene and my brother are not what I am thinking about, they are not far from me. Eugene is as essential to my version of John as my brother is. I wouldn't have known that before I became him. In any case, on this afternoon I've inventoried and straightened up the merchandise. I've tended to the six or eight customers who've strolled through. The only sign I've had that Sean was in the office all day was his occasional changing of the CD in the stereo system. At some point he traded out Sun Ra for Bob Marley, and then Bob Marley for the blues. We've been listening to a Muddy Waters record for I don't know how long when Sean emerges from the office.

"Oh, man," he says, stretching and rubbing his neck. He bends down to touch his toes, but his fingertips only make it to his shins. "Yow."

"You get everything squared away?"

"Good enough for government work," Sean says. "Bookkeeping is exhausting." Sean reaches up and takes an acoustic guitar down from the rack over his head. He props a foot on a shelf and tunes the instrument. He's got lean, elegant hands and calloused fingers, his nails yellowed from cigarettes. If he knew me as Jane, would he think I was just a kid, just this young thing? Who knows? Not me.

"Hey, Fields," Sean says, and I start. "Thanks for coming out last night. Thanks for sitting in."

"No problem, man," I say. "I was glad to. You guys are tight."

"It's a good crew. And they were impressed. Clint and I will talk things over this week, but I can pretty much say that you're in if you want to be. Leda liked you, which is way more than half the battle."

"She's amazing," I say.

"No shit," Sean says. He sighs and shakes his head. "Some guys, man. Some guys have everything."

"Right?"

Sean looks at me. He looks down at the guitar strings. "Speaking of," he says. "What's your story? You holler at April or what?"

"Yeah," I say. "I called her. We're meeting up this Friday."

"Listen, John. You guys can do whatever the hell you want. It's none of my business. But April likes you. You know? She's a good girl. She's a friend of mine."

"I know," I say.

"I'm saying, do whatever, but if you hurt her, I'll have to break your legs."

Sean still has his eyes on his hands rather than on me. He's working on a little blue grass riff.

"I wouldn't," I try to say, but Sean holds up a hand.

"Don't want to hear it," he says. He stands abruptly and hangs up the guitar. He steps just inside the threshold of the office and lights a cigarette, but doesn't close the door. "Marching band, right?" he asks.

"What?" I'm having a hell of a time trying to follow Sean.

"That's where you got started. In high school. Marching band."

"I led the drum line," I say. "It's not the only thing I ever did, but yeah, I played in the marching band. It sounds lamer than it was."

"Fascinating," Sean says, and then turns toward the desk to ash his cigarette. "Count your drawer, man. Let's get out of here for the night."

By the time John was in high school, Eugene was the marching band drum line instructor and the percussion coordinator for the whole school district. He didn't have time to be coming over to our house every Wednesday for lessons anymore. He never gave me any special attention when he worked with the junior high orchestra, but he taught me how to play the marimba, the xylophone, the bells, and the tympani. He taught everyone how to read music and read the conductor and read our own heartbeats. He taught us that even if our job was just to play the triangle, we were integral, that the whole orchestra hung in the balance of a single, perfectly struck note. He dangled the triangle from his long fingers to demonstrate, and it did seem a thing of beauty, that slender, silver shape suspended in mid-air, waiting to be rung. While I was learning how to play pit instruments in the orchestra, Eugene and John were building the high school drum line into a corps of statewide reputation. I felt as if I'd been waiting my whole life to start ninth grade so that I could join John's drum line during his senior year.

That year, Eugene started dropping by our house in early June to work on the marching music for the coming fall with John. He'd show up with sheaves of sheet music and charts of drill coordinates, and he and John would argue over every shot of a drum break. A week before drum line auditions, I overheard Eugene discussing me with John.

"What do you think?" he asked. "Janie on third or fourth snare? Would the other guys deal with that, or should we start her on quads like everybody else?"

John had started on the snare his freshman year and was named section leader by the time he was a sophomore, but John wasn't everybody. Protocol said you start a rookie drummer on quads, and I was going to be a rookie drummer, John's sister or not.

"It's not my call," John said. "You're the drum instructor, not me."

John and I went to drum line auditions together the next week.

"How're you feeling, Janie?" he asked as we neared the band room doors. He was wearing his dark curls spiked up with hair gel in those days. He wore sunglasses that made him look like a speed skater.

"Good," I said.

He ran one hand down my long ponytail, giving my hair a gentle tug at the end, and then pulled open the heavy security doors. We stepped into a wave of climate-controlled air. The band room was in chaos. All the folding chairs and music stands that usually lined the five horseshoe levels that descended toward the conductor's podium at the bottom of the room had been packed away somewhere. Various stations were set up around the room with pit instruments, snares, quads, bass drums and cymbals. The room teemed with loud boys. The juniors and seniors sat at the back of the room twirling drumsticks in their fingers and laughing. The sophomores looked a little less at ease. The freshman boys darted about the room, both nervous and cock-sure, behaving like children. There were a few other girls milling about, girls who played in the pit, chiming bells, shaking maracas, and sometimes joining in on a melody on a keyboard.

"Slay 'em, Janie," John said, and then marooned me in the middle of the room as he went to join his friends.

We worked in groups at each station, sight-reading music, learning basic cadences, sometimes playing together and sometimes playing solo. I was better than any of the other freshmen. I was at least as good as the best sophomore. Eugene never said anything more than, "Well done, Jane," or "Nice," but I knew he was proud of me. John wore his sunglasses all day, so I could never see what he was thinking. By the end of the afternoon, I'd been grouped together with all of the older boys as Eugene and Mr. Bartlett, the band instructor, made final decisions about the drum line. Third and fourth snare positions seemed open, as well as all four spots on the quads. The five meaty guys who played the marching basses sorted themselves out, more or less in order of size.

Those of us who were being considered for snare or quad had to audition on both in front of everyone. My arms ached and my hands were sweaty. I had ripped blisters on both of my palms. But it felt right to be in front of the whole room, to have everybody's attention as I played the drum break we'd been learning all afternoon. I knew it as if I'd been playing it my whole life. My wrists snapped and the drumsticks cracked, and I could feel every muscle from my fingertips to my shoulders flex and bulge. When I finished, the junior who ended up playing third snare said, "Holy shit, John," and whistled through his teeth. "That's one hell of a sister you've got." Eugene looked at me like he loved me, which was enough. I didn't care that I ended up marching second quad. It made sense. It was a matter of seniority. I'd been seen and heard, and the only two people who mattered in the world were Eugene and John.

"You're good, Jane," John said once we were headed home in the station wagon. My hands throbbed. I could feel ghost rhythms in the exhausted muscles of my arms. "I forget, sometimes," he said, "how it used to be when we were kids. I forget how you used to keep up with me."

I didn't know what to say, so I leaned my head back against the headrest and closed my eyes. The rush of air from our open windows filled the car.

"I mean, sure, you've been coming along just fine, but you kind of floored me back there. It's hard to see what someone's really about when they're hidden back behind an orchestra or concert band."

"Yeah, it's different," I said.

For some reason John laughed, and then snapped on the car

stereo. I didn't know if it was John or our father who had put the *White Album* in the CD player, but John turned it up and thumped his thumbs against the steering wheel.

After Eugene named me to the drum line, the first half of the summer went exactly as I'd imagined it. We had marching practice during the day and section rehearsals three nights a week to work on music. I was the only girl on the line, but it wasn't hard for me to find my place. I was everybody's little sister. I was teased but respected, bullied but protected. John set the tenor and the tone, and all the other boys seemed to go through John when deciding how to treat me. The only boy who never had anything to say to me was the second snare, Drew. He was shy and skinny, a junior, a boy so thin I wondered if I could loop my fingers around his bicep. He had white-blond hair and vanishing eyebrows. Drew looked as if direct exposure to anything might bleach him into oblivion. He loved my brother like I did. There were times—like when we'd be going over drill charts together, or once when he loaned me his drum key and our hands touched—that I thought maybe I was falling for him. I didn't know, yet, what falling was supposed to feel like. John must have seen something. The drum line was packing up our marching instruments one night after sectionals when out of nowhere John asked, "Drew, you got a thing for my sister?"

Everybody's head snapped up. Drew dropped his sticks, and they clattered against the tile floor of the instrument storage room. He crimsoned. John smiled, threateningly.

"No," Drew said. "What? No."

My heart hurt. My throat burned.

"Of course not," John said. "She's one of us, right? She's one of the guys."

"Yeah," Drew said. And that was that.

We hit our only snag of the summer when we began to merge the music we'd been learning with our choreographed field drill. We'd learned all of our coordinates and were beginning to smooth out our marching, and John started thinking about the drum break in the closing number. He and Eugene had written a spectacular four-minute break. You could feel it coming in the music, and even from the field I could imagine how the drill would look from the judges' box, each pattern shifting the drum line, set by set, toward the long rail of extra drumheads at the sideline. By midsummer we had the music for the drum break nailed. Even now I can feel that break in my skeleton, the way my arms ached two minutes in and we had two more minutes of furious rhythm, two more minutes of our hands flashing, of our sticks pounding on our own drums, on the rail drums, our arms crisscrossing, even, so that for two measures we were all playing on the man's drum to our left. The percussionists from the pit stood behind the rail and held up crash cymbals. They had to brace their weight on a back leg to keep from being knocked down by the drum line. The best part of the whole break was an eighth-note rest sixteen measures before the end of the break. We knew that sudden, blistering silence, a silence like hammered brass, could make the world stand still. We were working on the drum break, just the percussion section out on the field one night, when John had a brilliant idea.

"Our hats," he said, and we all looked at him. The sky beyond the stadium lights was neon, and in that bright, artificial light, my brother seemed to glow. "In the rest. Picture it. We're flying through the drum break like crazy, right? The stadium is already going nuts, and then, in that rest, we reach up and knock our hats back." He demonstrated, miming the hat. "An eighth-note rest is just enough time."

I could imagine it. The whole band wore hard, cream-colored cowboy hats. The drum line wore ours crammed down low and flat. When the drum heads fell still in that rest, and our quick hands snapped back to reveal thirteen sweat-drenched bare heads, and then the whole line came down with a hard, clean rim shot, the stadium would go wild. The judges would be blown away. I could see the same scenario playing out behind everybody's eyes. I could see that Eugene loved the idea, but then John's eyes fell on me, and disappointment darkened his face.

"What?" I asked.

"Never mind," John said. "It's no good. The idea sucks."

"The idea's great," Eugene said. "Kind of brash, but I think you guys can pull it off. What's the problem?"

John took me by the ponytail.

"Judges don't like girl drummers. Forget it," he said.

Eugene didn't protest immediately. He hesitated for a split-second, just long enough for me to see that he truly agreed with John before he said, "Come on. That's nonsense. She'll have her hair pinned up anyway. No one will notice from the judges' box."

"Sure they will," John said. "And if the judges up top don't, the field judges will. We'll think of something else. We'll give the break some other kind of pop."

No one could forget it, though. The move was brilliant. Without it, the whole drum break seemed diminished. The next morning, I took the bus out to a strip mall and got my hair cut at a SuperCuts. I sat thumbing through an old copy of *Good Housekeeping* until the hairdresser finished picking out the gray curls on top of an old lady's head. Once the lady paid and made her way out the front door, the hairdresser took a long sip from a fountain soda and turned to face me.

"You're up, sweet pea," she said. She was a large woman with soft, flawless skin. Her short hair was dyed an unnatural shade of purplish read. When she leaned my chair back to wash my hair in the sink, I could smell her face powder and her sweat. She righted my chair and smiled at me in the mirror. "What can I do for you?"

"Cut it all off," I said. "I want it short. I want to look as much like a boy as possible."

She ran her fingers through my long, dark hair. She raised one skeptical eyebrow.

"Are you sure? You don't want something like a bob?" I shook my head. "You want to go from this straight to a boy-cut? No little pixie curls over your ears or anything?"

"Nope, nothing," I said. "Give me a boy's haircut."

"It's not my head," she said, and took a comb and a pair of scissors from a jar of green disinfectant. She turned me from the mirror and worked methodically, her comb and scissors coordinating precisely. My smock rustled when she leaned against me to get a better angle at my ear, her breasts pressing softly into my shoulder. My hair fell away in thick, heavy locks. Eventually, she turned to her clippers. She tipped my head down so she could shave my neck and part of the way up the back of my head. Finally, she dusted my face and neck with a powdered brush.

"We're finished," she said. "You're going to have to look."

She swung my chair around to face the mirror, and my new head stunned me—the sharp angles of my hairline, the smooth curve of my skull. I looked alarmingly like John. My face was suddenly lean and hard. My eyes, even, looked different to me. I reached up and touched the prickly softness of this new hair. I pressed my hands to the close firmness of my scalp.

"Holy cow," I said.

"It's a number three fade, sweetheart," the hairdresser said. "This was your doing, not mine. I better not get a phone call from an irate mother."

"She'll understand," I said.

I paid the woman her twelve dollars and stepped out into the blinding light of the parking lot. My mother was tending the hanging spider plants on the porch when I got home. She stood with the watering can in her hand and watched me come up the front steps. I couldn't read the expression on her face.

"Oh my stars, Jane Marie," she said.

"How do I look?" I asked.

"Like you've gone crazy," she said. She reached out her delicate fingers and touched the top of my head as if my hair might be sharp. "Good heavens. What is this about, Janie?"

"Judges don't like girl drummers," I said.

"Did your brother set you up to this?"

"It was my idea," I said. "John didn't say a word."

"Other than that judges don't like girl drummers."

"Eugene said it, too."

My mother looked at me incredulously.

"He didn't say it," I said, "but he didn't deny it, either. Everybody knows it's true."

"You're incredible, Janie," my mother said. "Go on. Go find John. I'm sure he'll be thrilled."

I found John out in the backyard, sprawled across the grass in just a pair of basketball shorts, studying the drum line charts. I let the screen door slam behind me and stood on the steps. John looked up. He blinked, startled, and then a grin spread across his face.

"Holy shit, my little Janie," he said. "Holy fucking shit."

"We can knock our hats off, in the drum break," I said.

"Hell yeah," John said, rising to his feet. "Come here. Get over here. Let me look at you."

I crossed the patio to my brother and he rubbed my head as if it were a bowling ball. He laughed and hugged me, pounding a palm against my back. Little bits of my hair stuck to his hands and his bare chest.

"Right on, Janie," John said. "You are the best."

The drum break was everything we'd hoped it would be. The season unfurled before us. Eugene said we were the best drum line he'd ever worked with. We took home trophy after trophy for best percussion. I spent every waking hour outside of school with my brother. I thought I was at the beginning of everything. I was fourteen, and I didn't know anything.

I'T'S FRIDAY, AND JOHN KNOCKS ON THE BATHROOM DOOR as I'm shaving before work. I jump, nicking my jaw line just beneath my ear. I've been strung as tight as a piano wire all week. "Shit," I say, rinsing my razor beneath the tap. Blood blooms from the tiny cut, tingeing the lather around it pink.

"Johnny," John calls from the other side of the door. "Open up, man. I've got something for you."

"Give me a minute," I say. "I'm just—can't I have like five minutes to shower and shave?" I dab at my jaw. John is silent out there in the hall. He hasn't walked away. He hasn't moved. I sigh and open the door.

John looks like an enormous child. His liquid eyes are wide, and he holds a box between his big, soft hands. He blinks and I am as sorry for snapping at him as I've ever been about anything. It is my job to protect him.

"Oh, man," I say. "Shit. I'm sorry."

"You cut yourself," John says.

"Yeah."

John scratches and pulls at his beard. He's taken to cutting it with kitchen scissors, as he does his hair. It's patchy in places.

"Should I shave?" he asks. "Maybe I should shave. Maybe that's part of my problem."

"What's in the box?"

John looks down at the package in his hands. For a moment it seems he's never seen the box before, that he's got no idea how it's come to be in his possession. Then he holds it out to me.

"A penis."

"What?"

My brother grins, and the child version of him vanishes. He is wicked and proud of himself.

"I ordered it. From the Internet. At the library. You'd be amazed what you can buy, Johnny." He opens the box and extracts a peach-colored set of rubber genitals. "There's a strap. It's not functional. You can't pee out of it, and it's too soft to, you know. Those were more expensive." He waggles the penis and we both watch it flap back and forth. "It's a stuffer. It's just to fill out the front of your pants."

"Oh, god," I say.

"You don't like it?"

"John, we're screwed. We're totally fucked. There's no way on earth we can pull off this thing with April." I feel faint. My vision begins to sparkle and I steady myself against the bathroom door-jamb.

"Don't be nervous," John says.

"I'm not nervous."

"You are nervous. Don't lie. You suck at lying. Lesson number five thousand thirty-three, Jane-face."

"We're just..." I say. I take a deep breath. "John. Do you know how crazy this is?"

"I can make anything happen, little brother," John says. His voice is lilting. He's suddenly talking to me as if I were a little kid. "Don't be afraid. You've got yourself thinking you have to make this happen, Janie-Jane. Of course you can't. Don't be a fool."

I look at my brother. I'm not sure who's talking who into what anymore. Even now, years later, I can't tell you any more about that than I could tell you then.

"Trust me," John says, and I do.

"It's just this whole date thing feels so much more personal," I say. "You know? Like with Sean at the store, or even with his band, I just have to be some kid. Some random guy off the street. It's like I'd have to give them a reason not to believe. With April, I don't know. It's real up close and personal."

"Your shaving cream is melting," John says.

I return to the sink and the mirror and this thing I do to make myself feel as much like a boy as possible. The bathroom is steamy from my shower, even with the window open. I am slick with sweat beneath my chest binder.

"April would make you nervous even as your girl-self," John says.

"That's true."

If April and I had met in high school, back before John got sick and I still imagined myself a normal teenager, I would have been too terrified to talk to her. She would have been one of those girls who takes a lot of art classes and walks around with a portfolio tucked under one arm. The kind of girl who gets her nose pierced, who sneaks out at night to run around, who smokes more than cigarettes. I was tall and quiet and gangly with big hands and big feet. I waited, mortified, while I failed to develop real breasts. I had never really figured out how to be comfortable in my own skin, and then John got sick, and I stopped thinking about myself almost completely. He gave me someone other than myself to be frightened for. In its own way, that was a relief.

"And you're not just some guy," John says. The hard edge of his voice makes me take my eyes off the mirror. "You're not just a generic kid. You're John. You're me. Right, little brother?"

"Yeah, of course. I didn't mean I wasn't. That came out wrong."

"That's what I thought," John says.

I splash cold water on my face and dry off with a hand towel. Whatever cloud of suspicion has come between us is gone by the time I look back at John.

"Get dressed," he says. "Put on that penis. I'll be in the living room."

I take John's fake penis to my bedroom. I take off my boxers and strap the prosthetic penis over my girl underwear. It's more complicated than it looks at first, and it takes me a while to get all the straps in the right place and the whole thing tightened down, but once I do, the prosthesis is fastened securely. I turn from side to side and watch the penis wag. I have never felt anything stranger in my life. Perhaps I am feeling the exact opposite of the ghost pains and phantom limbs of amputees. I place a hand around my rubber genitals. John was right. I never learned how to touch a penis back when I was a girl. Once I've pulled on my boxers, I feel a little bit more like myself. I put on my favorite pair of John's jeans and have to zip them differently. I pat the bulge behind my zipper. Once my penis is hidden under my clothing, it feels somehow more natural, somehow more like me. I put on a t-shirt and a plaid button-down. I roll up the sleeves and buckle my watch on my wrist. I feel as much like John as I've ever felt, but when I duck into the bathroom for a quick look at myself, I see nothing but my girl features, my high cheekbones and curved lips and soft skin. Why no one else sees them, I don't know. I wonder what will happen to me when I go back to being myself. Who will people see?

"What's wrong with people?" I ask when I join John in the living room. He's splayed out on the floor, flat on his back.

"Mostly they're blind. And they're idiots," John says. He doesn't look at me. "You look great. Even if she were some super sleuth, April would never be able to tell the difference between you and me. Did you know we have fly eggs on our ceiling?"

I glance up. Our ceiling is cracked in a few places, and I've been wondering if a patch of water damage in one corner was there when we moved in. It is also lightly dusted with tiny black specks.

"I don't think those are eggs," I say. "I think that might be fly poop."

"Flies poop?"

"Of course."

"Huh," John says. "I've never thought about fly poop before in my life. It's disgusting."

"Yep," I say, and drop down on the couch. "Sean's going to make my life hell, you know."

"Of course he is. He's one of those."

"He said he'd kill me if I did anything to hurt April."

"He won't kill you," John says. "He's not capable of it. He's just a wool-head stuffed full of hyperbole."

"He didn't actually say he'd kill me. He said he'd break my legs."

"Oh," John says, as if that changes everything. "He might break your legs. I could probably break someone's legs if I had to. And if I had a hammer."

"You're a real friend."

"I do what I can do," my brother says. We sit together for some time, silently sweating in the summer heat. "Did you know people used to think eyes were lanterns?" John asks. He looks up at me and I shake my head. "They did. They thought eyes threw out their own light, and that people saw whatever the light from their eyes touched."

"Really?"

"Abso-fucking-lutely," John says.

A steady electric current hums through me, making my skin prickle.

"What if I don't know what to do?"

"You'll close your eyes and think about me. You'll imagine, and then you'll know what to be. I'll be watching you, Johnny. I'm always watching you. I was watching you even back before, back when we were kids. You didn't know it then, but I was. I can make almost anything possible. Do you trust me?"

"Yes," I say, because I do.

"That's the only thing in the world you need. Faith. It's amazing."

My watch says it's quarter after noon, which means I should leave for work. I both look forward to and dread leaving John like this. It's become normal, but only in that way that terribly painful things can become normal if you do them enough. I stand and stretch. I am halfway to the door when John stops me.

"One thing, Johnny," he says.

"Sure."

"Don't let Dad call. If he thinks you're not here, he might. He's still trying to get at me."

I place a hand on the doorknob. "Okay," I say. "I promise. I'll make sure he doesn't."

"That's all I need," John says. "The rest I can manage."

I don't know why it's our father who John's paranoia has latched onto. He was the last one among us to recognize John's break. Our mother was the second person to see what was happening to us. I was the first. But even I didn't know what path we were headed down when John left for college.

We all traveled downstate together to drop John off that first year. It was festive and sad. John was excited and anxious, and I'd skipped a whole day of marching band practice to go say goodbye to him. When he tried to ask me how things were going with the drum line now that he was gone and Drew was in charge, I just shrugged off his questions. "We'll be fine," I'd said, "but not great. Don't think too much about it. It would just depress you." Eugene's wife had gotten a job in Saint Louis the previous February, so he was gone too. Nothing was like it was before.

"Yeah, you're right," he said. "I wish you could hurry up and graduate and come to college with me. That would be better than having you stuck still in high school playing in a mediocre drum line."

"Tell me about it," I said.

But college didn't go well for John that first year. He said the chair of the music department had it out for him. He said the faculty all wanted to bring him down a peg. He failed a couple of classes in his first semester and lost his music scholarship. He said the other kids in his department were idiots or just plain pricks. He talked about transferring, but couldn't decide on where. He failed more classes in the spring semester, and changed his major to anthropology. I knew John wasn't just having a hard time. Something had changed inside my brother. I'd spent my whole childhood running after him adoringly. Something was happening in John that I didn't understand, but it scared me. When John moved home over the summer, the fact that he was losing his grip should have been obvious to our parents, but John is right that people only see what they want to see, and no parent wants to see their kid go crazy.

John got a job working third shift at a factory that stamped steel parts for cars, so we didn't see that much of each other, really. When he'd get home in the morning, he'd tell me fantastic stories about what happened on the line over night, stories that couldn't possibly be true—near deaths in the machinery, the shift manager and his girlfriend having sex in plain view, the messages embedded in the hidden musicality of the machines—and then he'd spend the day in the basement on the drum kit. I started sitting on the bottom step again, listening to my brother, like I had when I was a kid. John would play until he was drenched in sweat. He was even better than he used to be. I quit marching band so that I wouldn't have to go to summer camp or sectional rehearsals, so that John and I could spend our mornings together in the basement. Our parents protested, but seemed at a loss for what to do. When August rolled around, John applied to move back into the dorms two weeks early. He vowed to work harder, to get off academic probation, to be a little nicer to our mother the next time he came home. And then our father carted John off to school in the station wagon, this time on his own. I knew then that the John I'd always known would be gone by the next time I saw him.

As soon as John was out of the house, I started playing the piano again. I began practicing regularly, spending an hour or more every afternoon running scales and finger exercises, returning to the fundamentals before I took up even the easiest sheet music. At first our mother was surprised. She was cautious about my playing. She'd comment on my progress or compliment a certain phrasing I'd been working on, but she tried to keep a cool detachment about the situation.

"Would you like to play together?" she asked one afternoon.

I'd been thinking about John as I practiced and hadn't heard her come to stand in the archway between the living room and the dining room. When I looked up at the sound of her voice and saw my mother standing there, so corporal and solid, I smiled with relief.

"We could work on a duet, really play something together," she said. "You've got such a beautiful touch. I've been loving listening to you."

"What could we play?" I asked.

She turned to her music library, which occupied one section of the bookcase on the far wall. She pulled out a few books and a couple of folders, turned pages and thumbed through loose sheet music until she found what she was looking for.

"How's this?" she asked, offering me the first pages of Schubert's *Serenade*.

The arrangement was difficult. I was glad she'd chosen something too hard rather than too easy for me. She placed the music on the piano's stand and sat next to me. We read through it, talking over key signatures and time changes, and sang harmonies. We agreed on who should play each part. We sight read a little bit of the opening, and even in half time, even as we both stumbled and I bumped her hard in the shoulder on a crossover, I could tell the piece would be beautiful.

"Are you hanging in there, Janie?" my mother asked once we'd finished the first movement.

"What do you mean?" I asked.

"I don't know," she said. "It was a rough summer. Now that you're back at school and everything, you're still happy about your decision to quit band? You're not regretting that now that the season is underway or anything?"

I shrugged and looked out the French windows, at the sweep of our lawn rolling down toward the sidewalk at the bottom of the hill. "It wasn't fun anymore. It didn't feel right."

Mr. Bartlett had come to speak to me during study hall in the first week of classes. Then he sent Drew my way, but when I told Drew I really wasn't coming back, not for concert band or for the next season or anything, he said that was okay. He'd asked if I'd want to hang out some time anyway, and I'd said I'd give him a call, but I never did.

"Okay," my mother said.

"I just never thought about it, you know? How things would be without John. I spent all those years looking forward to the two of us getting to be in the drum line together and I just never looked beyond that. I guess that's stupid, but I didn't."

"It's not stupid," she said. "We're all pretty blind to what's coming down the pipeline. Especially when it's inevitable."

Still we did not leave the piano, and we did not look at each other.

"How's your brother?" my mother asked.

The question made me want to burst into tears, but I didn't. "I'm kind of worried about him," I said.

"Me, too. Your father says it's a phase. He's going through something and he'll come around. I'm sure that's probably true."

"What can we do?" I asked.

"Nothing," she said. "That's the worst thing about loving someone. You have absolutely no control over what they do."

John began calling home late at night. The first time, our father rose from bed with concern. He put his bathrobe on and turned on the lights in the living room. Our mother, too, emerged from the bedroom. The sudden commotion downstairs woke me, and I was halfway down the steps when I heard my father saying, "John? John, what's going on? Are you okay?" I sat down where I was and watched my father pacing, my mother trailing after him across the living room. In their pajamas, they looked older than I usually thought of them.

"Richard, what is it?" our mother kept asking.

I leaned my head against the spindles of the banister. Our father held one hand out to quiet our mother. His head was cocked toward the phone. He squinted in his attempt to understand whatever John was saying.

"Okay," he said, and listened. "No, that's fine. What did you want to talk about? Okay. Well, no, I mean we certainly could if you'd like to, but yes, I was asleep. Okay. Okay. I love you, too, son," he said. "Goodnight then, John. Okay."

"What on earth, Richard?"

"He was just calling. He was just up studying and lost track of time. He said he was just calling to chat."

Our mother narrowed her eyes at the clock on the mantle. It was three twenty-five. She ran a hand over her forehead. When she looked up, she saw me on the stairs.

"Go back to bed, Janie," she said.

I obeyed.

The phone calls continued. At first, it was every few weeks, just infrequently enough that it would seem John had abandoned the habit, but then he'd call again. At first, he would apologize and claim he didn't know what time it was, and then he would apologize and say he needed to talk anyway, and then he stopped apologizing and began demanding things. He had misplaced something and needed our mother's advice about where it could be. He couldn't eat at the cafeteria anymore because they were serving rancid meat. His roommate was moving out, and the dorm staff was going to let him take all of John's stuff. He demanded our parents do something. He often asked for me, but our father, who was the only one to take the midnight calls, said absolutely not. Our parents didn't talk about John going crazy—they talked about his failure to cope with college life. Our father called the health center and asked about how best to get to the bottom of what might be a drug habit. They sent our parents some brochures about how to talk to your college-aged kid, but said there was no possible way anyone could intervene or call John in at our father's request. He was an adult. He was beyond our family's reach.

Sometimes John would call on Saturdays when our father had gone off to his office to mark papers and our mother was out running one errand or another. When I'd answer, John would say, "Oh my god, Jane. It's you. Thank god I got through."

"Hi, John," I would say.

"What month is it, where you're at?" John asked one afternoon.

"October," I said. "It's the same month for me as it is for you. Months are like that. They're not like time zones."

"I know," John said. "Don't use that voice with me. I've got to be able to ask you questions, Jane. You're the only one I can talk to."

"I'm sorry," I said. "I know. What's going on?"

"I'm in some hot water, sister," John said. "I can't figure out what to do. If it's October, I don't know how I'll make it to December when this train pulls into the station. At first I thought I was here to learn a lesson about myself." I sat on the couch in our living room and listened to the rising tide of my brother's voice. "But now I know I didn't come here to learn a lesson about little old me. That was stupid thinking. I was so naïve, Janie. This is about something so much more important than that. I can't even talk about it. I can't even tell you. Do you mind? Does it hurt your feelings that I can't tell you everything?"

"John," I said, "are you going to pass any of your classes?"

"That's why I need you. I hate it when they won't let me talk to you. You're the only one who talks sense half the time. Classes? I don't think I'm here for classes. Some will fail me and some won't, I'm sure. That's how things go around here."

"Do you talk to anyone?" I asked. "Aside from me and Mom and Dad on the telephone?"

"Mom doesn't talk to me. And you? I have to move heaven and earth and our father figure to get you on the line."

"Who do you have, John?" I asked.

"No one in the whole, wide world. Not even you."

"Should I tell Dad to come get you?" I asked. It was a cold, rainy Saturday, and I watched water cataract down the French windows. "Maybe it's time. Maybe you should come home to us so we can figure out what to do."

"About the fact that by all reasonable accounts I'm going off the deep end?"

"Yes."

"Because you hate me?"

"No. Because I love you."

"How much are you telling them? How clued in are the parental units?"

"I don't say anything to them," I said. "And I won't until you tell me to."

"You're a brave girl," John said.

"Is it time?" I asked.

"Give me until the end. I might as well finish what I've started here. Don't turn Benedict Arnold on me. That's what college has given me. Hysterical history. Will you keep me in their good graces? Make sure there's a place for me?"

"You can always come home," I said.

"That's a fiction and a fantasy."

John hung up. I listened to the dial tone for a while before hanging up the phone. Our father was the first to return that afternoon. He came in through the kitchen and was still peeling off his damp raincoat as he wandered into the living room. He found me curled on the couch, an afghan across my lap, reading *The Scarlet Letter* for English class.

"Hey, Janie-Jane," he said.

"Hi, Dad," I said, without looking up.

"Where's your mama?"

"Don't know."

"What's up with you? Anything interesting going on in Jane's world this afternoon?"

I held up my book. "Just the tribulations of Hester Prynne," I said.

John held out almost until Thanksgiving. His phone calls grew even more unpredictable. Sometimes we would hear from him two and three times a day. Sometimes he would call, ask for me, and then set the telephone receiver down next to his stereo and blast our father's eardrums with Slayer and Pantera. One slushy, frozen evening, my parents got a phone call from the assistant dean of students. There was a disciplinary matter involving John, something having to do with vandalism. John had broken into the music department where he intended to set a number of fires, but he caved to self-incrimination and phoned campus security from the secretary's office. A small army of campus police found John asleep at the desk. He had pulled out all of the phone cords, but the only evidence of his attempted arson was a pocketful of matchbooks from a local bar.

There was talk of suspension or expulsion, but a student judicial body, moved by John's abject contrition at his hearing, sentenced him to fifty hours of community service, which he completed in one week by skipping all of his classes. The next Saturday, when I finally got the chance to talk to him, he said, "It seems I've run aground. Let the requiem begin."

"What's going to happen?" I asked.

"This institution and I have come to loggerheads. We will have to sever our bonds. They and their people will determine if we can do this amicably."

"College has improved your vocabulary," I said. "I only understand half of the words you use."

"College," John said, "has improved my ability to lie through my teeth."

"Are you sorry you went?" I asked.

"Janie-Jane, this path has been marked out for me. To be sorry I've come would be to be sorry I exist. We're stardust. We're bits of brilliance flashing briefly through the time-space continuum. I am me. Stars blink."

"What am I?" I asked.

"A soupy suspension, mostly water and trace metals, some other elements."

"What's going to happen when you come home?" I asked.

"Only our father who art hiding in his office writing a lecture about the Spanish Civil War knows," John said. "Will you love me when I come home?"

"Of course," I said.

"Imagine that I've been in a terrible car accident. I'm all disfigured with scar tissue instead of a face. Would you love me then?"

"Yes."

"Would you love me if I've become a criminal?"

"I'd love you if you were an axe murderer."

"Be careful what you wish for," John said.

"I'm not wishing," I said. "I'm just saying."

"Hold onto your hat, Janie," John said. "We're in for something."

Two weeks later, our father went to collect John. My mother and I moved through the house like apparitions of ourselves, waiting for them. We breathed air full of static and anxiety. Let it begin, I kept thinking. Let it finally begin. When our father returned late that night, he came in through the back door alone. He was ashen. My mother and I were sitting at the kitchen table in a pool of light. We'd been sitting there so long that night had fallen around us. We hadn't thought to go through the house turning on lamps, throwing out that standard signal that life was unfolding in our home. Our father gripped the counter and fixed a terrible look on my mother.

"Elaine," he said.

"Who should I call?" she asked.

"I don't know," he said. "I don't know how to do this. An ambulance?"

The car horn blasted from the garage.

"Can you get him inside?" she asked.

"I don't think so."

I left them talking nonsense in the kitchen. I was out the back door and across the patio before either of them could say word one. Shadowy light seeped into the garage from the security light in the alley. John was splayed across the front seat of the station wagon. He was writhing. I tried the passenger door, but it was locked. I banged on the window. John turned a face on me that I didn't recognize. I could hear our parents calling me.

"They're coming," I shouted at John through the glass. "Let me in, goddamn it. They're coming!"

"Jane!" our father shouted.

"Open up, John! For god's sake, let me in!"

John reached out and hit the power locks. I jumped into the front seat and hit the locks just as our father made it to the garage door. John pulled himself into a sitting position in the driver's seat and began banging his head against the steering wheel. The horn echoed in the garage. John swore—an unintelligible streak of words and anguish. Our father beat on the window, just as I had done. I kept one hand on the power lock and sat very still, staring straight ahead. I watched us all from a great distance, John snarling at the steering wheel, me sitting so remarkably still, our mother in the kitchen dialing 911, lights flicking on in neighbors' backyards, reasonable, quiet people stepping out onto back patios to see what on earth was going on, dogs picking up the panic, barking furiously at fences. I could see the whole neighborhood, and it would have been comic, as the absurd often is, if my heart hadn't been breaking. I saw the cop cars and the ambulance coming from a long way off, their blue lights wheeling in the night. I saw them long before I could have heard the wail of sirens over John's raving. I knew what they were bringing us. I knew they were bringing us our future full of psych wards and toxic medicines. I knew some would calm John's paranoia only to cast him into a black pit of depression. Some would stupefy him, punishing him into bleary-eyed oblivion. Some would afflict him with episodes of howling, which he would weather, locked in the bathroom. Some, which would do little else, would bloat his body like a dead fish. There would be a parade of doctors and hospitalizations and clinics. There would be in-patient and outpatient therapy. There would be four-point restraints. I couldn't have known any of this, but I saw it coming. I saw it hurtling down our empty neighborhood streets with the paramedics and the law enforcement, and I sat still as a stone with my hand on the car door's lock.

I get off the bus two stops early so I can make a quick call to our parents before I get to Stew's. It's a Friday afternoon, so there should be no one home at our place. I just want to leave a message. I want to warn our father off. When I called home last week to say John and I wouldn't be coming for dinner, I didn't say anything about not calling again. Our father was trying to be so brave, saying things like, "Sure, of course. No, we understand. You two are busy. Some other time, then. We just were thinking of you. We're always thinking of you, Janie. Let us know what we can do." I didn't have the heart to tell him his voice on the answering machine was just enough to bring down my brother. I feel for him, but I also can't have him thinking he's free to try to help. I don't blame him like John does, but I know our dad's help is the last thing either John or I need.

There's an Amoco on the corner four blocks south of Stew's. The payphone out front works. Over the summer I've learned the patchwork of payphones that dot the city between our apartment and Stew's. There's one in front of the grocery store in our neighborhood. All of the train stations have them, but some have the phone up on the platform where you'd have to pay a fare. Gas stations usually have payphones, but half the time they don't work. I've come to kind of love payphones. Who knows what desperate things get said into those receivers? I'd never thought about payphones before John told me not to call home on our own phone. Now the armadillo-tail cord that connects the receiver to the phone box is as familiar to me as an old friend. So is the heavy, greasy plastic of the receiver and the silver squares of the number buttons. I lift the receiver from its cradle and punch in the digits for my calling card and my parents' home number. People pump gas behind me. The sun is high and hot, and the curb I'm standing on is soaked with petroleum products and reeking. People approach the bulletproof glass of the cashier's kiosk to pay for the gas or buy cigarettes or lottery tickets or packs of gum. Our parents' phone rings in my ear, and my pulse picks up as I hold my breath for the voicemail.

I picture our empty house: John and my bedrooms at the top of the stairs, and the bathroom we shared at the end of the hall. The staircase that curves down to the living room. The archway to the dining room where our grandmother's rosewood dining set was hardly ever used. As a kid, I thought of the dining room as a strangely elaborate hallway to the kitchen, where we had meals at the table under a stained glass ceiling lamp. Our mother once told me that the bedroom she and my father shared, tucked down a hall behind the kitchen, was the cook's quarters when the house was built at the turn of the century. I've never known if that was true or not. I picture the phone on the wall in the kitchen ringing and ringing, and then finally, the voicemail picks up.

"Hey, guys, it's me, Jane," I say. My Jane-voice is different than my John-voice, a little reedier, centered a little higher in my chest.

I think it might make my throat hurt to talk like Jane for too long, now that I'm not used to it. "I just thought I'd check in and say hi and that John and me are doing fine. Sorry again that I couldn't come home last weekend. It would have been nice. But, so listen. I thought I'd mention that it kind of stressed John out when Dad called the apartment. I'll try to catch you again soon, but if you could remember that, it'd be good. He's fine. I mean, we're good, but you guys know how he is about the telephone. Why rock the boat, you know? But we're fine, okay? Don't worry about John and me. Bye."

I cut off the call with my thumb and then lay the receiver in the cradle. Then I hustle up the street.

Sean, it turns out, doesn't make my life hell. He acts normal, unnervingly so. We're busier than a typical Friday, which makes the afternoon and evening fly. At seven-thirty, a half-hour before I usually get off, Sean comes out of his office.

"So, Fields," he says. I look up from the drum catalogue I've been considering. Sean stretches his arms like he's warming up for something. "Today's the big day, right?"

"Yeah."

"You look like shit, man."

"Thanks."

"No, I mean it," Sean says. He bends down to touch his toes. "You've been sweating it all afternoon like you were headed for the guillotine. Like April's the French Revolution and you're Marie fucking Antoinette."

"Thank you for the historical reference," I say. My skin is clammy. Sean keeps the air conditioning turned way down low.

"Any time," Sean says, and smiles. "But you can take a hike if you want to."

"What?"

"Get out of here. Watching you sweat is making me nervous. I'll watch the shop and close out your drawer and everything."

"Oh," I say. "I can't, really. April's coming by here."

Sean looks at me like I'm not speaking English.

"You've got a strange way of romancing the ladies, Fields," Sean says. He shakes his head and retreats to the office, where he closes the door. He cranks up a little Parliament, which I assume is meant to mock rather than encourage me. I go back to looking at the Yamaha catalogue, which really means turning one page after another without actually seeing anything. The music is loud enough that I don't hear the bell over the door when April comes in. I just look up, eventually, and she's standing by the door, watching me. My heart does what a heart might do if you'd been dropped from an airplane without a parachute. April smiles. Her blond streaks have been dyed pink. She's wearing more eye makeup than I've seen her wear before, and a black t-shirt stretched tight across her breasts.

"Hey," she says.

"Hi."

"You ready?"

"Sure." My pulse is a wild horse in a dead bolt. "Let me just check with Sean."

Before I can knock on the office door, though, it swings open. Sean's got a lit cigarette between his lips. He takes one look at me and one look at April and ratchets down the music a decibel or two.

"Hello, kids," he says.

"We're going to hit the road," I say.

Sean looks like he's just about to say something to fuck with me, but April says, "Don't be an asshole, Sean." Sean looks at April, then shrugs.

"I'd never," he says. "I was just going to say have fun."

"Are you ready?" April asks again.

The street beyond the plate glass windows behind her is alive with artificial light.

"Yeah," I say, and April presses open the door. She smiles at me, and I think of what John said about girls, about how they keep you in your body, how they make the world possible, and then I follow April into the night.

I DID NOT THINK ABOUT HOW MY TELEPHONE MESSAGES might have made my parents feel. I tried not to think of them at all during that long, bright summer that John and I lived in the world of our own invention. I was thinking of April as I hustled toward Stew's after leaving a message. And I could not think at all as I walked with April to the bus stop on the corner. I could only hope that by throwing my body into motion I would be able to keep up with her. How could I have known that in the early afternoon on a Friday in July, as the telephone in her home was ringing, my mother was walking into a Cineplex on the outskirts of our town to catch a mindless matinee? The wheel of my own life was turning.

I can see her now, though. I can see her, two-and-a-half hours after my phone call, emerging from the overly air-conditioned lobby of a movie theatre into the muggy late afternoon as clearly as if I had been there with her, breathing the exhaust fumes in the parking lot. The summer sun is still high above the horizon, but its light has taken on the orange hue of evening. My mother enjoys the momentary time-confusion induced by stepping from a dark theatre into daylight. She also enjoys the sticky heat of a July evening. Instead of unlocking the station wagon and heading home, Elaine crosses the parking lot to a chain café in a strip mall. She buys a cup of tea and sits at a metal table on the sidewalk, even though the patio faces a busy street that's been widened three times in the twenty-odd years since she and Richard moved to this town. She sips her Oolong tea from a paper cup. She doesn't know what "Oolong" means, and she doesn't think the kids working behind the counter do either. She watches minivan after SUV after hatchback screech to a halt at a red light. Many of the cars are packed with reckless teenagers who hang out of passenger-side windows to shout things at other drivers, or bounce around in back seats, their music thumping loudly.

Elaine has to remember that her children are not teenagers. She thinks of them as adolescent. When she closes her eyes, she sees her daughter as a fourteen-year-old. The teenage girls at the table next to her, loud, brash things in shirts that bare their midriffs, do not remind her of Jane. Jane wouldn't have had time for girls like that back when she was in high school. She never had those girlfriends that make up the average adolescent girl's universe, for better or for worse. She ran with John's crowd. She seemed happy, in her own quiet way. She seemed to truly fit in. Elaine secretly wished girlfriends for Jane. "Teenage girls only give each other grief," Richard had said, once, when Elaine mentioned something on the subject. "They make each other's lives miserable. Jane has more self-confidence than ninety percent of the girls in this town, I'm sure of it." This was probably true; Elaine thinks so, even now. But it was a curious sort of self-confidence. Elaine thought it was a self-confidence that protected Jane a year later when John started getting sick, but on this account, she now believes she was wrong. What she thought was her daughter's resilience was something more like brittleness. Something got snuffed out in her daughter back then when her son got sick, but the world was so thoroughly unhinged Elaine didn't notice it. She didn't see the full spectrum of consequence until John took Jane away from her, until they both disappeared. Elaine thinks that John's influence over Jane is independent of his illness, but there is no way to know if that is true. There is nothing independent of John's illness. John's illness infects—if she were speaking to anyone else, even her husband, she would say, "touches"—her whole world. John's illness is the eastern sky in the morning and the sky in the west at sunset. It covers all of their lives. She knows she mustn't, but she can't help but blame him. John has stolen Jane, that's the truth of the matter. Elaine does not forgive him for this. She wouldn't even know how to try.

Even these Friday afternoons and evenings alone are a vestige of the early days of John's diagnosis. When Richard first brought John home from college and they woke into the nightmare of paranoid schizophrenia, she and Richard promised each other that come what may, they would not lose each other in this. They would not turn on one another, or neglect the other, or blame or accuse or demonize or divorce each other. They had heard horror stories.

Family support groups were full of them. Family support groups were miserable with stories of familial disintegration. Within months of John's first solid diagnosis, they'd quit going to family support groups altogether.

People said, "Go on dates. Remember to romance each other," but Elaine and Richard soon found what they missed most, what sapped them dry and left them dangerous to each other, was the lack of emotional space. For the first year of John's illness, they spent nearly every possible minute together, talking and talking and talking, sobbing, waking each other in the dark for no more reason than that one of them needed suddenly and desperately to be held by the other. After a year of this, Elaine was shocked to discover that she was beginning to hate her husband. They had talked about this. Richard agreed. He was very nearly sick of Elaine. John was entering the first of his brief, heartbreaking episodes of stability. His meds were controlling most of his psychotic symptoms. He had a rotation of therapists and doctors that seemed to be working. So Richard and Elaine had decided to try Friday afternoons and evenings alone. Richard rarely taught on Fridays and Elaine rescheduled her piano students for other days of the week. They went their separate ways and did their separate things. Now, these difficult five years later, Elaine misses Richard almost ardently after a Friday on her own. It makes her heart glad to feel this way.

Elaine stands and tosses her paper cup in a trashcan live with yellow jackets and crosses the parking lot. Crowds have begun to gather at the theatre for the evening shows. Elaine unlocks the station wagon and slips in behind the wheel. She feels satisfied to know someone will soon be glad to pull into her parking space. She feels as if she's doing something altruistic. She wonders what Richard is doing. She does not assume, but wouldn't be surprised to know, that he has dozed off in his office. That he often spends his Friday afternoons and evenings sitting quietly, just breathing, just listening to the halls beyond his door empty and the quad beneath his window grow calm, doing his best to think about absolutely nothing at all, until he nods off and enjoys light, dreamless sleep.

Elaine parks the station wagon in the garage behind the house. She takes her time in the backyard, perusing the patio and flower gardens, deadheading lilies, and considering the aftermath of spring's riotous peony patch. She sets her purse on the concrete back steps and walks around to the side of the house where Richard keeps their hose coiled. She unwinds the full length of the hose and turns the spigot on so that she can water the flowers in the backyard. The fancy nozzle Richard has screwed onto the hose sends an arc of perfect raindrops cascading through the cooling evening air. The day is waning into dusk. Elaine loves the smell of wet dirt. She sprays the cedar fence so she can smell wet wood as well. When the children were small, they loved to help water the flowerbeds after dinner. Helping water meant stripping down to their underpants and flinging themselves in front of the spray as Elaine thumbed the open end of the hose. "Oh my goodness," she would say. "Oh, I'm sorry! I didn't see you there! Oh, dear, Johnny, for heaven's sake. I sprayed you. So sorry!" And he would shriek and howl and squeal. He would run in wild circles, Janie, no more than two or three, chasing after him on fat little toddler legs. They'd be so splashed with dirt and mulch and cut grass that they'd have to go straight to the bath. Tonight, Elaine listens to the patter of water on wood and leaves and concrete. She can hear the crickets beginning to sing. There is the high lilt of children's voices, but they are far away. They must be in a backyard some ways down the block. Elaine and Richard's street has become a street occupied by middle-aged couples. There are not so many children left.

Once the flowerbeds are sufficiently soaked, she turns off the spigot and rewinds the hose. She gathers her purse and car keys from the stoop, and lets herself into the house. She does not immediately turn on any lights. She enjoys the familiar shapes of her home cast in great wedges of light and shadow. Rooms with western exposures—the kitchen, dining room, and living room—are still luminous, everything glowing deep red or orange in the final moments of daylight. Upstairs, John's room would be lit as well, but Jane's would already be dark. She gets the first rays of morning light. Out of habit, Elaine steps into her and Richard's bedroom and picks up the telephone to listen for messages. The dial tone pulses, which makes Elaine's stomach drop. She says to herself, it's just Richard, or maybe a telemarketer. Someone offering to consolidate our debt or give us a great deal on replacement windows. It's just some stranger leaving us an unimportant message. She says this to herself every time she has to dial the number for their voicemail. Elaine is both relieved and disappointed each time that she is right. Tonight there is one unheard message, and Elaine runs her fingertips along the molding of her bureau as she waits and listens. Tonight, of course, the message is from me.

"Hi," her daughter says, and Elaine has to cover her eyes with her hand. "Hey, guys, it's me, Jane." The message is brief, as they always are. There's traffic or some other street noise in the background, and Elaine tries to picture Janie standing at a payphone. Jane says that she and John are doing fine. She always says this. She says she is sorry that she did not come home for dinner. She says to please not call her and John's home phone, that Richard's call upset John. She says that she will try them again soon. Jane addresses the message to the plural you. Elaine wishes she could have heard her daughter say Mom.

Elaine clicks off the phone, sits on the bed, and cries, her wet face in her hands. Her nose runs and her whole body shakes. She sobs so hard that her chest and throat ache. She cries like this for perhaps five minutes, although the passage of time seems irrelevant. This grief, Elaine thinks, exists outside of her. It is as close to her as her shadow. It lurks at the edges of her vision. It is in the very air she breathes. It is nothing short of her full force of will that keeps despair at bay for any portion of any day. It makes her physically sick, and though she doesn't tonight, sometimes after an episode of weeping, she vomits. She tries, so far as she is able, to never let Richard see her like this. When she is quiet, she picks up the phone from the bed and returns it to its cradle. She fluffs the comforter. In the bathroom she turns on the first light of the night, which hurts her eyes. She avoids her reflection in the mirror. She blows her nose, pulls her hair back into a girlish ponytail, and washes her face. She is just emerging from the bathroom when she hears Richard coming in the back door.

"Hello?" he calls, flipping on the light in the kitchen. "Elaine?"

"I'm home," she calls to her husband.

Elaine goes to him in the kitchen. The sight of Richard, just now setting his bicycle helmet on the kitchen table, propping his right foot on a chair to unroll his pant leg, his hair messed, makes her throat constrict. The very thought of life without Richard is impossible to her. She kisses him on the shoulder on her way to the refrigerator.

"Do you want anything to eat?" she asks. She pulls open the door and squints at the jumble of leftovers on the shelves.

"What is there?" Richard asks. He comes to stand behind Elaine. She pulls out a Tupperware container of a pork roast she made earlier in the week. She peels back the lid and considers the hunk of meat.

"Cold pork sandwiches?"

"Yes," Richard says. "That sounds great."

Elaine takes the bread and mustard from the refrigerator, and Richard takes down plates.

"Jane called," Elaine says as she slices the meat into strips.

"She did?" Richard asks. Elaine doesn't look up. "What did she say?"

"Just hi, really. The usual. And she told us not to call the apartment. It frightens John. I left the message in case you'd like to hear it."

"I think so," Richard says. "I think I would."

There is a phone on the wall in the kitchen, but Richard goes to the bedroom to listen to Jane's message. Elaine makes sandwiches. She returns to the refrigerator and gives each plate a scoop of cottage cheese. She slices a tomato, gives half to herself and half to Richard. She pushes Richard's helmet, a newspaper, and a stack of junk mail out of the way to make room for their plates at the table. Richard doesn't say anything when he comes back into the kitchen. He just looks at the plates and then goes to the silverware drawer for forks. He puts a hand in the small of Elaine's back, and she turns in to him. They stand like that for a moment, arms loosely wrapped around one another, feeling whatever it is they're each feeling, without speaking.

"Okay," Richard sighs, and they both sit down to eat.

Once, when Jane was in her senior year of high school, Elaine came home and found her asleep at this table. The house was dark save for the lamp over the kitchen table, as it is now. Elaine had come home alone from the hospital where John was being admitted for the second time that month. He had been flushing his meds for weeks. He'd gotten in a huge argument with his father when Richard had informed him he wasn't allowed to blast Pantera during dinner, and John had put his fist through the kitchen window. There was a chaos of blood and cursing, and Elaine had wrapped John's gushing hand in a dishtowel before the three of them had sped off to the emergency room. Elaine has no memory of what was said to Jane in all that bedlam. Jane had been standing in the kitchen. She'd watched it all happen, and as far as Elaine can remember, she'd watched it silently—the argument, the broken window, the bloodied fist, the panicked dash for the garage.

Elaine had stayed with John and Richard until John's hand was stitched, but it might have been morning before anyone came down for his psychiatric evaluation. John had tried to bite one of the E.R. nurses, which would help get him admitted. Richard stayed with John, and when Elaine arrived home it was midnight. Jane was face down in her calculus book at the kitchen table. The casserole Elaine had been baking for dinner was sitting untouched on the stovetop, covered in tin foil. A plate with breadcrumbs and a half-drunk cup of milk sat on the table near her daughter's head. Jane had cleaned up the broken window glass and the blood. Elaine touched Jane's shoulder, but her daughter did not wake. She cleared the plate and cup to the sink and then sat down next to Jane. Jane was breathing softly from the mouth, drool warping a page of calculus problems. Elaine lay her own head down on the table next to her daughter's. She put her hand gently on Jane's back. She just wanted to sit with Jane for a moment, but she, too, fell asleep. When Elaine woke, the kitchen damp and cold due to the gaping window, Jane and her calculus book were gone. At some point in the early hours of morning, Jane had taken herself off to bed.

"What are you thinking about?" Richard asks.

Elaine's right hand rests on the table, her fork buried in her cottage cheese. She looks up at her husband. He reaches out and strokes the back of her hand with his thumb.

"Nothing," Elaine says. "I'm just feeling. Just feeling sad."

"Me, too," Richard says.

"I know," Elaine says.

She lifts Richard's hand to her lips and kisses his fingers. He smiles, touches her cheek, and then picks up his sandwich.

APRIL AND I STAND UNDER A LAMPPOST AT THE BUS STOP. This is perhaps my favorite memory of us: her round face tipped up toward me in the orange glow of the streetlight, her dark hair pinned back in barrettes. She is twenty and thinks she's wise to the world, and she is used to the way guys get nervous around her. She has utter faith in her charm. She gives her attention like a gift, and though I know now that her cool was a veneer as thin and brittle as anyone's outer self, I do not know it then. Then, I feel as if the sun is shining when she looks at me. I have my anxious hands buried in the pockets of my jeans. I can feel every layer of me, from my internal organs to my girl skin, to my clothes to the boy version of me that April sees. I watch the river of traffic flowing past us on the street. I am two inches taller than April, just tall enough to have to drop my gaze to meet hers. I am John from high school, the guy I waited for after school. He'd be talking to some girl at the end of the hall, her back pressed up against a bank of lockers, her face tipped up hopefully. If they kissed, I would always have to look away. April and I are young and full of promise, as is the night. The beginning is always so much better than the rest of anything.

"So, has Sean been making your life difficult about all this?" April asks. She's got a hand wrapped around the post for the bus stop sign. She leans her weight out over the curb, and the pole swings slightly with her.

"Not too bad," I say. I can feel myself blushing and we both laugh. "He threatened to break my legs at one point, but apparently that's about par for the course."

"Sounds like Sean," April says. "He likes you. If he didn't, he'd threaten something a lot worse."

"How long have you known him?"

"A few years, I guess." April makes a pivot of one foot and swings herself a half-turn around the pole. I glance down at the bolts holding the thing to the sidewalk. "We kind of ran in the same crowd for a while, back when I first moved to the city. Now I just see him at the store, mostly. And I go to his shows. He dated a friend of mine for a minute."

"Yeah?"

"Which was weird," April says, "when you think about it. I feel like he's a little old to be dating somebody my age."

"I guess so," I say. "With Sean, I kind of don't think about it, though. He's my boss, sure, but I forget he's thirty or something."

"None of them seem like they're old," April says. "Have you met Clint and Leda?"

"Yeah. They're something else. I sat in with them last weekend."

"That's right! I totally forgot. Sean's been after you to sit in for a while, hasn't he?"

"I guess," I say. I can see our bus in the distance, lumbering slowly our way. "They're tight. Super tight. It was a good time."

"I bet you're good."

I shrug. I toe the curb. Those are my feet, I think. These are my legs and arms and hands, not my brother's. "I can hang."

Our bus arrives with squeaking breaks and hissing hydraulics, and we have to stand back to let two old ladies disembark with their shopping carts before we can board. The old ladies are wearing raincoats and clear plastic caps over their gray curls even though it hasn't rained in days. They wrestle their carts off the bus and then shuffle slowly up the block, leaning close to each other and speaking an eastern European language I'd have to guess at. April steps up and slips her bus card into the machine.

"Hello, young lady," the bus driver says, and April dazzles him with a smile.

"Evening," she says.

I pay my fare, and we make our way to the back of the bus, both of us losing our balance as the bus lurches away from the curb.

"You've got a fake, right?" April asks as she drops into a seat by the window.

"What?"

"An I.D. For Phyllis's. I just figured. You know it's a bar, right? Twenty-one and up."

"I don't need a fake I.D."

April raises her eyebrows skeptically.

"I'm serious. I'm older than I look. I've got a baby-face, I know. I get it." John suggested this strategy. Whenever questioned about my age, I should look as bored as possible. I should act like the question is so old it wears me out. April still doesn't look like she's willing to believe me. "I'm twenty-four."

"For real?" April asks.

I take my wallet from my back pocket and hand her my driver's license. She studies it, turns it over a time or two, and glances back and forth between the picture and my face. I turn my palms up.

"This is a real I.D.," she says.

"Of course it is. Would I lie to you?"

April bites her lip and cocks her head. She looks me up and down before she says, "I don't know yet. I don't know you." She looks back at my John R. Fields driver's license. "It's a nice picture for a driver's license. You look tough."

She hands me my license and then rummages for her wallet in her shoulder bag. She hands me her driver's license. It's from Wyoming, and it says she's twenty-two.

"You're from Wyoming?" I ask.

"I've never been to Wyoming in my life," April says. "And I've never run into a door guy who's from there. Which is good. I think there are like half a million people in the whole state. I get the feeling they stay put."

She hands me a second driver's license with a local address and a birth date that makes her seven months shy of twenty-one. She's older than me by three weeks.

"You're twenty?" I ask.

April nods. "Yep."

"You seem older than that."

"Maybe it's because I didn't go to college," she says. "Something happens to people whey they're cocooned for four years. I'd still be in college if I was trying to get something normal and useless like a sociology degree. That was never my thing. I graduated high school, moved out of my dad's place, and got trained as a dental assistant. It took, like, eighteen months, and the money's good. And it's easy work if you don't mind looking into strangers' mouths, which I don't. I wanted a real life, not a brochure life with college sweatshirts and frat parties, you know?"

"That makes sense."

"How about you? Did you go to school? What's your story, anyway?"

"I went to college for a year," I say. "Down state. My dad's a history professor, so school was kind of a big deal. I was working on a degree in fine and performing arts. That was the department. Then I figured if I wanted to make music, I didn't need to pay thirty thousand dollars a year to someone else to let me do it. Knocked around for a couple of years and then moved up here. I'm not planning to work at Stew's for the rest of my life, but I'm still sort of figuring things out."

"It takes time," April says.

I agree.

"Did your dad go ape-shit? When you dropped out?"

"Not really." I think about how my dad reacted when I dropped out of community college to move up here with John. Leaving school was so far from the most dangerous thing I was doing, I don't even think it came up.

"That's good," April says. "Dads can be difficult."

"Yours?"

"He's okay." April looks out the window. "I'll give you the family low-down some other time, but my pops is all right."

I realize I've relaxed. We're just two people talking. We're just two kids with false identification in our wallets, out on a date. Two kids on the bus. April tells me about the dentist's office—funny stories about what children do and even funnier ones about adults. I like the way she looks away from me when she's talking, the way I can see her picturing the whole scene in her head. I lean into her at one point, putting my ear close to her mouth when she's said something I didn't hear. I try to think how to describe her smell to John. She smells like candle wax and something sweet and something woody and girls' deodorant. When we step down from the bus, a few blocks still from Phyllis's Nightclub, April slips a hand between my ribcage and my thin bicep. I push my hands deeper into my pockets to keep her hand pinned there. I wonder if she can feel the seam of my chest binder. I wonder if she wonders what it is. Just before we reach the door to the bar, April sidesteps into an alley, pulling me after her.

"What's up?" I ask. It's dark enough that I can hardly make out her face. My brain is suddenly flooded with too much blood. April slips two fingers through my belt loops. She tips her face up and before I know what's happening our mouths meet. I can feel the fine, soft down of her upper lip, and then her tongue slips past my teeth. I catch her by the shoulders to keep her body from collapsing into me.

April drops her hands and steps back. "Sorry, John. I didn't—"

"No," I say. "Don't be. I just—"

"I know that's supposed to be an end-of-date thing. I'm sorry. I thought we could both, I don't know. Get it out of the way already?"

"Yeah, no," I say. "I mean, yeah, yes. That was a good idea, I think."

April laughs, and then I laugh, and then she puts her hands back on my belt and leans her forehead against my sternum. I cup her head in my hands.

"Come here," I say, and this time I kiss her. I let her wrap her arms around my waist. The alley spins, and I think of how this must have felt for John. For a minute I wish that I really were John. Not because I want to give him this, but because I want to really have it.

"Want to go in?" April asks. Her mouth is still close enough to mine that I can feel the words on my lips.

"Yeah, we better," I say.

April turns and leads the way, taking me by the hand. She knows the bouncer, who hugs her rather than asking for her license. He's a huge man with a scraggly beard and a leather vest. The backs of his hands are elaborately tattooed.

"This is my friend, John," April says. I am three steps behind her. "Hey, John, this is Christoph."

When we shake, my hand is swallowed in Christoph's massive palm. I would expect a man like that to crush the slender bones of my fingers, but instead, Christoph cradles my hand the way you might hold a baby bird to prevent it from struggling and hurting itself.

"A pleasure," Christoph says.

"We'll see you," April says, and then we're through the door and pushing our way into the dark, crowded, and overheated bar.

"Christoph's great," April shouts at me. "Gay as Christmas."

I nod. A jukebox blares Bon Jovi. April grins. She snakes her way through the crowd, inching us toward the curved bar. I keep a hand on her shoulder. I feel like a foreigner, but April clearly loves the role of showing me the ropes. The bartender looks old enough to be my grandmother, except she has short silver hair, and her tank top reveals broad, muscular arms. She's wearing eyeliner. The glass shelves of liquor are backlit in orange, and an antique mirror behind the taps reflects a wobbly, inverse image of the crowded bar. I recognize April immediately in the reflection. She's leaning on the smooth wooden rail of the bar, waiting to catch the bartender's attention. I don't recognize myself at first. April catches my eye in the glass. Her cheeks glow. I think about what John said, about eyes as lanterns. I return April's smile in the mirror. She reaches back and grabs hold of my shirt. When the bartender finally turns to April, her face breaking into a beautiful smile, April orders us both Jack and Cokes. The bartender floats maraschino cherries in April's but not mine.

Drinks in hand, April and I weave our way toward the stage where she introduces me to her friend. He's busy setting up, but he comes down to the foot of the stage and claps me on the shoulder. April shouts stuff at the both of us, but we can't really hear her over the jukebox. Her friend nods and looks at me impassively from beneath his baseball cap. I wonder if this is common, April dragging in some boy she's met and showing him off. The friend, who turns out to be the bass player, goes back to plugging in his pedals and amp.

April leans into me and puts her mouth very close to my ear. "He's not the friendliest friend I've got."

"I guess not," I say, and she shrugs.

We have two quick rounds of drinks before the jukebox is switched off. I'm feeling the whiskey and the body heat. Sweat runs from my hairline down my check. The sound system crackles and pops, and then kicks with bass. April drains her drink and sets her glass on the bar.

"You have to dance, John. I know you can shake that skinny ass."

For a split-second, the prospect of dancing fills me with dread. I don't know how guys dance, but I'm suddenly certain there are a million ways my body in motion could give me away. I've spent hours thinking about how John walks. I've studied the fluid movements of knees and arms and hips. My memory spins for an image of my brother dancing, but it hits on nothing. My hand is in April's. She's wiggling her way into the center of crowd. The band launches into a cover of once famously lip-synched lyrics, and the bodies around me explode into motion. April turns away from me with glee. I am saved by the crush of the crowd on the dance floor. No one could possibly know if I can dance or not, or if I dance like a girl or a guy. I am just one sweaty body bouncing chaotically to a rhythm, jostled and elbowed and smiling with relief. I have to work to stay in close proximity to April. Half the time she seems to just be dancing with abandon, dancing with no one but herself, but the other half she's clearly dancing with me. Other guys are watching her. I can feel it. Just when it seems that April's forgotten me, her eyes clear and she grins and touches me. I put a hand on her hip. I brush my fingers across her forearm. I don't try to hold her.

I imagine we're in a movie about beautiful young people having a good time. I am not her boyfriend. I'm just a boy this girl has decided to like for a minute. The song ends, and the girl tucks her sweat-wet hair behind her ears. Her barrettes have come loose and she sticks them in her pocket. She leans into the boy, says something into his ear, and he nods. She stays where she's at and he snakes a path away from her. The fact that I am that boy in the movie is remarkable to me—it is remarkable to me, even now. I maneuver my way to the bar and order another drink for April and a straight Coke for myself. When I get back, April downs the drink in under a minute and sets the empty glass on the foot of the stage. The ice melts into a brown puddle. April knows half the people at the bar. She catches one glance after another that causes her to smile and wave. Sometimes she shouts a name at me and turns me toward a face in the crowd. When the band's set is finally finished and we've clapped and April has whistled through her teeth, a couple of her friends come find us. I stand back, let her hug people and say hello.

They all look alike to me—utterly interchangeable—with their shaggy hair, flushed faces, cigarettes pinned between slim fingers. I say hello and shake some hands without catching any names.

"Hey," April says. She steps directly in front of me to get my attention. "We're gonna step out for a minute. Maybe take a walk around the block." She looks at me to be sure I understand. "You wanna come?"

"No thanks," I say. "I'll just grab a beer."

"Is that okay? If I go?" She's looking up at me from under her bangs rather than tipping her face toward mine. It's a look that's already familiar to me.

"Yeah, totally," I say. "Have a good time."

April kisses me on the cheek and heads out into the night with her friends. I watch her moving through the crowd until she disappears from sight. I am alone and anonymous and the world suddenly feels enormous. If John can hold it together, I might start going out more often. It might be good for both of us—expand our horizons, expand our cast of characters. I am about to turn toward the bar—reminding myself not to bury my hands in my back pockets, something I've always done when I'm nervous and something that would give me away as a girl in an instant—when I realize that I have to pee. I am usually careful to avoid public restrooms altogether, which is not difficult when my world stretches no further than from Stew's Music to home, but John and I have practiced for this. Mostly in public libraries and all-night diners. My pulse picks up and my joints go weak.

"Walk with confidence," John had said when we were practicing. "Don't look like you don't know where you're going. Keep your eyes down. Don't look another guy in the eyes and don't ever look at his dick. Are you listening, Johnny? They'll be pissing in the urinals and you just walk straight to a stall. Some guys are shy. Some guys have to shit. Do your business and get out of there, got it?"

I try to pretend that I'm at a public library and the only people I'm likely to meet in the restroom are homeless men and reference librarians. I head toward the hall that cuts back behind the left side of the bar. I can hear blood rushing in my ears. My breath comes ragged. The hall is crowded with girls waiting for the women's room.

I duck my head and step around them, avoiding lit cigarettes, and press open the door to the men's room. The light is bright, the floor dirty, and the place smells like bleach and piss. There's one guy at a urinal and one stall with a functioning door. I step in and latch the door behind me and fumble with my belt. A wave of something like euphoria sweeps over me. I can go on a date. I can walk into a men's room. I can do almost anything. But under my jeans and my boxers I have a stuffer strapped over a pair of girl underwear, and the whiskey has made me clumsy. "Shit," I mutter, struggling with the straps. I am an unbelievable idiot. The guy at the urinal zips up and leaves. Once I'm alone in the bathroom, my panic subsides enough that I can unfasten the stuffer and pee. I squat over the toilet, arms braced against knees, my warm rubber prosthetic penis in my hands. I don't know if I'll tell this part to John, if he'll find the whole situation funny or just pathetic. I keep my eyes on the cracked linoleum floor and the puddle spreading from where the toilet tank is leaking.

I'm just tightening my stuffer back into place, but before I can finish and get out of there, someone else comes into the bathroom. The other guy's shoes click against the linoleum, and I wonder who on earth would be wearing leather-soled shoes in a bar like this. I flush the toilet. The paper rotates lazily, but finally the bowl drains. I step out of the stall and walk straight to the sink to rinse my shaking hands in cold water. In my peripheral vision, I see the other guy approach the sink.

"John?" he asks.

My head snaps up and in the mirror I look directly at Eugene. The bathroom tips and reels. There's an enormous change of air pressure around me, and I reach for the sink. My vision sparkles and narrows, threatens to go black, but then Eugene grips me by the elbow and keeps me on my feet.

"Jane?" Eugene asks. I stumble backwards. "Janie?"

I wrench my arm free. I hit the hand dryer and the bathroom is suddenly full of the racket of the motor and the rush of hot air.

"John," I say. Eugene is between me and the door. I try to smile that menacing smile John could wield back in high school. "You're mistaken, Eugene. I'm John."

The door swings open. A guy looks at the two of us, and then steps up to the urinal. The dryer goes silent as his piss hits porcelain. Eugene doesn't believe I'm John for a second. He looks straight through me. He's the first person to see the Jane me in months.

"John, my god," Eugene says. His eyes say, *Okay, Jane. I'll play this game.* "So good to see you. It's been a long time."

I can see the clockworks of his brain turning. He's figuring what to do in this situation. It's clearly complicated by our location. Eugene holds out his hand—the way he did on the night we met him—and we shake. I don't know what to do but put my hand in his. I wonder what happens to a person when he hyperventilates. My extremities are numb, and I think that might be a symptom.

"Let me buy you a drink, John," Eugene says.

The guy at the urinal snorts, shakes off, zips, and leaves without washing his hands. Eugene takes me by the upper arm and guides me out of the bathroom. He steers me toward the corner of the bar. I could run. I could wrench free of his hand and be out the door in seconds, but how would I find April? What would I say to her? And what damage is Eugene capable of? I do not struggle. I simply let Eugene's grip on my arm guide me. His touch says, *I know who you are.* It says, *Don't be afraid of me.* There are no free stools, but we wedge up to the bar by the wall. Eugene orders us both a beer. He has me trapped between his body and the wall. My heart beats so rapidly that my sternum aches.

"Breathe," Eugene says. "It's okay. Just breathe."

Eugene doesn't look at me as he says this. He watches the bartender opening our beers. When she slides two paper coasters in front of us and hands us our drinks, Eugene angles his bottle toward me.

"Cheers, John," he says.

I tap my bottle against his.

"Cheers, Eugene."

The years that have passed since I last saw him hardly show on Eugene's face. A few fine lines crease the skin around his dark eyes. There are tiny kinks of gray in his close-cut hair, but mostly he looks to me like the man he's always been.

"Are you okay?" he asks, after I've brought my ragged breathing under something close to control. I nod. "What's going on?" he asks. Now, his face reveals nothing. I look at him for a long while, but he is impossible to read.

"Nothing," I say. "I'm on a date. This girl brought me to hear her friend's band play." Eugene turns and scans the crowed. "She stepped out. I think to smoke."

"Oh." Eugene peels the label on his beer bottle with his thumb. "And where's Jane?"

"She's none of your fucking business," I say, and the curse causes Eugene's eyes to dart up at me.

He nods slowly. "Okay."

"What are you doing here?" I ask. "If you don't mind me asking a question or two. What the hell are you doing here? I thought you moved to Saint Louis."

"We did," Eugene says. "You're right. But Brenda was transferred to the office up here a couple of years ago. It's a good city for me, you know, professionally. And Brenda's job's secure, the girls are in a good school and everything."

I try to picture Eugene's wife. We were invited to his wedding when John was in middle school and I was still in elementary. His daughters were born when I was in the seventh grade. I remember Eugene's twins as fat toddlers with their hair combed up into identical pompoms on the tops of their heads. Brenda brought them to a couple of marching band competitions during the year I marched in the drum line with John. And the whole family came to dinner after John graduated, the night Eugene told me he'd be leaving the school district. I'd known forever that after my freshman year I'd have to imagine my life without John. I hadn't known I'd have to imagine it without Eugene, too. His daughters, who were just toddlers then, are people now, girls in school.

"I heard through Frank—Dr. Hartman?—that you guys had moved up here. I've been thinking about trying to get in touch," Eugene says.

"But you haven't."

"No," he says. "I should have. I'm sorry."

"What are you doing here?" I ask, indicating the bar.

Eugene nods in the general direction of the stage. "Playing," he says. "I've recently picked up with this band. It's nothing too serious, but it's a whole lot of fun. They're going to be pissed if I'm not setting up in a minute."

His gaze rests on the stage for a moment, and I watch him watching his band mates. I want to say, Eugene, it's me. I know you know. It's me, Jane. Ask again and I'll tell you the truth. But then April is suddenly sliding up next to me. She wraps one arm around me and rests her other hand on the bar.

"Are we still drinking?" she asks.

Eugene looks from the stage to me to April, and then back to me. He smiles faintly.

"April, this is Eugene," I say.

She turns languidly to consider Eugene. She is lovely and high. She looks like a very happy child. She puts her hand in Eugene's and sways on her feet.

"He was my teacher," I explain. "He was my drum instructor a lifetime ago."

"Nice to meet you, April," Eugene says.

"Likewise," April says.

"I've got to go," Eugene says. "We're about to go on, but here, take this." He takes a card from his wallet and hands it to me. I glance down to see that the card identifies Eugene as a session musician and composer. It lists his cell phone number. "Be in touch, John," Eugene says. "Please."

"Sure," I say and slip the card into my back pocket. I might drop it in the river when we walk across the bridge to the bus stop. Eugene and I shake hands, and he pulls me to his chest. I didn't know I knew what he smelled like until I'm overwhelmed by the scent of him. He thumps me hard on the back with his free hand.

"It's good to see you, man," he says. He looks at me as if I should read some other message in his face, but the message must be coded. It's undecipherable to me. Eugene nods to April and then makes his way back toward the stage. The room spins and roars in his wake. April leans into me. Her friends have disappeared.

"Let's go home, John," she says. "I know I said I wanted to see this band, but maybe we could catch them another time? I'm not feeling so steady."

"Okay," I say.

I usher April toward the door just as Eugene begins testing and adjusting his hand drums—a set of congas, a doumbek, a tabla. I turn back to see Eugene's hand slap a bongo. Eugene looks great under the stage lights. We hit the sidewalk, and I turn up the block toward the bus stop, but April steps into the street and hails a cab.

"Let's go," she says. A taxi slows and pulls toward the curb. Instead of stepping up onto the sidewalk she remains in the street, right in front of the cab's hood, one hand held up in that universal gesture meaning stop. Her frame is washed in headlights. I open the rear door and she crosses around to climb inside. The leather seats smell like hair oil. April leans forward and gives the driver her address through the Plexiglas window. The driver pulls a u-turn and guns it across the bridge.

"So that Eugene guy seems nice," April says. She wiggles in her seat, trying to get comfortable, and I put my arm around her so she can lean against me.

"He's a good guy," I say.

"He was you teacher?" she asks, and I nod. "He's kind of hot."

"I know," I say.

"Yeah, well, whatever," April says. She sighs and tucks a hand under my thigh. We ride in silence, me watching the pavement and streetlights roll toward us through the windshield, April with her eyes closed. Perhaps she sleeps. I don't know. When we reach her apartment I pay the cabbie and gently rouse her.

"Here we are," I say. "Okay, April. You're home."

The cab pulls away just as I swing the door closed. April watches it go. Her hair is matted and stringy. She pins back her pink stripes with the barrettes from her pocket and then digs in her bag for keys.

"Listen, John," she says, once she has her keys in her hand. "Do you want to come up? I don't mean we have to do anything. It's late. You could just stay."

She shifts her weight from one leg to the other. I put my hands in my pockets, my gaze cast past her, avoiding her eyes.

"You know, I, well," I say. April waits. I swallow. "I should go."

"Okay," April says. "No problem. That's cool. I've got, you know, stuff to do in the morning and everything."

"Me, too," I say.

April doesn't move.

"So how should we do this?" she asks. "Should I call you or will you call me or what? Do you just want to say see you later, and I can find somewhere else to buy strings?"

Without warning, I realize if I try to speak I might cry. I want, more than anything, to lie down somewhere and sleep. I want April to take me by the hand and guide me upstairs. I imagine nothing but her soft hands soothing my head and then the merciful void of sleep.

"Are you okay?" April asks.

"Yeah," I say.

"I don't like a whole lot of bullshit, John. I'm a big girl. It's pretty clear that I'm interested, so the ball's in your court. I can handle a little honesty."

I lay my hands on her throat. Her skin is cool and damp. She closes her eyes, and I kiss her cheek, then her neck. She wraps her arms around me, and I can feel her soft breasts against my tightly bound chest. She rests her head against my collarbone. I think she's right. I could tell her almost anything. I kiss the top of her head and taste hairspray—sweet and bitter, chemically.

"I can't stay," I say. "But I'll call you. You can stop by Stew's or whatever, but I'll call you."

"Okay," she says. "That sounds good. I saved your number, so, you know, I can give you a ring if I have to."

I think suddenly of John pacing the living room, the telephone ringing. I can see him prowling, distressed, sneaking up to take furtive glances at the caller I.D. I can imagine the machine picking up, my own voice on the outgoing message followed by April's saying who knows what.

"That number," I say.

"Yeah?"

"It's actually not going to do you much good. It's a landline, and I'm behind. You know, on the bill. Significantly. They cut it off this week."

"Oh," April says. "Do you have a cell?"

"No," I say. April looks at me like I might be lying.

"Really?"

"Really," I say. "I know, I'm sorry. I'm not the easiest guy to get a hold of. But you know where to find me. And I will call you. I promise."

"Okay," April says.

"I had a nice time."

"Me too," April says. She turns, fumbles with her keys, unlocks the security door, and shoves it open with her shoulder before she turns back to me. "God, I could use a cigarette. You don't smoke, do you?"

I shake my head.

"Okay," she says. "That's good. Night, John. Get home safe. Don't get mugged or anything."

"I'll do my best," I say, and then she turns and lets the door slam behind her. Through the glass, I watch her make her way up to the first landing where the stairs double back. I hail a cab instead of walking to the bus. On the ride back to our neighborhood I take Eugene's card from my back pocket. I could slip it out the window and the card would be as gone from me as if it had never existed, but I don't. Instead, I slip it in my wallet. The card with April's number is tucked behind my driver's license, but I hide Eugene's in a pocket in the compartment for folding money And then I think about John. I try to think of how I will tell the story of tonight. I'll tell him everything that happened, the kiss in the alley, April's body so close to mine as we danced, the difficult trip to the bathroom, even, the cab ride home, watching April through the security door as she climbed her stairs. But I will not tell him about Eugene. I will spare my brother that.

When I step out of the cab in front of our apartment building, there is a woman leaning against our security door. She buzzes one of the apartments and then steps back onto the sidewalk to look up at the windows above her. She doesn't seem to notice me. She is blond and dangerously thin, and her jean shorts—cut off and frayed at the crotch—reveal a wide, purple bruise on the back of one thigh. She steps back up to the door and presses her thumb to the buzzer. She curses softly. I watch her for several seconds before I realize she's pressing the buzzer to John and my apartment.

"Hey," I say. She goes on pressing the buzzer. I can hear it now, the corresponding electric buzz from the intercom box in our hallway. "Hey, what's going on?"

"What?" the woman says. She turns toward me. "Who are you?"

"I live in that apartment. What do you want?"

The woman digs a slip of paper out of her pocket. She angles the paper toward the light and then holds it out to me. It's a scrap of lined notebook paper with our address and apartment number, in John's handwriting. A chill skitters through me.

"You live here?" she asks. "With John?"

"Who are you?" I ask.

"Who the hell are you?"

"I'm John's brother," I say. "What do you want?"

"His brother?" She shakes her head. "He's never talked about a brother. He's talked about a sister, but like maybe she's dead."

"Fuck off."

"Hey, hey, hey," the woman says. She holds up her hands, and a strange smile creeps across her lips. "Take it easy. I'm just here to visit a friend. Tell John hello for me. Say Penny says hi."

"Get out of here," I say.

"You're as crazy as your fucking brother," she says, "but more of a prick." She hefts a tote bag over her shoulder and heads up the street.

My keys rattle in my hand, and it takes me two tries to get the right one in the keyhole and open the door. I run up the steps, calling to my brother before I'm even on our landing. "Hey, John," I say. "John, it's me. Open up, okay? Get the door for me." But the door is locked. I drop my keys, and this time it takes me three tries to get the right key for the lock. Our door swings open into the dark apartment. "John?" I call. I listen, but I don't hear a thing. I flip on the hall light and then the living room light. I listen at John's door. "Hey, John," I say, rapping twice before I open the door. His room is empty of him. John isn't in the bathroom and he isn't in the kitchen. The back door stands open. Beyond the screen door are our back stairs and beyond our back stairs is the alley and beyond the alley is the vastness of the city and the darkness of the night. My brother could be anywhere.

I STAND IN OUR KITCHEN FEELING AS IF I AM MADE OF aluminum. Blood pumps inside of me—I can feel the labor of my heart—but my body doesn't feel real. I do not know where John is. That is one problem. The bigger problem is that I don't know where he has been or what he's done. He has a friend named Penny, which means I don't know the first thing about what John is up to while I'm at Stew's. He has never said anything about Penny. I have never considered the possibility that he has a life beyond me, the he doesn't tell me everything as I do him. What if I don't know who John is? If I do not know my brother, I don't know who I am supposed to be.

A breeze wafts in through the open kitchen door. The night breathes. Our planet hurtles through the void of the cosmos. We are utterly alone. I cross to the door and step out onto the porch. The wooden catwalk descends to the alley, where there is no sign of John. If the sky were not so washed out by light pollution, I could see the pinprick light of distant and long-dead stars. I miss stars in the city. I miss a sky that serves as an enormous window out to the galaxy. I lift my hands just to see if there is any communication between my brain and the furthest reaches of me. They rise and turn. I consider my palms, my fingertips.

"Okay, John," I say. "I give. Where are you?"

But I know my brother isn't around to answer me.

"What's this about? A little test? Is this a game, John? Is this where I ask what would I do if I were you?"

What John would do now is a harder question than what John from back in high school would do. I've got that guy down pat, but John now? He's crazy. There's no telling what he's likely to do. I return to the kitchen in search of clues. The table is empty, and the counter and sink have no more, and no fewer, dirty dishes than they usually do. Nothing is out of the ordinary in the hall. I don't usually go in John's room, so I don't know if the mess of magazines and blankets and clothes is normal. If there's a clue here, it's not a clue I could interpret without John's prompting. His room smells like him, like sweat and flesh and unwashed hair. I should think that John's smell stinks—I know a normal person would—but it just smells like my brother to me.

As far as I can tell, my room is untouched. It's not much cleaner than John's, which makes me think I should do something about that. I can't tell if my room smells like anything, but I'm pretty sure it doesn't smell like a girl. I scan my dresser and bed and window-sill, all of the obvious places John might leave something for me to notice, but nothing catches my eye, and I still don't know what I'm looking for. I cross the room and pry open the window to let in a cross breeze.

At first I don't see anything in the living room, either. The drum set sits glittering dully in the streetlight that filters in. The couch stretches across one wall, the armchair sulks in the far corner. John's pulled the blinds up, maybe that's something. Usually he keeps the blinds down, sometimes going so far as to peer between them, parting the slats with his fingers if he wants to look down at the street. But tonight they're scrunched up toward the top of the windows and the cords dangle to the floor. Was he watching for me? Or was my brother anxious for Penny? She'd never been to our apartment before. She had our address on that piece of notebook paper. She kept stepping back to look up at the windows. For some reason, this comforts me. She was here tonight, but she didn't get in. I gaze down at the sidewalk and street. Cars stream past. Teenagers climb the fence around a playground behind a Catholic church a couple of blocks up. I can see why John likes looking out this window. The world is like TV, except without the improbable plots.

When I turn from the window, I see what John has done to the telephone. He's destroyed it—popped off the number keys, smashed the receiver, pulled out and shredded the wires. A claw hammer with the Ace Hardware pricing sticker still on the handle lies on the floor next to the couch. The remnants of the telephone are piled neatly on the end table with a green and silver circuit board balanced carefully on top. Something cold slithers through me. I glance around, half expecting John to materialize, grinning, menacing. But I am alone. He's taped a note to the wall above the wreckage of the telephone. Paint flakes as I peel back the tape. I unfold the lined notebook paper. *I hope you've been telling me the truth, little brother,* it says. *I hope you know what's good for you. Love, JRF, your creator.* A vice grip closes around my chest, and I can't catch my breath. John has gone to Stew's. I don't know how I know it, but I'm as sure of that as if he'd written it here in his note. Fear and anger bloom inside me in equal measure.

I take John's note to the kitchen where I find a Sharpie in our junk drawer. On the blank side of the paper I write, *I've gone looking for you. If you get home before I do, stay put. I'm not joking, John.* I leave the note on the kitchen table and all the lights burning in the apartment. I follow John out the back door, but I close it behind me instead of leaving it wide open as he did. April's apartment is just a few blocks from Stew's, so for the third time today I head north toward that neighborhood. I took the bus on my way to work, as I always do. I took a cab with April an hour ago. Now, I'll walk. Whatever damage John's done won't be mitigated by how quickly I find him and I'm too humming with fury, now, to stand patiently at the bus stop. It is somewhere between midnight and one o'clock. I don't check my watch. I don't care what time it is.

The alley echoes with my footsteps. A stray cat wraps itself around a fence post, meowing hungrily at me, but I ignore it. I cut through a neighbor's side yard to the street. I glance in the dark windows of the coffee shop on the corner. Chairs are perch upside-down on tables, waiting for the early morning shift to come in, sleepy and grumpy, bed sheet patterns still creased into skin. The side streets are eerily empty. On one block I see a couple sitting on the steps of a two-flat, sharing a cigarette. On another, a lone woman strides purposefully, her heels clacking on the sidewalk, her keys gripped so that they protrude like a jagged weapon from her fist. Part of me expects to run into Penny around each new corner, but I don't.

Soon I'm not in our neighborhood anymore. I walk through streets I've never heard the names of, even though I travel in this general direction five days a week. I steer clear of the major thoroughfares and opt for angled, one-way, neighborhood streets, where the windows of the apartment blocks are mostly dark. This is probably dangerous. I could get mugged, I'm sure, but I don't care. A dark part of me thinks it would serve John right if I got beaten to a pulp tonight and left on some sidewalk in a pool of my own blood. Now, it occurs to me how strange that sounds, how my body felt more like John's than mine, how the things done to it might reward or punish my brother instead of me, but I do not think of that then. Then, I walk with my hands in my pockets and my shoulders thrown back. Each step closer to Stew's makes me angrier with my brother.

I arrive on Stew's familiar block unaccosted and unmolested. From down the street, I see what I knew I'd find as soon as I read John's note. The store isn't dark and empty as it should be at this hour of the night. The grate over the door and front windows is pulled down halfway but not locked. The neon signs have been clicked off, but even from down the block, I can see that some light is on in the store. Not the full illumination of the overhead lights, but maybe the lamp in the office at the back. I approach the store as if I'm moving through water, and when I'm close enough to see through the windows, I see John engaged in animated conversation with Sean. Sean has an unplugged electric guitar slung around his neck. His hands move on autopilot, fingers plucking strings and working the neck, while he responds with obvious passion to whatever my brother has just said. John laughs, revealing all of his teeth and his wet, pink tongue. I am humiliated. For him? For me?

John looks like a person you'd have to avoid on the street. His eyes bulge and dart. His thick, matted hair sticks out in all directions. His hands, which I still think of as elegant and sure, twitch and fidget and tug at his hair. His sweatpants are stained, and he's wearing untied sneakers without socks. His big, bulky frame heaves with each breath. I have not seen him outside of our apartment in weeks and weeks. Away from the rest of the world, John looks normal to me. Even if he didn't look like the beautiful teenager I idolized for all those years, I could still see that kid in him. Here, in front of Sean, my brother is a fat, possibly homeless, nut job. Even I wouldn't know we were brothers. My anger melts. My heart breaks.

Before I can think what I should do, Sean's eyes stumble over me. His face lights with recognition and surprise. He hustles to the door.

"Hey, John," he says. He props the glass door open with his foot. One hand rests on the guitar, and he links the fingers of the other hand through the security grate. "What's shaking?"

"Nothing," I say. My ears ring as if I've suffered a blow to the head. I back up, but I bump against a parking meter. Sean heaves the grate up a few more feet. John joins Sean at the door. He looks sinisterly pleased to see me.

"Come here," Sean says, stepping far enough out onto the sidewalk to collar me. He's laughing. "Are you fucked up? Are you high? You always play your shit like you're straightedge or something."

I think my knees might buckle, but Sean tugs me into the store. The Strokes are on the sound system. Sean lifts the guitar from around his neck and hangs it, out of place, from the rack above our heads. He takes my shoulders in both of his hands.

"You in there, kid?" he asks.

"Yeah," I say. I try to smile the way he's smiling, as if I've been caught, as if this is funny and foolish instead of terrifying. "I'm fine, Sean. I'm just a little…" I let my voice trail off and my eyes wander. "Gone."

Sean chucks me in the shoulder, which sends me staggering. We both laugh. John considers me over Sean's shoulder. I cannot predict him. He puts a finger to his lips to hush me.

"What the hell are you doing here at this hour?" Sean asks.

"I was just," I say. "I just dropped April off at her place." I shrug. In some ways, it's even the truth. "I was just walking. I saw the grate. What the fuck are you doing here? And who's that?" I ask, turning my attention to John.

John grins. He holds up both hands as if he's just been told to stick 'em up. His eyes are somewhere between friendly and menacing. "No one is where he's supposed to be, is he?" John asks.

"This," Sean says, clapping a hand on John's shoulder, "is my new friend. This good man and I have spent the night discussing important matters of music. I'm glad the two of you could meet."

"We've been arguing about whether music is discovered or made," John says.

"Arguing is a strong word," Sean says. "Debating, maybe."

"I haven't actually been talking to Sean," John says. "I've been testing him. He's just too thick to see what's really going on."

Sean is unfazed by my brother's rebuke.

"My good friend has inside information that would indicate all music exists already, has always existed, in fact, like our alternate selves in alternate realities, parallel universes or some shit like that, except unlike those parallel universes that seem to have no connections for traveling back and forth, we can tap into those other musical realities, if not at will, then at least with regularity." Sean raises his eyebrows, soliciting corroboration.

"Well spoken," John says. "You've learned something. I didn't think that was possible."

I can't tell who is humoring whom. John looks me up and down. He grins at me, an aggressive display of teeth, and then bites the thumbnail of his right hand.

"I came here for answers," John says. "I got them, and now I'm going back where I came from." He holds out one sweaty hand to me. My heart races, but I put my hand in his and John squeezes. "John?" he asks. I nod. "A pleasure to meet you like this. I'd hoped you'd come."

"Do you two know each other?" Sean asks.

"I know everything and everyone," John says.

Sean gives me a wide-eyed look that says something like, *Can you believe this shit?* He holds out his hand to John, but my brother doesn't take it.

"You're welcome back any time," Sean says. "It's been real, my man."

"Don't hold your breath, wool-head," John says. "I'll see you, but that doesn't mean you'll see me."

It's killing Sean not to laugh. John has to duck under the security grate, his bulk blocking the whole exit for a moment, and then he strides off in the appropriate direction for catching the bus. I want to fly after him. I want to apologize, but I don't know for what.

"Crazy motherfucker," Sean says. "Mad as a motherfucking hatter. That was unbelievable."

I could kick his teeth in.

"I should go, man," I say.

"He showed up like one second after you and April hit the road.

I was all set to shut this place down and then that guy comes strolling in."

He was watching us. John was watching April and me.

"Did he say what he wanted?" I ask, trying to keep my voice even and casual, trying to sound like I have only the typical dark curiosity about the crazy dude who just walked out of here. I try to think of where he could have been standing, what he would have seen as April and I walked out of Stew's Music and down the block to catch the bus.

"At first he was asking questions like he was going to make Stew an offer for the place or something. All these questions about how long we'd been in this location and monthly receipts and if there were other employees than just me. If he'd been a normal guy I would have told him to fuck off, but he was just kooky enough that I pretty much answered him. I'm mean, who gives a shit if some crazy dude knows what's up around here?"

"Did he say anything about himself?" I ask. "Anything about what he was after?"

Sean gazes at the blank windowpanes behind me. "Not really. It was just one of those things. This led to that, and the next thing I know we're talking music. Deep shit. He's probably super smart. One of those crazy geniuses, you know?"

I want to be home with my brother.

"I gotta go, Sean," I say, making a move for the door. "I'm beat."

"You and me both, but right now," Sean says, leveling a finger at my chest, "you are going to sit down and smoke a joint. Clint called this afternoon. Everybody's talked it over and we want you in if you're willing. Say yes, man. Okay?"

"I need to think about it."

"What's there to think about? That's the dumbest thing I've ever heard."

"I'll let you know this afternoon, okay? I just need to think things through. I've gotta go, though. Really."

"Chill the fuck out, " Sean says. "Relax. What's the matter with you?"

"I'll see you this afternoon, dude," I say, and I duck out the door leaving Sean standing, palms up, in the middle of the floor. I hit the sidewalk just in time to see John stepping onto the bus two blocks down from the store. I run and shout, but the driver doesn't wait for me.

I could catch a cab, but I don't want to beat John home. I don't want to sit in our empty apartment listening to trucks rumble past on the street or the couple down the hall shout at each other. I don't want to feel the seconds dragging by like molasses as I wonder whether or not John's going to get off the bus he got on. My head throbs and my eyes burn. Instead of waiting at the bus stop, I walk along the route until I can see the next bus on its way toward me. When I let myself into the apartment, I hear John humming in the bathroom. He's turned out all the lights I left burning, so the place is dark except for the wedge of yellow light spilling out from where the bathroom door stands ajar.

"Is that you, Johnny-John?" my brother calls.

"Of course it's me," I say.

"Come here," John says. "I've got something to show you."

I hang my keys on the hook on my way down the hall. John shoves open the bathroom door with his foot as I approach. I blink in the glare of the lights. John stands shirtless in front of the mirror, chopping at his hair with our kitchen scissors. He's been cutting his own hair for years now, but this is different. The tile floor is covered in thick, twisted curls. Great clumps of hair cling to his shoulders and chest. He pulls one of the last remaining locks of long hair away from his head and chops into it with the scissors. In some places he has cut his hair so close I can see his scalp.

"You didn't tell me, Johnny."

"What?"

"How badly I needed a haircut." He drops the scissors into the sink and runs his hands over his head. Snippets of hair rain down. His hair sticks to everything—his face, his hands, the sink basin, and the mirror. "Do you remember when you first got your girl hair cut off, Johnny?"

"Yeah."

"You were transformed," John says. "You did that for me, didn't you?"

I shove my hands in my pockets. John's head looks like the belly of a poorly shorn sheep, but even so, it's amazing how much more like his old self he looks without that chaos of dirty hair.

"I did it for the band," I say. "For the drum line."

"I was the band. I was the drum line."

He picks up his shirt and gives it two good shakes, then he pulls it on without even dusting off his shoulders and chest.

"You should shower," I say. "You're going to be itching like crazy."

"I'll shower later." John considers himself in the mirror. He touches his head and his face. He was vain of his beauty back when we were kids. "What do you think, Johnny?" he asks, turning to me.

"What's this about?"

John bites his lip. "The plan. You and me. Getting better. You're not supposed to be me forever, remember?"

"I know." I go to the kitchen for the broom and dustpan and begin sweeping up. John and I trade places. He stands in the hall while I work in the bathroom.

"You're mad at me, aren't you?" John asks.

I dump the dustpan full of John's hair into the trash. "Where were you?" I ask.

John's eyes widen. "At Stew's. I was there the whole time. I wanted to check up on you. I knew you'd know where to find me."

"Before. When April and I left. Where were you?" I return to sweeping. It'll take more than one go to get the floor something approaching hair-free.

"Across the street. I knew you wouldn't see me. I was standing right there. She's pretty, Johnny. You were right. I mean, she's nothing special. She's just a pretty girl. They're a dime a dozen, but for now, for starters, she's all right."

I empty the dustpan and take it and the broom back to the kitchen. I'd like to break the broomstick over my brother's head when I pass him, but I don't. I return with paper towels to wipe down the sink and the walls.

"And the phone?" I ask. We don't have bathroom cleaner under the sink, just Windex, so I spray that on the mirror and the walls and the sink.

"That was just a precaution," John says. "You can't be too careful with telephones. I know you think you can talk sense to our parents, but I know things you don't know. And the last thing I needed was trouble from them." John glances in the direction of the living room. He twists to scratch his back and pull at his shirt. "Will you get us another one? Maybe I should have just taken the receiver off the hook."

"You went to the hardware store for the hammer."

"Yeah. We didn't have one. Now we do. Think of all the ways we can use it."

I throw the filthy paper towel into the trashcan and wash my hands. John pulls at the collar of his shirt. I push past him and head for the kitchen where I get a glass of water. I lock the back door. John hasn't followed me.

"Hey, John?" I call.

"Yeah?"

"Who's Penny?"

John is silent. The whole apartment is silent. I drink my water and fill my glass again at the tap. I wait. Eventually, John comes creeping down the hall. I hear him enter the kitchen. I don't see him because I'm turned toward the sink, rinsing my glass out and placing it in the dry rack.

"What was that?" John asks.

I turn and lean against the counter. I wipe my wet hands on my jeans.

"Penny," I say. "Who's Penny? You heard me."

"How do you know Penny?"

"The question, John, is how do *you* know Penny?"

John fingers the molding on the doorframe. "That's none of your business," he finally says.

"None of my business? There's a hooker on my doorstep looking for you and it's none of my fucking business?"

"She's not a prostitute," John says. "She's my friend."

"Really? She looks a hell of a lot like a prostitute."

"You don't know the first thing about anything, Jane-face."

"I know what a fucking hooker looks like. Are you paying her?"

"She's my friend!" John roars. He knocks over a chair, sending it clattering across the linoleum floor. I'm not afraid of my brother, not even in all this red-faced rage.

"Up until tonight, I would have believed you. Now, I don't know what to think. Why didn't you tell me about her before?"

"Because it's not my job to tell you things," John says. "It's your job to tell me things. You're Jane-John. I'm not John-Jane, you fucking hamster-face."

"I tell you everything," I say. "I've given up everything for you. And you go trailing me like I'm some sort of criminal. What the hell is going on around here?"

"I had to know, Johnny. I had to see for myself."

"You could have..." I say, but stop. What could have happened is too disorienting to think about.

"I could have what? Blown your cover? Ruined everything? Yes, I could have. But I didn't."

"What did you do, John? What did you say to him?"

"Nothing. I pretended to be someone anonymous. I just wandered in off the street. You're not the only one who can make people see someone imaginary. It's not that hard, Johnny. You're not doing anything extraordinary. Remember that. Or at least try to." John rights the chair he knocked over and settles into it. "Would you get me a glass of water, please?"

I take a glass from the cupboard and fill it at the tap. I hand it to my brother.

"You don't trust me," I say.

"Now I do," he says. He takes two gulps of water and holds the glass up to the light. "Sean's exactly like you say he is. I could have drawn a picture of him. Part of me wondered if you'd started to make him up."

"Now you know," I say. I slump into the other chair at the table.

"Now I know," John repeats.

"How do you know Penny?" I ask. "I'm not trying to make you tell me. I'm just asking. Like a brother."

John tugs on his ear. He rocks side to side in his chair. I can't tell if he's trying to make something up or if he's just taking his time deciding whether or not to tell me anything.

"I met her at the grocery store," John finally says. His eyes skip across my face and then seem to focus on the back door. He shrugs. "It's a common enough occurrence. I helped her choose a rat poison. We were both in the aisle with those sorts of things. You know, bathroom cleaner and fabric softener, and silver polish, and other chemicals. She asked what happens to the rat after it eats the poison. Like what happens to the body. She wasn't asking me, or anybody, really. She was just asking the way people ask things sometimes. Just out of curiosity. But I told her the body gets all liquefied. The insides just turn into soft goo. She said she thought that'd probably kill something, to have its organs turned to goo. She asked if it would lie there stinking, you know, behind the walls or somewhere in the bathroom plumbing, wherever it crawled off to die. But I said I thought there was something in the chemicals that keeps the body from putrefying. Don't you think so, Johnny? The person who came up with the chemicals must have thought this through. What good is a rat poison if you end up with the smell of dead rats stinking up your apartment, or even a whole house with a basement and an attic and everything, for years and years? That doesn't make any sense. You'd have to rip out all the drywall to get at the dead rats. You'd have a different problem than the problem with the living rats, but that might be better than the problem of the dead rats. We talked about that. She said her rat chewed a whole in her kitchen wall, and that it came in from the next apartment over where this old guy lives in squalor. That's how she ended up with a rat."

John smiles at me. It's the most honest smile I've seen from him for years. I have no idea if he's telling me the truth. I have no idea if he knows, either.

"Okay," I say. I nod. I rub my eyes.

"Penny is her real name. It's not a nickname or anything. It's not even short for Penelope. I asked. It made me think of that movie with cartoon mice that rescue a little girl who's being kept in a cave. Do you remember that?"

"I do," I say. "The little girl's name was Penny."

"Yes," John says. "And the mice rescue her. But this Penny was buying rat poison, which is funny, when you think of it." John laughs.

"Is this a...I mean, is this friendship with Penny something that might get, you know, romantic? I'm just asking. Like a brother."

"A brother would put it another way," John says. "You're asking like a girl who doesn't know anything."

"Are you interested in her?" I ask. "Are you going to try to date her?"

"How could I, Johnny-John? I've got April to think about."

"April," I say. So much of last night feels warped like a dream.

"I've been thinking about her. I know it might not seem like it after all this confusion, but I've been thinking about April and what we're going to have to do. Did things go well? I know you're a sleep zombie at this point, but can you tell me? Please?"

"Yeah," I say. "Things were, um, good. Things went well, I think."

"You guys left Stew's and you caught the bus. I saw that much. I saw you standing under the bus stop and the way she looked up at you. What did you talk about?"

"Let's see. Let me think." I put my hands over my eyes and try to remember. Last night might as well be a thousand years ago. "We talked about Sean, how he's an okay guy and wasn't the jackass about all of this that he could be. We talked about how she moved to the city—right out of high school, it sounds like. She's younger than she looks. She's twenty. My age. She's got a fake I.D. It sounds like she lived with her dad in high school. She didn't say anything about a mom, but who knows. It takes time to learn everything about someone. She's a dental assistant, have I told you that?"

"Yeah," John says. He smiles. He scoots down in his chair and leans his head back. He closes his eyes. "I can picture her with all those little tools."

"She asked to see my I.D. and I showed her. She was surprised it was real, but she bought it. That was easy."

"John Richard Fields," John says.

"Yep, she believes."

"I told her how we moved here."

"We?" John raises his eyebrows but doesn't open his eyes.

"You," I say. "Me. The guy she thinks is John, right? I told her I went to college for a minute but it didn't work out. I told her we moved up this way to see what might shake out."

"We?"

"John. You."

"Right," John says. Then he asks, "What's she looking for? Why'd she pick you out?"

"I don't know," I say. "I've been wondering that. She could more or less have whoever. Sean for one, but I bet pretty much anyone."

"She thinks Sean's some old dude."

"That's true. He dated one of her friends. That's how they met."

"And then what happened? I don't want to hear about Sean. I'm sick of that guy for one night."

"We got off the bus right by the river. We had to walk a couple blocks, and just before we got to the bar, she pulled me into this alley and kissed me."

"Oh," John says, softly. "What did that feel like?"

"Fireworks," I say. I'd never been kissed before, not as John or as Jane. I hadn't known it would be so slippery, although maybe I should have imagined. John and I both have our eyes closed again. "It felt like it looks like it feels in the movies. So we go in and she knows the bouncer and the bartender and half the people in that place. She's got a whole world she lives in."

"How was the band?"

"Lame. But good. You know, they don't take themselves too seriously. Sean's band is a million times better."

"Skip it," John says.

"I used the men's room," I say.

"Yeah?"

"Yeah. I nearly had a heart attack, but everything went okay. Just like how we practiced. The stuffer complicated things, but I got in and out of there in one piece. No one all night knew I wasn't you."

I think of Eugene's face in the mirror, his confusion and recognition and surprise. I think of his card in my wallet that I haven't thrown out yet. I cut him out of the story as carefully as I might cut someone out of a photograph with a matting knife.

"How was the second band?"

"We didn't stay. April went out to get high with some friends, and then she didn't feel up for sticking around."

I open my eyes, and John is looking at me out of one eye.

"What kind of high?"

"Weed," I say. "Nothing."

"Drugs will fuck you up," John says. "I'm speaking mostly about psychotropics, but I don't trust that hippie shit, either."

"I know."

"Keep an eye on that. The last thing we need is a drug addict on our hands."

"She's not a drug addict," I say. "She's a party girl. She over indulged, and I took her home."

"You're quite a gentleman."

"There's not much else I can be," I say.

We both sit, thinking about April, or maybe thinking about me. Or maybe John is thinking about Penny. I suppose I know very little about what my brother thinks. The night beyond our back windows is still pitch dark, but the birds that nest in the eaves of the building begin to chirp. Morning is coming, even if it doesn't look like it.

"You're going to need a story," John says. "For April. She's not going to wait around. This isn't like the old days where a girl would keep you waiting, trying to protect her honor and all that. This is a new millennium."

"She asked if I wanted to stay tonight. What are we going to do, John?"

I look at my brother, but he's still slouched down in his chair, eyes closed, hands folded across his belly.

"You're going to call her. You're going to ask if you can see her again. Maybe somewhere where you can talk. Like her place." John smiles. He wipes his nose and lips with the back of his hand. "Then you're going to tell her this story I've made up."

"What is it?"

"Just a small work of genius," John says. "Just a story that's going to work miracles."

"Are you going to tell me?" I ask.

"Are you awake? Are you ready?"

"Yes," I say.

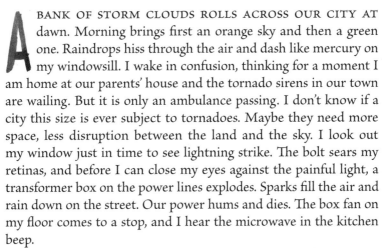

A BANK OF STORM CLOUDS ROLLS ACROSS OUR CITY AT dawn. Morning brings first an orange sky and then a green one. Raindrops hiss through the air and dash like mercury on my windowsill. I wake in confusion, thinking for a moment I am home at our parents' house and the tornado sirens in our town are wailing. But it is only an ambulance passing. I don't know if a city this size is ever subject to tornadoes. Maybe they need more space, less disruption between the land and the sky. I look out my window just in time to see lightning strike. The bolt sears my retinas, and before I can close my eyes against the painful light, a transformer box on the power lines explodes. Sparks fill the air and rain down on the street. Our power hums and dies. The box fan on my floor comes to a stop, and I hear the microwave in the kitchen beep.

"Holy shit," I say, pressing my fingers to my eyes. John snores. I collapse back into bed and am dragged down into feverish sleep.

The rain does not let up. My bedroom window is a cataract when I finally get up. A new wave of thunderstorms is muscling its way over our city when I leave for work. The wet sky crackles, and when lightning isn't ripping from cloud to cloud, the streets look as if dusk has fallen hours early. My sneakers are soaked and my jeans have wicked water to the knee by the time I get to work. Stew's is empty except for Sean doing push-ups behind the last aisle. He jumps up when the bell above the front door rings as I enter.

"Sean," I say, and Sean salutes.

"Welcome back," he says.

"Shitty-ass weather, huh?" I say. My umbrella streams water across the store floor. I toss it into the office.

"Dude, it's perfect," Sean says. He crosses to the front of the store and peers up at the sky around a neon Yamaha sign. "I love it. I wish we'd get a tornado or something. If this were still a prairie, we could see this weather happening for miles."

"I was wondering about that."

"What?"

"Tornadoes," I say. "Do tornadoes ever hit the city?"

"Not that I've ever known about," Sean says. He's still watching the sky. "Something about how all this concrete affects the ground temperature, I think. Up drafts. That sort of thing."

"Okay," I say. I take down the guitar that Sean hung up in the wrong place last night and return it to its rightful position before taking my place behind the counter. "We're going to be dead all day."

"Here's the story, Fields," Sean says. "I've told the band you're coming this Sunday. Everybody's stoked. You're in, right?"

John and I didn't talk about Sean's band last night.

"I'm in," I say. "I'm good to go."

"That's what I'm talking about," Sean turns toward the office but turns back to me before taking a step. "While I'm thinking of it, let me give you Clint's digits. He's the brains of this operation. You can talk to me, I mean, I'm kind of responsible for you, but you should know how to get in touch with Clint, too, just in case."

"Sure," I say. "Of course."

Sean pulls his wallet from his back pocket and roots through its contents. He pulls out a dog-eared business card.

"His cell and home." Sean holds the card out to me. "Don't bother them unnecessarily, but if you call Clint at home every now and again, you might get to flirt with Leda on the phone."

We both laugh. This is clearly something Sean likes to do. I take the card. I take out my wallet and slip Clint's card behind my driver's license, with April's.

"Hey, listen," Sean says. "Do you mind if I get out of here for a minute? I want to take a spin around the block if you can hold down the fort. Check out what this weather's doing to the lake."

"Be my guest."

Sean shoots a finger at me and walks out the door. No jacket, no raincoat or umbrella or anything. He squints up at the clouds. Rain strikes his head and shoulders. I watch Sean until he disappears from view. That is one odd dude, I think. The store is silent. I hadn't noticed before that Sean didn't have the sound system on. The fluorescent lights buzz. Rain hits the windows. A flash of lightning illuminates the street and, seconds later, thunder cracks. I pick up the telephone by the cash register. My pulse is light and quick. I know April's number by heart. I dial it, just like John told me to, my heart keeping pace in my chest as I watch the door for customers. April's cell rings and rings, and then her voicemail picks up. "It's April," she says. "You know the drill. Leave me a message and I'll give you a holler when I get a minute."

"Hey, hi, April. It's John," I say. "I was just calling to say I had a really nice time last night, and, you know, I'd like to do that again. Hang out, you know? Give me a call at the store, or drop in, or whatever. Let me know. Okay, talk to you later. Bye."

I click off the phone and breathe. The store is still. This is an action I cannot account for, not even now: I take my wallet from my back pocket and pull out Eugene's card. I have three numbers squirreled away in my wallet now. April's, Clint's, and Eugene's. Eugene's is the only one that's dangerous to me. I turn the card over several times, touching the raised ink of his name and number. Before I give myself the chance to think about it, I dial the number. I just want to listen to Eugene's voice on his voicemail. I just want to listen to his outgoing message and then I'll hang up, but Eugene answers after three rings. "This is Eugene," he says. I'm so startled by the sound of his voice that it takes me a moment to realize it is him and not a recording. "Hello?" he asks. My heart races and I click off the phone. I drop the receiver on the countertop as if it were hot.

"Oh, god," I say. I watch the receiver, expecting at every second for it to ring, but it doesn't. After several minutes my pulse calms down and I manage to hang up the telephone and go about my usual empty-store routine. I jump again at the sound of the bell over the door, but it is only Sean returning from his sortie to the lake. He is drenched, his curly hair streaming water down his back.

"How was the lake?" I ask.

"Amazing," he says, heading straight for the office. "I watched a front pass over the city and out onto the water. I saw three lightning strikes between the clouds and the lake. You'd think it was an ocean the way the waves were crashing in. You should check it out."

"I'd rather stay dry," I say.

"Of course you would," Sean says from behind the closed office door. A moment later he swings open the door. He is dressed in a dry set of clothes. He towels his hair. "I keep a change of clothes in the office for just this sort of occasion."

"Really?"

"It's true. I was a Boy Scout, man. Always be prepared." He tosses the towel on the folding chair by the desk. He slaps his hands against his stomach, and then steps just inside the threshold of the office and lights a cigarette. I shake my head.

"I don't know about you sometimes, dude," I say.

"Crazy like a fox," he says. He points his cigarette at me and then turns to put on music. The Jazz Messengers blast through the speakers for a moment before Sean turns down the volume to a more jazz-like level. "I've been thinking about these cats. Hey, you're an Art Blakey man, aren't you? I remember that, from your interview."

"Yeah," I say. Sean's put on the first jazz album Eugene ever played for me and John.

"The crazy guy who was in here last night had some things to say about the Jazz Messengers."

"Really?"

"Oh, yeah," Sean says. "It was like he had some personal vendetta. Like he came here to let me have it about these cats. He talked like he knew the guys, like Art Blakey used to be his best friend and now he hates his guts."

"That's weird," I say. I can't remember John ever expressing such an opinion. Eugene never managed to turn my brother on to jazz, but I don't remember jazz ever being a point of contention between them. I just remember being disappointed when Eugene stopped playing it for us.

"Everything about that dude was weird," Sean says. "He was fantastic. I wish you could have been here for the whole thing."

"I saw enough," I say.

Sean looks at me for a moment, but before he can say whatever he wants to say, the bell over the door rings, and we both turn to see April shaking rain from her jean jacket. Her work scrubs are slashed with wet streaks.

"Speak of the devil," Sean says even though we'd been talking about John and not April. He steps into the office and closes the door.

April smiles at me. She looks awfully adult in her work clothes and without any eye makeup. She stays standing by the door, and I hold my ground behind the counter. April nods toward the office door.

"Sorry about that," she says.

"It's nothing," I say.

"It's awful out," April says.

"Sean was just out in it, for the fun of it. He says the storm is doing amazing things to the lake."

"All I saw was how it's flooding the storm drains. It's like you need a canoe to get from the sidewalk to the bus." We both laugh, awkwardly. "So," April says, "I'm not trying to make your life difficult with Sean, but I figured stopping by was easier than returning your call. You're on my way, anyway."

"Oh, yeah, of course." She's waiting for me to say something more. I clear my throat and try to look directly at her, but find I can't. "I had a nice time last night."

"Yeah, you said that. Me, too," April says. She smiles. She continues standing quite still, blinking at me. She has very good posture. I straighten my own shoulders.

"I'd like it if we could, you know, hang out again some time."

April's eyes crinkle at the corners. She's enjoying this. She's willing to wait. "Sure," she says. "Did you have anything particular in mind? I kind of did the leg work the last time."

"I thought we could, um, do something low key. Do something where we could talk," I say. These are John's lines. I don't know if they'll do what he says they're going to do.

April looks at me like she's deciding something. She bites her lip and then nods.

"What time to do you get off?"

"Eight."

"Why don't you just come by my place next week some time. Tuesday? We can just hang out. It doesn't have to be this ridiculous dog and pony show."

"Okay," I say.

April laughs and shakes her head. "I'll see you next week, okay, John? Pick up take out. I'll pick up movies. It'll be fun."

"Yeah," I say. "Absolutely."

April slips on her jacket instead of holding it over her head as she had been when she came in. She waves, and I wave back as she pushes open the door.

"You can come out now, Sean," she calls. "I'm out of here."

"Later, dudette," Sean calls from the office.

April ducks her head against the rain and shoves her hands in the pockets of her jacket. I watch her wait at the light to cross the street, and then she disappears up the street.

"You, my friend," Sean says when he swings open the office door, "have got zero game."

"I know."

He points the lit tip of a cigarette toward half a dozen crates of records stacked on the floor in the far corner of the store. "Stew just bought some old guy's stash sight unseen. Can you go through them? See what's what. Get 'em ordered and inventoried and everything?"

"No problem," I say.

Sean disappears into the office and puts a Cat Stevens album on.

We spend the rest of the afternoon and evening in relative peace. The electrical storms ebb into summer rain showers. A handful of customers come in. They are serious musicians after something in particular, people with questions I can answer and needs Stew's Music can meet, for the most part. The rain keeps the foot traffic down, but foot traffic doesn't mean business in a place like this; it means kids who want to jack around on borrowed instruments. When it's quiet, I sort through the crates of records, dust off jackets, pull out the actual vinyl to see how scratched up it might be. The guy was a jazzman. The records are pristine. I sort and alphabetize them, check prices on the Internet, slap on our store's price tags. I am just about to finish integrating the new records into our jazz section when Sean says, "I bet we can call it a day, John. Go ahead and cash out the register when you're done with that." It's ten of eight. I turn off the neon signs in the windows to discourage any last minute customers, but I don't lock up. I'm dropping the last two albums in their alphabetical spots when the door opens and someone comes in. I flip two more records to finish what I'm doing before I look up.

"Are you closed?" Eugene asks. My head snaps up. There isn't even a flicker of surprise behind Eugene's eyes. He's come here looking for me. I'm holding a Thelonius Monk album. I set it on top of the other records.

"Hi," Eugene says. He waits for several moments, but I don't say anything. "You called. Earlier today. From this number. I took a wild guess that it might be you."

Neither of us has moved. Eugene stands just inside the door. His hair glitters with caught raindrops. Rain patters against the windows behind him. Eugene presses his hands against the front of his slacks.

"John?" Eugene asks.

"What do you want?" I cannot manage anything more than a whisper. There isn't enough oxygen in the air.

Eugene glances around the store, seems to register the door to the office where Sean sits pecking at a keyboard. I can hear the keys clicking in the silence between tracks on the current CD. Eugene slips his hands into his pockets and approaches me, letting his eyes travel along the instruments and the aisles, taking everything in. He looks for all the world like a customer. He stands next to me, thumbing through our records. We're so close together I can see the stubble on his cheek. He probably shaved this morning, but he could afford to do so again.

"I don't want anything," Eugene says. He's not looking at me. "You called me. I came to see what you might need."

"I don't need anything," I say. "I shouldn't have called. It was a whim. I thought I'd get your voicemail."

"You don't have to be afraid of me," Eugene says. He leans a hip against the record boxes and crosses his arms over his chest. Part of me can imagine taking two steps forward and letting him wrap those arms around me. He put an arm around me once after marching band practice. We'd had a couple of rehearsals since the day I cut my hair, and as everyone was loading up the pit instruments onto trailers to haul them back to the band room, Eugene put an arm around me and said, "Walk with me."

"You didn't have to cut your hair," he said, once we were out of earshot of the rest of the band. Night had fallen. The world was dark beyond the stadium lights of the football field. Bats dove for mosquitoes in the bright shafts of light. Fireflies flickered across the baseball diamonds. "John was being unreasonable. Judges don't have anything against girl drummers."

"It's no big deal. I like it short."

"I know you can hold your own," Eugene said. "You're a good kid. Don't let John run over you, okay? He wouldn't mean to, but you know, you don't have to let him get away with bullying you."

"You know John really well," I said. "But I know him better than you do."

Eugene let his arm drop from my shoulders. He glanced down and gave me a smile I couldn't read.

"That I know," he said.

I left Eugene standing by the fence and trotted back across the field to my brother and the rest of the drum line.

"Jane," Eugene says, his voice so soft I can hardly hear him.

"Don't call me that," I say.

"I'm not trying to scare you. I'm not going to do anything, okay? I promise. I just want to talk to you, Jane."

"I said don't call me that."

"What should I call you?"

"Nothing," I say.

"Can we get together sometime soon? Let's just go somewhere where we can talk. Anywhere you feel comfortable."

"I'm busy this week," I say.

The office door swings open. "Fields, you little shit," Sean says, and then realizes Eugene is there. "Oh, sorry." His eyes dart from Eugene to me. I don't know what I must look like.

"It's okay," I say. "He's not a customer. This is Eugene. My drum instructor from back when I was a kid."

Eugene reaches out to shake Sean's hand.

"Sean," Sean says. "It's a pleasure. John's talked about you. He says you taught him everything."

"I did my best," Eugene says. His smile is friendly and at ease. I don't know how he manages it. "But John's a talented kid. I can't take credit for much."

I assume Eugene's talking about my brother rather than me.

"I was just going," Eugene says. "I just stopped in to say hello and see if I could take John out to lunch sometime next week."

"But I can't," I say. "I have to work."

"Good god," Sean says. "We're just selling musical instruments around here. We're not curing cancer. Take some time on Friday. Come in an hour or two late."

"Friday would be great," Eugene says. "How about the Fleetwood? You know it? It's just a couple of blocks from here."

"I love that place!" Sean says. "They serve buffalo burgers. Now there's an animal that's meant to be eaten."

"Right?" Eugene asks. He and Sean look delighted to have this opinion in common. Eugene looks at me. "Let me take you out to lunch."

"Okay," I say.

I did not know Eugene's face showed the strain of anxiety until I see his expression relax.

"I'll see you there," he says, and claps his hands. "I'll see you then."

"Good to know you, man" Sean says.

"You, too," Eugene says.

I watch Sean watch Eugene leave. It strikes me that Sean knows everything. He just doesn't know what he knows. He pulls a pack of Camels from his pocket and lights one without stepping back into the office.

"Let's get out of here," he says. "Cash out that drawer and hit the road, Fields. I need a beer. See you tomorrow, right? Practice?"

"I'll be there," I say.

On Sunday, it almost feels like John and I are back to normal after his trip to Stew's and my encounter with Penny. We go to the grocery store together, where John stalks the aisles and peers around corners and eventually convinces me to buy two packages of his favorite kosher hotdogs. He also demands pickled beets, which I refuse to buy at first since I've never seen him eat pickled beets in my life. But he says that he loves them and doesn't know what I'm talking about because he eats them all the time. I give in, and by the time I'm getting ready to leave for Sean's rehearsal space in the late afternoon, John is following me from room to room eating pickled beets straight out of the can. He stabs each purple orb with a fork and eats it in two bites.

"What do they call themselves?" he asks while I'm in the bathroom putting on extra deodorant. I've already got butterflies in my stomach.

"The Lifted," I say.

"Lifted as in stolen, or lifted as in raised higher?" John asks.

I cap the deodorant and put it in the medicine cabinet.

"Huh?" I say. "I don't know. Never thought to ask."

"You don't think it makes a difference?"

"Not especially. Not in terms of whether I want to play with them or not."

"You don't think very deeply," John says. "You've got a serious lack of curiosity."

I tuck a pair of drumsticks in my back pocket and grab my keys from their hook by the door. "I'm out."

"Do you mind if I eat all the hotdogs?" John asks. "Not that I'm intending to. Just if I get really hungry."

"That's fine," I say. "Eat all the hotdogs you want. Knock yourself out."

I realize I've forgotten my watch, and I have to step around John to get to my bedroom where I've left it on the windowsill.

"If I'm not here when you get home, I'm with Penny," John says. He's blocking the doorway to my bedroom.

"Okay." We stand there, looking at each other.

"I'm just telling you because you get nervous."

"Yeah, thanks," I say. "I do."

"I'm not saying that I will be out," John says. "Just that if I am out, that's where I am. I'm with her. I'm not anywhere else."

"Duly noted," I say.

John still doesn't move. He glances over his shoulder toward the living room.

"You know what we need? A new telephone. You haven't gotten a new one. The old one's still broken."

"You know what we need?" I ask. John looks at me. "We need you to stop smashing things we need with a hammer."

John laughs loudly. "That's funny, Johnny. You don't make many jokes."

"I gotta go," I say. "I'm going to be late."

"I am never late," John says. He steps out of the way. He opens the front door with a flourish. "John Richard Fields is always punctual."

I pat my brother on the shoulder and head out into the afternoon.

Band practice is much like it was last week, although this time we play more of their own songs. I listen just long enough to get the groove of what they're up to, and then I jump in. Clint keeps us organized. He's made a list of songs to work on. He and Leda talk through a possible playlist. Sean and Roger seem happy enough to follow their lead, and I just try to keep my head down and my ears open and soak everything up. We play for hours, far longer than we could last week because the metal band upstairs fails to show up. We play until I'm sweaty and my arms and hands are sore. Everyone's exhausted by the time Clint calls it a night. He rolls a joint and everyone collapses without packing up our instruments. Leda and I sit on the sagging couch, and the other guys sit on the floor.

Clint takes the first long drag on the joint, then offers it to Roger. Clint stretches as he holds his breath. I can picture him doing yoga.

"Hey," Roger says, as he passes the joint to Sean. Smoke curls out of his mouth as he speaks. "Anybody free on Tuesday? A buddy I work with is playing Shubas."

"Is he any good?" Sean asks.

"Yeah, in a song-writer kind of way."

"Is it free?"

"Is anything free, Sean?" Clint asks.

"What the hell. Sure, I'll go," Sean says. "Want to come, Fields?"

"I've got a thing," I say.

I glance around the rehearsal space. The bare light bulbs above us cast dramatic shadows across our faces. Leda raises one eyebrow.

"A thing?" Clint asks.

"Like a date?" Sean suggests. "With your girlfriend?"

"Johnny's got a girlfriend?" Leda asks.

"April," Sean says. "You've met her."

"Ah, yes. But that's so sad," Leda says. "I'm heartbroken."

"We've gone out once," I say.

"But now you have a thing," Roger offers. "On Tuesday."

"Fuck you, Roger," I say, and everybody laughs. As if on cue, Leda rises from the couch and begins unplugging microphones and amps. She coils cords around her slender arms. Everyone follows her lead and begins breaking down and packing up.

"Want to be a friend, Sean?" I ask. "Give me a lift?"

"Sure," he says. "As long as you load up my guitar and amp."

"It's a deal," I say, and I hoist his guitar over my shoulder and head down the back steps.

Sean and I say goodbye to everybody else in the alley after all the equipment has been loaded up into Sean and Roger's cars and Leda and Clint's minivan. We all slap hands, and then Sean and I belt ourselves into the front seat of his car and speed north. We drive without talking.

"Thanks, man," I say, as he pulls the car over to the curb.

"No problem-o," Sean says. "See you tomorrow." He peels out as I'm slamming the door.

I glance up to see John's face in our front window. I startle, even though I shouldn't be surprised. John waves, and I lift my hand. By the time I let myself in the front door and climb the stairs, John is waiting for me on our landing. He's agitated, but more excited than angry, I think.

"Hi," I say.

"Don't be afraid, Johnny," John says. He holds our apartment door closed with one hand on the doorknob.

"What's going on?" I ask.

"Close your eyes," John says. "I have a surprise."

"What's going on, John?"

John cups his hands around his mouth and whispers loudly, "Close your eyes. I have a surprise."

I do as my brother tells me to. I close my eyes and sway with vertigo. John grasps my hand. His palm is hot and damp. The world is dark and unpredictable. I don't trust the floor to be beneath my feet each time I take a step. John tugs at my arm, and I follow him slowly. We cross our threshold. We veer to the left toward the living room. I hold my free hand out in case he guides me into a wall. I don't know why it doesn't occur to me to simply open my eyes. John has told me not to, and so I don't. We come to a halt in what I assume is the middle of the living room. My brother takes me by the shoulders and turns me, but I am confused. I don't know if he's turned me toward the windows or the wall.

"Look," John whispers in my ear.

I open my eyes. Penny smiles up at me from the couch.

"Oh my god!" I cry. "Oh, shit. What the fuck?"

"Nice to see you, too," Penny says. John still has me by the shoulders, otherwise, I'd bolt. No one is supposed to see me and John together. Our world would not work. "Jane, right?" Penny says. "That's your name?"

"Holy fucking shit, John," I say.

"She swears like a sailor," Penny says to my brother.

"It's a bad habit she's picked up from that idiot, Sean," John says.

"You had me fooled," Penny says. "And I can usually spot a tranny."

"John, what's going on?" I ask. "What's she doing here? What the fuck is going on?"

John finally turns me loose. My upper arms throb from his grip. I'll probably be bruised by morning. John settles into the armchair by the window. He smiles beatifically up at me.

"Penny brought us a new telephone," John says. He motions toward the end table. A black cordless phone sits upright in a charger.

"I know a guy who works at Radio Shack," Penny explains. "You can chill out, Jane. I'm a friend. I know girls who do things way more fucked up than pretending to be their brothers."

"Did you see my hair?" John asks. He sits up and runs his hands all over his head. "Penny fixed it."

I can see that now. His hair has been evened out, although there are still a few nearly bald patches where he cut too close to the scalp. Aside from that, John looks like a guy with a normal haircut instead of a lunatic version of Samson.

"Delilah," Penny says.

"What?"

"Delilah, that's who cut Samson's hair."

"I didn't—" I look at my brother. "I didn't say anything."

John shrugs. "Penny's good like that. The bathroom's a mess. You're going to have to clean it up again." He has showered. His clothes are clean. I see for what feels like the first time that John's been losing weight. His cheekbones show again. He has a jaw line.

"You've got good bones," Penny says. "That's the thing. That's what gives trannies trouble. You can't do anything about bones. It helps that you don't have tits, but even big tits can be hidden. You've got the right kind of shoulders, the right kind of hands. You've got a guy's structure. I know boys who would kill for a frame like yours."

"John," I say, turning to my brother. "Please tell me what's going on."

"I told Penny everything," he explains. "I let her in on our little game. She thinks it's crazy, of course. She thinks we're a couple of whackadoos. But she's used to crazy. She's seen a lot of it."

"He told me the story you're going to tell April," Penny says.

"She knows about April?"

"Of course," John says. "April is part of everything. Get it together, Johnny. Good grief."

"It's a good cover," Penny says. "And from what John's said, April is just the sort of girl to buy it."

"You've never met April," I say to John.

"Oh, Johnny," John sighs. He leans back in his chair, his eyes searching the ceiling for patience. "I am with you all the time. I know what you know. I see what you see. There is a trap door in your brain."

"I don't know about that," Penny says. "But you tell him, Jane. You tell him everything." Penny reaches for a jacket that's been draped across the back of the couch. She pats the pockets until she finds a pack of cigarettes and a lighter. She slips a hand under the front of the couch and pulls out an ashtray. She lights a cigarette, licks her lips, and exhales. "You want to practice, Jane? I'll be April. You be John."

"No," I say. I look at my brother. I look at his friend. "No. I don't. Please leave."

ENNY CAN'T—COULDN'T—READ MY MIND. I KNOW THAT now, and I knew that then. John couldn't read my mind, either. This is not a story about telepathy. Penny was just some tough girl who'd gotten knocked around on the streets. She'd had a hard enough go to look at my brother and see a friend. I don't know what they did for each other—I don't know now and I didn't know then. She left when I asked her to. She leveled a steely gaze at me, shrugged, and pinned her cigarette between her lips. She gave my brother a secret smile and a little wave, and then she said, "I'll be seeing you, Jane." She sauntered down the hall and let herself out through the back door. I could hear the screen door squeak open and slap shut.

I am standing, paralyzed, in our living room. I can't breathe. The way Penny said "Jane" was enough to make a pillar of salt out of me.

"You're crying, Johnny-Jane," John says, his voice full of wonder.

I choke. I swipe at my face with the back of my hand. My whole body shudders with each breath.

"You're afraid." John circles me, getting a good look from every angle. "Of Penny? Or of me?"

"I'm not afraid," I say. "I'm angry."

"That's not true. You're not the kind of girl who cries when she's angry. I know you."

"You have to tell me if she's going to be here," I say.

"How am I supposed to know that? How am I supposed to know what Penny's going to do? She's a free agent, just like you."

"You can see the fucking future, right John?" I ask. "See that. Give me a heads-up, at least."

"Okay. I'll do it. For you. You're a good kid, Johnny. I'll humor you." John lies down on the couch. He stretches his arms over his head. He twists and sighs, getting comfortable. "I think I'll stay right here, all night. I don't want to go to sleep. I want to lie right here and think about things."

"Has she been here before? In this apartment? Has she been here when I didn't know about it?"

"No," John says. He puts his hands over his face. "We usually go out and do things. Sometimes while you're at work, but sometimes when you're asleep."

"Like what?"

"We walked downtown one night while you were sleeping."

I am too tired to stand. I don't sit in the armchair by the window—that's John's spot—so I sink to the floor where I am. I lean against the archway between the hall and the living room. From here, I can just see the top of John's head resting against the arm of the couch. The living room is dark but the hall light burns to my right.

"All the way downtown?" I ask.

"Sure," he says. "It's not that far. It's just a few miles. It was the middle of the night, but all sorts of stuff was happening. This guy on rollerblades almost ran Penny over. People put wheels on their feet, and they forget how to use their eyes. We got chased by a dog that was off its leash. Penny tried to put a stick in the spokes of this guy's bicycle. She said he was a bike messenger who hassled her once, but she wasn't quick enough with the stick and he just whizzed on by without even noticing us."

"All in one night?" I say. "Dogs and rollerbladers and enemy bike messengers?"

"Yeah."

"While I was asleep?"

"You sleep like the dead, Johnny."

"Did you walk home?" I ask.

"No. We got enough spare change from people to buy coffee and doughnuts and take the bus home. I came creeping in before your pretty little eyes opened for the first time. I was sitting there in the kitchen, and you didn't suspect a thing!"

John is close to glee.

"When?"

"What?"

"When? When did all this happen with Penny?"

"I don't know, Johnny. It could have been any night. We do all sorts of things, me and Penny. I can't keep track of everything."

On Tuesday at Stew's, once an afternoon rush has subsided, Sean takes down a banjo. He plucks a few strings and begins to tune the instrument.

"I've been thinking of taking up the banjo," he says.

"Really?" I ask.

"Mountain music, dude," he says. "Hillbilly tunes. Bluegrass is the white man's soul music." He tries out a little riff on the six-string.

"Whatever makes you happy," I say.

"Right-o-la," Sean says. He turns toward the office, taking the banjo with him. "Let me know if you need anything, Fields."

A half-hour before we close, the phone rings.

"Can you get that, John?" Sean calls. "Unless it's Stew, I'm not available for comment."

I pick up the phone behind the cash register and say, "Stew's Music. How can I help you?"

There's a moment of breathing on the other end of the line. "John Richard Fields?"

I hold the phone to my head. "John?" I ask.

"Good detective work," John says. "I wanted to try out the phone Penny got us. It works!"

My eyes dart to the door of Sean's office. He's still fiddling around on the banjo.

"What's up?" I ask, lowering my voice. "What's going on?"

"Did you know you're in the phone book? All a person has to do is go to the S section of the white pages and there's Stew's Music. It gives an address and everything. Have you had a good look at a phone book recently?"

"What do you need?"

"We're not in there, though. I looked under both our names, just in case. Not that Jane and John would be that far apart. I checked, just in case you put your old name in as a signal. But we're anonymous, aren't we?"

"Yeah," I say. "It's called unlisted. We have an unlisted phone number."

"That's a good idea," John says. "That's just what we need. But how did that father figure of ours find out how to call us? That's what I can't figure out."

"We gave him the number. He's our dad. Our parents wanted to know how to get a hold of us. That's not crazy. You know, in case of emergencies."

"Oh, I know all about emergencies," John says.

"Did Dad call?" I ask. "Is that what this is about?"

"No," John says. "Does he ever call you there at Stew's? It's not that hard to do."

"No," I say. "Never. You're freaking me out, John. What's going on?"

"Where's the wool-head? How come you're talking to me without using code?"

"He's in the office. But he could come back out here at any moment."

"Risk and danger," John says. "Isn't that fun? I like using the telephone."

"Are you okay?"

"I'm fine. I'm better than one hundred percent. I was just checking in before the main event. You're not getting cold feet? You probably should have practiced with Penny."

"I'm all set," I say.

"Did I scare you, Johnny?" John asks.

"You don't usually use the telephone."

"Don't worry. I won't make a habit of it."

"Do you want me to come home?" I ask. "I could cancel if you're worried about something."

"The plan is the plan, Johnny-Jane. Don't deviate. Don't go inventing things. Do you hear me?"

"I hear you," I say.

"Don't be afraid, little brother. I'm okay. Everything is a-okay. I just wanted to say hello before you left for the night."

And then I am suddenly listening to the dial tone. My joints feel weak. I lay the receiver in its cradle.

"What's the deal?" Sean calls from the office.

"Nothing, man," I say. "It was just April. She wants me to pick up Chinese. I'm going over to her place after work."

For some reason, Sean laughs.

It's a short walk from Stew's to April's—two blocks down the main drag and three more down a side street. I do stop at a corner Chinese place and pick up takeout. I watch for dog shit on the sidewalk on April's street, as she's instructed me to. Her building looks different than I remember it from when the cab dropped us off. The entryway looks more derelict. I hadn't noticed the eerie purple light seeping from the first-floor apartment windows, but perhaps that apartment was dark the other night. A pipe vents steam and the scent of dryer sheets from the basement. Someone's playing reggae. I find April's name on the list of buzzers and press the button. I can't tell if anything has happened. I wait and listen, but hear nothing. I'm wondering if I should ring her buzzer again, when I hear a screen scraping in its tracks. April sticks her head out of a window three stories above me.

"I thought that might be you," she says.

Every time I see her, I feel as if I've forgotten what she looks like. Her face is both familiar to me and surprisingly pretty every time I see it. This is true even when she's hanging out of a window.

"Hi," I say.

"What did you bring me?" she asks.

"What?"

"The takeout. What did you bring me?"

"Oh," I say. "Chinese. Shrimp lo mein or General Tso's chicken. Take your pick."

April leans her forearms on the windowsill, her whole upper body stretched out over the sidewalk. Her hair falls forward.

"You look pretty," I say.

April laughs. She disappears from the window, and a moment later, the security door buzzes and I let myself in. I feel increasingly faint as I climb the stairs, increasingly far from myself, so that by the time I reach April's landing and find she's leaning against the doorjamb, her hands buried in the pockets of her jeans, I feel as if I'm watching myself from a great distance. I am a nervous kid—John from back before, but a shyer John, a John who is less sure. April doesn't move from the threshold, and this John stands on the landing, his pulse rushing in his ears.

"You don't need to tell me I look pretty to get up to my apartment," April says. She takes the plastic bag from my hand. "I'm hungry. I would have let you up just for the takeout."

"Hi," I say. I don't know how to have the conversation she's having.

"Hi." She smiles. "You look terrified."

"I'm okay."

April puts a finger to her cheek. "Kiss me here," she says.

I do. I brush my dry lips against the softness of her cheek. I wonder if she can hear the roar of my heartbeat. She steps back into the apartment, and I follow her.

"So here we are," she says, making a sweeping gesture with her free hand that takes in the living room. Dripping candles burn on the coffee table, the top of the TV, and a bookshelf, filling the room with the scent of beeswax. One wall is covered by a large piece of cloth with a blue and green tree printed on it. Strange animals and complicated flowers crowd the branches. A poster of an old photograph of ballet dancers is tacked to the opposite wall. The dancers are on a break, their long bodies draped over battered couches and chairs, their feet and legs bound in dance slippers and tape. Some are stretching. Some languidly smoke cigarettes. April shoves magazines, catalogues, and unopened mail out of the way to make room for the takeout on the coffee table.

"Nice place," I say.

"I like it," she says, looking around. "Let's do the tour."

She takes me by the hand and leads me down a narrow hall. "Bathroom." She pushes open the door without pausing. "Bedroom." She flips on the light, but we don't go in. Her bed is a full-sized mattress on the floor in the middle of the room. It's covered with pillows and a billowing down comforter. Clothes and books are strewn across the floor. A pipe sits on the windowsill. Her guitar rests on a stand in the far corner. A beaded curtain hangs in front of her closet. "Sorry it's a mess. I thought about picking up, but didn't."

"I've seen worse," I say.

She looks at me sideways and flips off the light.

"I mean, in general, you know. Not like some other girl's room, specifically."

She kisses the back of my hand. "You crack me up." She looks at me seriously for a moment. "It feels like a long time."

"I know," I say. "I've missed you." As I say it, I know that it's true.

She smiles. She leads the way to the tiny kitchen at the back of the apartment. It's hardly bigger than a pantry, just enough room to turn around between the two-burner stove and sink on one side and the tiny fridge and cramped counter on the other.

"Beer?" April asks.

"Sure," I say.

When she opens the refrigerator, I can see it's nearly empty. A couple cups of yogurt, a wrinkled grapefruit, a box of Pop-tarts, and a case of beer litter the inside. We return to the living room and settle ourselves on the couch with our cartons of Chinese food— April chooses the chicken—and chopsticks. April is better with hers than I am with mine. She is, I know, better than me at almost everything. She eats with precision, one slice of chicken, one baby corn, and one curl of green pepper at a time. I struggle with the lo mein and end up dropping a greasy pile of noodles in my lap. April laughs. She's nestled herself into the far corner of the couch, her legs stretched out toward me, taking evident pleasure in watching me dab at myself with paper napkins.

"Sorry," I say. "I think I got some on your couch."

"Whatever," April says. "Clumsy is cute. So what's new? Tell me something."

She's got an egg roll between her chopsticks, and she bites it in half.

"Um, well," I say. "Nothing's new, I guess. It's been a pretty normal sort of week."

"I hardly know you. Everything about you is new to me. Tell me something."

"Sean says the band wants me in," I say. "Clint and everybody talked it over."

"That's news! Did you say yes?"

"Yeah," I say. "I think I fit. It was super fun."

"I bet you're good." April considers me, her head cocked to the right.

"I'm all right. I learned from the best."

"That Eugene character," April says. I think of April leaning against me, placing her soft, damp hand in Eugene's. He is a secret she doesn't know we share.

"Yeah," I say.

"Can I ask you something?"

"Shoot," I say.

"This quiet-guy thing isn't an act, is it?"

"How do you mean?"

"When you first started working at Stew's, I thought you might be one of those blowhards who's so full of himself that he thinks he can get away with this head-down, who-me routine. It takes a lot of nerve to assume you're so awesome that you don't have to do anything to be noticed. But that's not you, is it?"

I look at her. I look down into my carton and fish out a pink, butterflied shrimp.

"No."

"I haven't quite figured you out." April scoops rice onto her chicken with her chopsticks. "What have you figured out about me?"

"Nothing," I say.

"That's a lie," April says. "Girls like me are easy to read. Everything's on the surface."

"I'm kind of new at this, April," I say. "I'm doing my best."

She looks at me, an incredible tenderness in her eyes.

"I believe you. I haven't met anyone who was new at this in a long, long time. I think it's what I like about you."

"That I'm clueless?"

"That you're harmless," April says. "I'm not afraid of you."

We look at each other across the couch. I wouldn't have known that fear had anything to do with it.

"No offense," April says as she turns her attention back toward her General Tso's chicken, "but I could totally take you if I had to."

We both laugh.

"I know."

When we've finished eating, April takes the empty cartons to the trash in the kitchen and comes back with two more beers. She hands one to me, puts a DVD in, and kills the lights. The candles throw great shadows against the walls. She picks up the remote and presses a few buttons, then tosses the remote on the couch.

"How do you feel about *The Breakfast Club*? What's your opinion of the 1980s?"

"I've never seen it," I say.

"What?"

I shrug. "Never saw it."

"You're the strangest person I've ever met. It's like you're from a foreign country or something. This movie, and *Heathers*, pretty much saved my life in high school. You are now required to like them."

"I do," I say. "I like them both already."

April steps around the coffee table and sits very close to me. Images flash across the screen and sound blares from the television, but all I register is sound and light. April rests her hand on my thigh. My stomach drops and my heart rate picks up. She runs her fingernails along the inseam of my jeans. She has to feel all my muscles stiffen. I can hardly breathe. My heart bangs painfully against the walls of my chest. I've practiced saying, April, I have to tell you something, so many times that the words hardly make sense. I still her hand with my own, but she shifts my hand to her own knee. She seems content to sit like this, our hands on each other's legs, our bodies warm and close on the couch. We watch the opening credits. April's hand is warm on my thigh. She turns and kisses me on the neck. I have no idea what's happening on the television.

"April," I say. My lips are dry enough to split. My system is swamped with adrenaline. April puts a hand on my chest and I press it to my sternum.

"Shhh," she says. She doesn't struggle against the way I've pinned her hand. I feel her breath on my neck and then her cool teeth on my ear.

"I can't." My voice is so thin. I can't imagine how she hears me.

She slips her hands out of my grip. "You can't or you don't want to?" she asks.

"I want to," I say, "but I can't."

She turns and props her feet up on the coffee table. We're both staring directly at the flashing images on the TV. Teenagers are harassing each other in detention.

"You can't like you don't know me well enough, or you can't make-out with the TV on, or you're secretly married or something?"

"I can't like I have to tell you something," I say.

April reaches across the couch and grabs the remote. She clicks off the television, and now only the candles light the room. One has flared up and started to smoke. I turn, and we sit cross-legged facing each other on the couch. She runs her hands through her hair and takes a deep breath. Her pink streaks have faded to a salmon color. They look orange in the candlelight.

"I'm ready," she says.

I look at my hands in my lap. I turn them palm up and consider their thick calluses. I conjure John.

"I can't because I've never," I say. Words evaporate. I'm floundering as I search for my next sentence. I can see that April thinks this is the end of the story rather than the beginning.

"Hey, John, hey," she says. We're both whispering. "That's okay."

"I know," I say. "But it's not. I've never because I can't. I have to tell you the whole thing, okay?"

"Okay."

We're too close together. Our legs touch. I stand up and cross to an ottoman in the corner, leaving April on the couch. I sit, legs spread, elbows on knees.

"So," I say. "There was this accident when I was a kid."

April sits with her hands folded in her lap. She nods. She waits patiently.

"I was eleven, just this kid," I say. "And there were these older boys in my neighborhood—you know, skater punks, really cool. And they kind of gave me a hard time, but I liked it, you know? I was one of them in this junior varsity sort of way. That's how I thought about it. I don't know. They probably thought I was just some twerp kid to hassle. So these guys, these kids, they sometimes blew stuff up. High school shit. They made little pipe bombs and blew up mailboxes and trashcans and stuff. I wanted to impress them, so I figured out how to make a gasoline bomb with a Mason jar. I know how stupid it sounds, but I was just a kid. I was a fucking idiot kid. So I make this little bomb. In my dad's garage—gas from the lawnmower and everything, right? And I'm really proud of it, this little glass jar of destruction, and the next time I hear their skateboards in the alley, I go out back to find them. I don't think they knew what to do with me. They're giving me shit, you know? Saying it's not real, it's just water in there, and I'm saying no, it's real, I made it. And this one guy keeps flicking his lighter at me, keeps saying if it's real we should blow the fucking thing up. I keep backing off, trying to stay out of his way, and he's saying, Come on, Johnny. What's the problem? What, are you afraid? He grabs me and gets me in this one-armed half nelson. He's still flicking his lighter and I'm twisting and turning, and I don't think he meant to, but the next thing we know, the thing's lit. It's a rag fuse. I'm standing there with a Mason jar full of gasoline, and these guys go white as ghosts and bolt. I'm frozen. I don't know what to do and then somebody yells, Drop it! And somebody else yells, Run! I drop the thing, but it's glass, right? I mean, it's a fucking Mason jar full of gasoline and when it hits the asphalt at my feet it explodes."

As I speak the words, it's as if I remember the trauma. I remember the searing light and heat, the glass shards ripping into me. I could tell April about the blood and the burns and the ambulance and the hospital. John looked up everything I could ever need to know about a burn unit, but it's not just John's story. It's mine. It's not just a story, even. I don't feel like I'm describing something that could have happened to someone else. I'm telling April about me. I look up at her. Her fingers are pressed to her lips. Even in the yellow, uneven light of the candles I can see that she's pale, that her nose and eyes are red. I don't know what my face looks like. When I blink, tears wet my cheek. I lick my lips.

"I don't remember a whole lot," I say. "Just this blinding hot pain and this bright light and the sound of people screaming, and then I blacked out completely until the ambulance showed up."

I tell her how the glass shards ripped into me from groin to chest, the third degree burns that stretched from pelvic bone to sternum. I explain how I must have thrown my arms wide in terror when I dropped the jar, exposing the trunk of my body to the full force of the blast. I give her a few details about the surgeries that followed, the open wounds and the skin grafts. I tell her that I still wear compression garments because of the scarring across my chest. I pull my t-shirt and undershirt away from my throat and show her the top of my chest binder.

"And I'm, I mean you can imagine, I'm pretty mangled down there," I say.

April nods. She's gone totally silent. She doesn't take her hands away from her mouth.

"I've never had a girlfriend. It's always been easier to just pretend I didn't have those feelings than to try to figure out what to do about them." April's shadow dances wildly behind her. She is beautiful. She looks so frightened. I try to smile, but I don't think it does any good. "I don't know what you want to do. I'm kind of messed up in ways you never bargained for, so I'd get it if you didn't want to keep seeing me. I could go back to being how I was before. I wouldn't blame you for anything."

"Come here, John," April says.

I cross the room and sit on the edge of the coffee table in front of her. I feel like I could do anything. I could touch her. I could tuck a lock of hair behind her ear. She takes my hand and holds it in her lap.

"Does it hurt?" she asks. She blinks. I meet her wet gaze.

"Not nearly the way it used to," I say. "But sometimes. Sometimes everything aches."

April leans across the space between us and presses her wet mouth against my chapped lips. We stay like that for a long moment—our mouths pressed hard together—and then I rest my head on her shoulder.

"I'm afraid," I say. This is part of the story too. John and I have practiced this.

"Why?" she asks. "Of what?"

"I'm afraid of you." We look at each other, and I don't even have to pretend that this part is true. "I'm afraid you'll want to see me. You'll want to touch me. That you'll say you don't care how bad it is, that if I trust you I'll let you see all of me. I don't know if I'm ever going to be ready for that. I'm afraid you'll eventually want something I'm not capable of."

"I'd never," April says. She takes my head in her hands. "Okay, John? I would never. I'll always take your lead. Always. I promise, okay?"

"Okay," I say. I am miles from whoever I used to be. I am dreaming us. I watch as April strokes this frightened, damaged boy's head. He touches her face with his fingertips. They are both crying. "Can you show me how to touch you?" he whispers. "I don't know what to do."

April is silent. She lays the boy's hands on her neck, lets them rest there. He strokes the soft skin behind her ears. She tips her head back to enjoy the touch. She tips her face to the right so that he'll run his fingers over her throat. She shows him how to slide his hands into her hair. She takes him gently by the wrists, as if taking his pulse, and guides his hands down, over her chest, just over the outside curve of her breasts. She puts his hands on her hips and lets him slide his fingers under the hem of her shirt. She shows him how to stroke the soft roll of her stomach, how to run his thumbs over her ribs. When she places his hands on her breasts, she lets go, and the two of them look at each other, feeling the way her chest rises with each breath. She peels off her t-shirt. Her skin is almost gold in this light. He lets his hands rest where they are, and she reaches behind her back to unclasp her bra. He sighs when she slides the bra out from under his hands and there is nothing between her skin and his. She puts her hands over his and he lifts the weight of her breasts in his palms. For the first time, April closes her eyes. He leans forward, wanting to feel her warm, soft skin against his lips.

"Are you awake?" April asks, and I realize I must not have been by the way I start.

"What? Yes," I say. My heart is suddenly hammering. I don't know what I must have been dreaming. April is curled in front of me on the couch, her back to my belly. The curve of her shoulder looks like a sand dune in this light. "I should go," I say.

"Don't go," April says. "Stay."

My watch is on the coffee table. The candles have all burned down to nothing. I don't know what time it is.

"Tell me something," April says. "I want to feel close to you."

"You already know more about me than anybody else does."

"Tell me more," April says. "If you can tell me about the accident, you can tell me anything. Tell me something you're afraid to tell me."

We both lie very still.

"Why don't you tell me something first," I finally say.

April pushes both arms under her head, pillowing her cheek on her elbows. I touch her shoulder blades.

"I lost my virginity at thirteen," she says. "I always lie about that. Doesn't that make me sound like a terrible person?"

"No."

"I don't even have a good excuse," April says. I pull myself up so I can look at her face, but April doesn't turn toward me. I can only see her profile. "Nobody made me. I wasn't tricked or duped or coerced or anything. I just decided to do it, and then I found somebody and did it. I told the guy I was fifteen, so that's what I say when anybody asks how old I was, you know?"

"Oh."

"It's still young, right? But not, like, criminal or something. I've never told anyone that."

I stroke April's shoulder. I stroke her hair. She shrugs, and because I don't know what to say, I lie down again beside her and wrap an arm around her.

"Your turn," April says.

I lie perfectly still, my eyes on the dark windows in front of us. An upstairs neighbor clomps loudly above us. When we are this quiet, I can hear the traffic on the main street three blocks away. I wait so long to speak, and April breathes so evenly, it would be possible for me to believe she's fallen asleep.

"I have a brother," I say.

"Mmmm?"

"I don't talk about him because he went crazy back when I was in high school." April doesn't say anything. She just wiggles one hand free and strokes my wrist. Her touch is so light, all I feel are her bitten fingernails. "Looking back, we should have seen it coming, but we didn't. We packed him off to college where things got more and more out of control until he had a complete psychotic break. He totally flipped. He was my big brother, you know? He was my whole world, and it's like that kid I grew up with just checked out and hasn't been heard from since."

"What's his name?" April asks.

My mind is blank. It's as empty as the lake in the morning on a rainy day, the sky and water indistinguishable from each other, just a diffuse, depthless gray.

"James," I say.

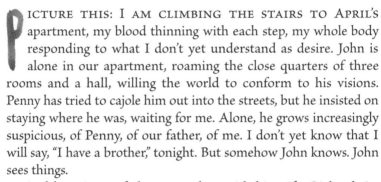

ICTURE THIS: I AM CLIMBING THE STAIRS TO APRIL'S apartment, my blood thinning with each step, my whole body responding to what I don't yet understand as desire. John is alone in our apartment, roaming the close quarters of three rooms and a hall, willing the world to conform to his visions. Penny has tried to cajole him out into the streets, but he insisted on staying where he was, waiting for me. Alone, he grows increasingly suspicious, of Penny, of our father, of me. I don't yet know that I will say, "I have a brother," tonight. But somehow John knows. John sees things.

And here is our father, on a date with his wife: Richard sits across from Elaine at an upscale Italian restaurant near campus, a restaurant frequented by faculty and visiting speakers. Undergraduates occasionally save up to take each other on dates here, and it always touches Richard's heart to see those young kids wearing ties and high-heeled shoes, on better behavior than they have been in weeks, paying a great deal for fettuccini alfredo. A little oil lamp flickers between Richard and Elaine. The warm light deepens the fine lines around his wife's eyes, which Richard finds beautiful. Elaine is a little flushed with wine and excitement. She has spent the day attending a master class with a visiting pianist at the university's music conservatory. Richard saw the flyer tacked up on a bulletin board in the student union, and brought it home to his wife.

"It sounds wonderful," he says.

"It was," Elaine says.

At first Elaine refused to consider registering for the master class, although she immediately ordered a ticket for the pianist's evening performance of Grieg's *Piano Concerto in A minor* at the university's concert hall. As the date approached, and Richard learned from friends over in the music program that the master class was not yet full, he suggested it again to his wife.

"I'd feel ridiculous," Elaine had said. "I'd be double the age, at least, of every other student there."

"So?" Richard had asked.

"I haven't played like that in years and years."

"Nonsense. You play concert pieces all the time."

"Here, at home," Elaine said. "I'm a piano teacher. I give music lessons. I haven't been a pianist since before the kids."

"Do you want to go? Would you enjoy the class?" Richard had asked.

"Very much," Elaine said.

"Then go, honey," Richard said.

And so Elaine registered for the class. Richard had suggested that they meet for dinner between the class and the concert, and Elaine had agreed. Richard felt oddly nervous and excited all day. He spruced up for dinner, putting on a starched shirt and a green tie that Elaine had recently bought for him. He took the bus to campus since Elaine had the car, and as he approached the music school, he spied Elaine waiting for him on the steps. He used to meet her similarly when he was in graduate school and she was a conservatory student. She was a young woman of such serious concentration and dark beauty that she often looked furious. It took Richard months to cease being surprised when her dark aspect would suddenly melt into a warm smile at his approach. "I'm not angry, Richard," she would say to him. "I'm just thinking."

This evening, Richard feels as if all the years that have passed between them have vanished and they are young and tender and tentative again. She took his arm as they walked to the restaurant. Richard doubts Elaine has any idea what such a gesture means to him. She told him with great heat and passion about the master class, about how the famous pianist—a name Richard had never heard before—praised her phrasing and her touch, how he called her fingers perfectly delicate and deft. She held her free hand out in front of them so they might both examine those fingers. She described the music—Chopin and Wagner and Rachmaninov—with similar verve. He laughed, and when Elaine asked, "Why are you laughing at me?" Richard said, "Because I love you so much."

Now they gaze at each other in the low light of the restaurant.

Richard lifts his wine glass, although they've both already drunk most of a glass.

"A toast," he says.

Elaine lifts her wine glass.

"To you," Richard says. "To music."

They clink glasses.

"Come here," Elaine says, and when Richard leans across the table, a hand pressed to his chest to prevent his tie from falling in the oil lamp, Elaine kisses him warmly on the lips. "Thank you for suggesting I go," she says. "I wouldn't have, without you."

Without him, Richard thinks, perhaps Elaine would currently be a lauded concert pianist. She would be the one arriving on university campuses to give concerts and master classes. She would sweep into recital halls and rehearsal rooms in dramatic long dresses, her heels clicking on polished floors, her gorgeous, silver-streaked hair pulled back in a bun, thrilling the students who have been waiting, anxiously, for this moment for weeks. Richard has wondered over the years if marriage and children have held his wife back, if somewhere along the line she chose those roles over a career as a professional musician, and if some small part of her heart resents him and the children for it. Richard finds it easier to wonder than to know. John and Jane, Richard thinks. His children, whose troubled lives are heavy stones he carries and cannot put down.

Richard feels suddenly tired. He is a man in his middle-fifties. His joints ache and his muscles, once full and plump beneath his skin, have grown sinewy. He has provided adequately but not spectacularly for his family, and his children have rejected even what small measure of protection he once could provide. He has achieved a limited and rather anonymous success. His beard is graying. He could go on with this list of complaints against himself for days.

"Why so suddenly quiet?" Elaine asks. They are eating their entrées now. The waiter has been by once to refill their wine glasses.

"Oh, you know," Richard says. His eyes burn, threaten to tear. He blinks twice. "Sometimes being happy makes me sad."

"Yes, I do know," Elaine says.

Elaine puts her hand under the table and touches his knee. Elaine speaks more about the master class, the personality and predilections of the pianist she has long admired. She says that she cannot quite describe his presence, the way the rehearsal hall seemed to brim and spill over with him. This reminds her of a droll anecdote from graduate school. Soon, they are deep in the past, reminding each other of all the romance and drama of their worlds when they were in their twenties. Dinner ends with a great deal of laughter. When the check comes, Richard tips their server extravagantly.

Out on the sidewalk on this fine summer night, Richard holds Elaine's hand. He walks her to the steps of the concert hall and then asks her to check her purse for her car keys and cell phone, just to be safe. She doesn't have any cash on hand, so he gives her a twenty, which she tucks into the coin purse of her wallet. Concertgoers stream up the steps and into the brightly lit performance hall. Richard kisses Elaine on the cheek and sends her off. Through the open doors he can see the red-carpeted vestibule and the throng of well-dressed classical music enthusiasts. He had asked Elaine if she'd like him to join her for the concert, but she'd said no, that she wanted to simply steep herself in the music and then come home and tell him about it. Richard slips his hands in his pants pockets and permits himself to whistle as he strolls up the street to the bus stop.

Richard is pleasantly tired when he arrives home. He admires their house as he approaches it from the front, which he so rarely does since he parks both the car and his bike in the garage out back. He thought to leave a light on for himself, and the front windows glow invitingly. He tries to see the house as a stranger might as he mounts the sweep of flagstone steps that will carry him to the porch steps and then the front door. He trimmed the grass yesterday, and the sloped yard still smells of it. He used to approach the house from this vantage point back when the children were in school and Elaine needed the car for errands and after-school activities and such. That was back before he started riding his bike to campus in an effort to preserve the capacity of his heart. He loved climbing his own front steps at the end of the day. When the children were quite small, they were as likely as not to be tumbling about getting into some sort of mischief in the front yard. They would shriek with delight when they caught sight of him. Even then, he was struck by the wonder of it, the pure, unadulterated pleasure of being their father. As the children grew older, of course, they were far less likely to greet him, but all through her high school years, perhaps more so even after John grew ill, Jane would occasionally be sitting out on the front porch reading a book when he came home from campus in the evening. Sometimes, even in the late fall, she would be sitting bundled in sweaters and a scarf, reading by the yellow porch light in the early dusk of autumn. She would look up as he climbed the last few steps and say, "Hello, Dad," and he would say, "Hi there, Jane." He wouldn't bother her with conversation. He would just go straight on into the house, and a few moments later, she would follow him in. He never knew if she came in so directly after him because of the dim light and the cold or if she truly had been waiting for him.

Tonight, of course, the house is still when he lets himself in. There's almost a chill to the living room. Elaine keeps the central air set a few degrees cooler than he would. Richard drops his keys on the end table by the couch and goes into the bedroom, loosening his tie. He slips his shoes off by the bed. He hangs his tie on the tie rack behind the closet door. He picks up the phone and listens to the dial tone. There are no messages. He had hoped to come home to his daughter's voice. They have not heard from her since her message chastising Richard for calling out of turn. He has been fighting the urge to phone the children ever since. He wanders from the bedroom through the bathroom, down the back hall to the kitchen, and then back around through the dining room to the living room. He can't think of anything he'd particularly like to do. He goes to the stereo, and after a search through Elaine's CD collection, puts on a recording of the concerto she's currently hearing. Grieg's concerto is accompanied by Schumann's *Piano Concerto* on this album, both recorded by the Cleveland Symphony Orchestra. The music bursts through the speakers, and after the initial shock of sound, Richard finds the recording soothing. He adjusts the volume and then takes up a book of *New York Times* Sunday crossword puzzles. When his wife is anywhere in the house, Richard does the crosswords diligently. When she is not, as she is not tonight, he turns to the answers in the back. When the phone rings, he sets the book of puzzles face down on the couch and instinctively tucks his mechanical pencil in the breast pocket of his shirt. He crosses the room, takes up the cordless telephone, and says, "Hello, Richard Fields speaking."

His son breathes on the other end of the line. Richard would know that labored breathing anywhere. Richard feels struck on the head. Staggered. Stunned. John breathes.

"John," Richard says. "Hello, son."

"Good guess," John says. "I wondered if you'd recognize your namesake."

"Yes," Richard says. "Of course. I recognize you." His knees threaten to buckle, but Richard feels bolted in place.

"Is this a shock?" John asks. "Am I surprising you?"

"We haven't heard from you in a long time. We usually only hear from your sister. How are you, John?"

John ignores Richard's question. "My sister," he says, pouncing on each sibilant. "Yes, I've called to have a chat with you about her. I'm sure that's all topsy-turvy in your head, old man. You're used to whispering about me with her. I know you two are in collusion. Our own personal Madonna has other ideas for Janie-Jane, but you, you're the one who thinks he has a pipeline to her brain."

"We haven't heard from Jane in a little while," Richard says. "Is she okay?"

"That's all relative," John says. "It depends on what you mean by Jane."

"John, you're frightening me. Is Jane in trouble?"

"Of course I frighten you. I'm the big bad wolf, aren't I? Are you alone, or is your other-double lurking in the shadows?"

"Your mother isn't home right now," Richard says. Already the conversation is spiraling beyond his ability to navigate it.

"That's good. You're easier to handle without her. You don't have to be afraid. Jane hasn't gotten herself into anything I can't get her out of. Although she's trying to. I think we can say that with certainty. Did you have trouble with her when she was in high school? I can't remember for the life of me. Did she run around a little bit during the dark days?"

"John," Richard says sternly.

"Listen, man," John says. "We have to speak honestly."

"Your sister has never been trouble."

John laughs, the sound amplified and distorted over miles of telephone wire and great leaps of radio waves.

"She's not the little girl she was once," John says. "You're going to have to give up that dream if you want the truth revealed to you. Our little Janie is up to things that could make your head spin. She's attempting a grand transformation. It would be spectacular if it weren't doomed. She thinks she's getting away with something, but I know better. Here's one thing you should know—that daughter of yours can't lie to save her own life. Is that comforting? I see through her, which is curious. I see right down into her bloodless heart. What I need to know is, has she talked to you about any of this?"

"Any of what? I'm having trouble following you."

John's paranoia and his incoherent wanderings are somehow comforting to Richard. Richard remembers John on the telephone from back in the old days. The more John talks, the more Richard feels reassured that he's incapable of saying anything true about Jane. John lives in a world entirely of his own invention.

"You look but don't see," John says. "You listen but don't hear."

"Where is Jane right now?" Richard asks. "Would it be possible for me to talk to her?"

"Jane will one day have to account for tonight herself."

"Does she have a boyfriend?" Richard asks. "Is that what this is about? Is your sister seeing someone?"

"If up were down and down were up, if everything were the opposite of itself, you could say that would be an approximation of the truth. There are some things your daughter is going to have to tell you herself."

The idea thrills Richard. Jane needs a world that is bigger than her brother. It didn't take a therapist to convince Richard that Jane and John were too close. He has a sudden wave of sympathy for his son. His poor sick son, frightened and alone.

"Are you okay, John?" Richard asks softly. Sometimes, even in the middle of John's most blinding psychotic rages, Richard could quiet him with gentleness. Richard could melt him with love. "It must be hard to feel you've been left on your own."

"I don't need your sympathy, Richard," John says. "But what you don't say reveals what you know. You're an idiot, hamster-face. You can't even grasp the scope of what you don't know."

"I can hear that you're angry," Richard says. "You're angry with your mother and me, and now you're angry with Jane. But your sister deserves her own life, don't you think? Don't you want Jane to be happy?"

"You, apparently, learned nothing from all those doctors you dragged me to, Daddy-dad. I'd laugh if you were funny in the least."

"What can I do? What can I do to help you?"

"Hold onto your hat, old man. I'll let you in on a little secret. You think you've been to Never-Never Land, but you've only had the sneak-peek. You think I've gone off the deep end. Just wait for what happens when it's your favorite."

"John," Richard says. He wishes he could physically touch his son. "I love you. You're my son. I would give my whole world for you."

"That's a pretty speech," John says. "Fuck you."

He hangs up the phone and is gone. Richard stands, blinking and dizzy, in the middle of his living room. The phone in his hand is silent for several seconds, and then clicks over to a rapid busy signal. Richard presses the off button with his thumb. He feels as if his skull has been scoured out. He can't think how to think, and he certainly can't think how to feel. He walks mechanically back to the couch and sits down. He is sitting in exactly the same position when he hears the garage door opening more than an hour later. He fumbles with the crossword puzzle book and pulls his pencil from his pocket just as he hears Elaine coming in the back door.

"Honey, I'm home," she calls.

"In the living room," he says.

His wife sweeps into the room and collapses onto the couch beside him. She flings her legs over the arm of the sofa and sprawls across Richard's lap.

"It was wonderful," she declares. "It was exquisite." She beams up at her husband, and then cocks her head. "Schumann? Were you listening to Grieg?"

"What?" Richard asks. He hears the music again for the first time since John called. "Oh, yes, the recording. I wanted to hear what you were hearing."

"You are a wonderful man, Richard Fields," Elaine says. Richard strokes her hair. She closes her eyes and hums along with the recording. "It was a thousand times more exquisite than this."

"Mmmm," Richard says, as if he were deeply engrossed in his crossword puzzle.

"Is this what you've been up to? Is this how you've spent your night."

Richard gazes down at his wife. He rests his hand with the pencil on her chest.

"Yes," he says. What would he say to her if he tried to tell her about John's telephone call? What could he possibly say that wouldn't upset her terribly? It seems almost cruel to say anything. Especially tonight, when she's almost floating. He will contrive some way to speak with Jane in the near future. That is what he'll do. He will just make sure that he's around to answer her call the next time she phones home. He'll ask her a few direct questions and get a sense of what's what. There is no need to distress his wife.

"Quiet," Elaine says. "That sounds nice."

"Yes," Richard says. "It was. I just sat here waiting for you, love."

I DON'T KNOW WHAT I DON'T KNOW. WHEN I COME HOME from April's in the early hours of a Wednesday morning, John doesn't tell me he's phoned our father. He doesn't tell me he's begun to mistrust not only my ability but also my intentions. He asks me how the night went, and I tell him. He asks me how April responded to his story, and I say just as he predicted she would. I tell him April believes, that we have a clear path in front of us, and that for the time being, at least, my girl body is safe within our boy story. I tell him how her skin felt and what her lips tasted like. He says, "I remember. Yes, that's how girls are." I do not tell him that April lost her virginity at thirteen, and I don't tell him that I told her I have a brother. Instead I think of all the things I can tell April now that I have made up James. When I tell John about the two of us dozing off on the couch—the two of them, he corrects me, April and John—John asks, "Is that it? Is that everything?" I look into my brother's glittering eyes, and I lie. "Yes," I say. John tells me he spent the evening with Penny. They went to a park where she sometimes picks up johns and swung on the swings while addicts shot heroin in the bushes. We are storytellers, John and me. Even I know we are living in the land of make-believe.

When I arrive at Stew's later in the day, I find Sean pacing the floor, his cell phone pressed to his ear. He gives me a thumbs-up, then retreats to the office and closes the door. The store gets busy for a Wednesday. Some college kids come in and noodle around on instruments they have no intention of purchasing. A woman asks about piano lessons for her daughter, and I give her the number of a friend of Stew's. We've got someone to recommend for lessons on almost every instrument. I sell a few used records. A guy walks in who wants to check out banjos. I take down a few of our middle-of-the-road instruments. But he's a serious musician, and pretty soon

I grab a high-end six string. He tunes the banjo, and as soon as he starts to play the whole store gets quiet. Sean even pokes his head out of the office door. "Mountain music," he says. "That's what I've been talking about. John, take care of our friend." I sell the guy the banjo for its asking price, but throw in a better case and a couple sets of strings. By late afternoon, we get our first lull of the day. As the last customer in the store heads out the door, Sean turns to me.

"So that was Clint on the phone when you came in."

"Yeah?" I ask. "What's he got to say?"

"Oh, just that he's lined up a couple of gigs for us."

Sean's playing it cool. Pretending to dust the saxophones and French horns displayed along the back wall.

"Are you serious?"

"As a heart attack," Sean says. He grins.

"That's awesome."

"I know. And the best part is that Leda's going to bake us Hungarian wedding bread to celebrate."

"What's Hungarian wedding bread?"

"Deliciousness," Sean says. "Cake-like perfection. You'll see at rehearsal. Leda bakes when she's happy. She's like the sexiest den mother ever."

The bell above the front door jingles. The evening sun casts its light from across the street, and April stands in its path in front of the door, a silhouette of herself.

"Hi, strangers," she says.

She's wearing her work clothes. Her blue scrubs are worn so thin that in direct sunlight her pants are transparent. I can see the curve of her thighs within them. April approaches the counter, and as she steps out of the light the outline of her body vanishes. Her scrubs are substantial again, her body concealed.

"Hi," I say.

"Hello, lady," Sean says. "Long time no see. Are you here as a customer or just as John's girlfriend this evening?"

"What's it to you?" April asks.

"Not a goddamn thing. Just curious. I'm just a guy with an inquiring mind." Sean turns his attention toward me. "John and I were just talking about Leda and her baking abilities."

"Legendary," April says.

"You know about her Hungarian wedding bread?" I ask.

"Yeah," April says. "Doesn't everybody?"

"If she weren't married to Clint, I'd marry her myself, just for the cake, even if she weren't the hottest thing on two legs. No offense, April," Sean says.

"I think Leda's the hottest thing on two legs," April says. "No offense, John."

"None taken," I say.

April's eyes laugh. She turns to Sean. "I think I am a customer tonight."

"What can I do for you?" Sean asks.

"I've been thinking of investing in a new guitar. My dad is desperate to buy me something. He's talking about a car, but I think I can satisfy him with a guitar."

"Right this way, little lady," Sean says and leads her gallantly the fifteen steps across the store. He lifts down a couple of different acoustics, and April pulls up stools for the two of them. They sit swapping guitars, tuning, playing chords, and talking. April tries out most of the decent guitars we carry. When she decides on the one she likes best, she settles in to play, her fingers light and quick on the strings. I have not, until this moment, heard her play. What a shame, I think. How stupid of me not to ask her to. I watch Sean watching her, and then he surprises me by picking up a guitar and joining in. I finally recognize the Allman Brothers' "Blue Sky." Sean's range never stops surprising me. April glances up and smiles, and then they both begin to sing. I wouldn't have known April's voice sounds as it does, a rich alto. I wouldn't have guessed Sean's tenor, either. Clint is the only one who ever backs up Leda. I wonder if Sean and April knew these things about each other, if maybe they've had reason to sing together over the years. The pleasure of watching them is almost painful. I watch them as if they were characters in a film, pretty and ordinary people made magnificent, thrown up larger than life on a screen.

"Make her our best offer," Sean says when he and April are at the end of a song. "Sell her the box at ten percent over cost."

"Thanks, Sean," April says, looking up at him through the slash of her bangs.

"Whatever, kid," Sean says. "I like you just about as much as I like

Leda." He sets the guitar he's been playing down next to the others. I'll hang them all back up before we close tonight. Sean retreats to the office and closes the door, leaving me gazing at April across the store floor. She works through a chord progression.

"You've got a nice voice," I say.

"Not really." April shrugs. "I just like to sing."

"How's your day been?" I ask.

"Ridiculous," April says. She brings me the guitar so I can ring her up, and leans a hip against the counter. "We had this kid in for his first cleaning. He was like five or something, and he'd never been to the dentist. My office specializes in pediatrics, right? I mean, we're used to kids, but this little guy is a terror. He ends up biting down on the hygienist's finger, going straight through the glove and breaking the skin and everything. There was blood. His mom freaks out and the hygienist freaks out and I think everybody's threatening to sue everybody."

"My god," I say. "What did you do?"

"I just stood back and tried not to laugh."

April crosses around to my side of the counter and begins to check things out. She pushes buttons on the cash register and slides open the glass door to look at the collection of odd buttons, guitar picks, and harmonicas on display.

"What about you?" April asks. "What's happened here?"

"Nothing as dramatic as all that."

I put a hand on April's shoulder and she turns toward me. She wedges herself between the cash register and the stool I'm sitting on. She puts her hands on my knees and we kiss.

"No girls behind the counter, Fields," Sean says from the office door.

I jump and smash my lip against her teeth.

"Good grief, Sean," I say.

"I'm just saying," Sean says. "What kind of establishment do you think we're running around here?"

April ignores Sean. She rubs her palms on my thighs.

"I've got the day off tomorrow," she says. "Come over after work?"

"Sure," I say. "I'd love to."

"You kids are going to make me puke," Sean says.

"You're going to get me fired," I say to April.

"Nah," she says. "Sean likes you. And he also likes me."

She kisses me again, her tongue flashing behind my teeth.

"See you tomorrow, Johnny," April says.

"Yeah."

I zip her guitar into its case.

"I'll see you later, alligator," she says to Sean.

"After a while, crocodile," he says.

I don't ask John for permission to see April after work on Thursday. I tell him. I say she stopped by the store and played music with Sean and bought a guitar and I'm going over to her place tomorrow. Simple as that. John says, "Ah, I see. I understand." He smiles at me in a way I can't quite read, but I ignore it.

"Good," I say. "I'm glad."

"Oh, you won't be," my brother says. "Soon you won't be glad about anything, but have fun tomorrow."

He leaves me in the kitchen where I am heating up a pizza.

"Hey, aren't you hungry?" I call after him.

"Don't you worry about me," John says. He disappears into his bedroom, cranks up a Queen album, and I don't see him for the rest of the night.

In the morning, John is nowhere to be found and there's a note taped to my bedroom door. It says, *Later, later, alligator. Please don't smile, crocodile.* It's a children's rhyme, I tell myself. It's the sort of thing people say all the time. Sean and April didn't make it up. John and I probably said it to each other when we were kids. Life is full of coincidence.

After work on Thursday, I am once again standing on the sidewalk in front of April's building. This is how life happens, I think. You do something often enough and it becomes a part of you. In the beginning, every new action is an act. But eventually, you are no longer acting—you are just being. I press the button for April's buzzer, and moments later, she leans her head out the window. Her face is as bright as a streetlamp above me.

"Hello," I say.

"Now the buzzer's broken," April says. "I'll be right down to let you in."

I wait on the sidewalk in front of her glass security door. A cat presses itself against the screen of the open first-floor window. I try to get a quick whiff to check my pits. April trots down the last flight of steps, unlocks the door, and pushes it open with her hip. She's wearing a sarong and a white tank top over what seems to be a pink bikini. Even in the dim light of the foyer, I can see her nose and cheeks and ears are sunburned.

"Hello, sir," she says and holds the door wide for me.

When I step into the vestibule, April wraps hers arms around my waist, and we kiss. I finger the knot of her bikini top.

"What's this?" I ask. "Were you at the beach?"

"Yep."

"You don't strike me as a beach person."

"I'm full of surprises," April says. "I assume you're not? A beach person, I mean?"

"Not in years and years," I say.

April nods. Through my t-shirt, she kisses me on the clavicle. She runs a finger along the seam of my chest binder where it crosses over my shoulder. I can imagine what she's thinking.

"Come on up," she says.

Once we're in her apartment, April leads me straight to the kitchen where we each open a beer. A battered boom box sits on the counter. The band sounds familiar, but I don't recognize the track.

"Who's this?" I ask.

"Portishead," April says. "'Glory Box.' It's hot in here. You want to sit on the porch?"

"Sure," I say.

We sit on her back stairs watching the stillness in the alley and the strange pantomime of other people going about their lives through kitchen windows. The moon is just a nick in the sky above us. From some pocket in her skirt, April produces a small glass pipe. I shake my head when she offers it to me. We both lean back against the thick beams that support the wooden catwalk of her back stairs. I sip my cool beer while she gets stoned. We talk softly, knowing our voices must carry far in this alley, bouncing off the brick backs of buildings, amplified by all the concrete and blacktop.

I tell April about agreeing to the two gigs with Sean's band and how nervous this makes me since I haven't played seriously in years. She tells me about how her father is picking her up tomorrow afternoon before he leaves the city so they can go to her grandmother's ninetieth birthday party. Her dad is taking half a day off work, and she's promised to stay with him in the suburbs. Hers is not the typical family story. Her father worked his way out of childhood poverty on the Irish south side, eventually becoming an investment banker. "Whatever that means," April says. Her grandmother moved in to take care of her after her mother died of a freak brain hemorrhage when April was a child. Her father left their house at four in the morning for his commute into the city and rarely returned in the evening before seven or eight. "I could count the number of times I've seen that man out of a suit on one hand," she says. I nod. I say I understand. She says he's still offering to pay for college, but she doesn't feel like taking him up on that yet. We talk and drink until we're both buzzed and sleepy. April's legs are stretched out toward me, her long skirt hiked up to her knees, and I have a hand resting on her ankle.

"Do you want to go to bed, John?" April asks.

"Yes," I say.

We kiss in the kitchen after we drop our beer bottles in the sink. We kiss in the hall, and in her bedroom without turning on the lights. I can taste the bittersweet weed. I run my hands under her tank top. She wraps one arm around my midsection and buries her other hand in the back pocket of my jeans. I kiss her jaw, her throat. I reach up and untie her bikini top before I peel off her shirt. April sighs, tips her head back, and closes her eyes.

"Where can I touch you, John?" she asks. "Where can I put my hands?"

I take her hands in mine and place them on my head. She strokes my hair, runs her fingers over my ears. She blinks, her green eyes alive in the dark. I cradle her and bring us both down on the bed.

April hardly moves in the night, her body heavy, her ribcage rising and falling rhythmically, but I have trouble falling asleep. I drop in and out of shallow, stressful dreams. As soon as I doze off, I'm gripped by the certainty that we are not alone in the apartment, but I cannot wake to investigate. I hear doors opening and closing, footfalls in the hallway, windows rattling. My body is immovable, my eyelids leaden. I can feel April sleeping in my arms, utterly innocent to what's going on in the apartment, utterly vulnerable. Each time I struggle awake, I lie in the dark with blood hammering in my ears, certain, this time, that what I've heard was not a dream. But each time I wake the apartment is still. Everything is as it should be. Near dawn I fall into an exhausted, stupefied sleep. This time I dream that I am introducing April to my parents. I cannot explain to them that I am John and John is John, that John has not become me. I jerk awake with April leaning over me.

"Hey," she says. "Are you okay?"

"What time is it?"

Daylight glows behind the drawn shade at the window.

"Morning," she says. She leans across me and picks up an alarm clock from the floor. She clicks it off. "Just about eight. You were dreaming. Are you okay?"

"Yeah," I say. I'm out of breath.

April kisses my damp forehead.

"I'm getting up," she says, "but you should sleep."

"Work?"

"Don't you know it. There are children out there whose teeth must be cleaned!"

April runs her hands through her hair. She looks like she's strategizing. I start to sit up, but she stills me with a touch.

"Lie there. Stay in my bed until after I've gone so that I can picture you while I'm waiting for the bus."

"That I can do," I say.

April stands and stretches. I watch her untangle herself from the sarong she's slept in. She stands naked in the diffuse morning light as she rummages through her drawers for a bra and underwear. She pulls on her work scrubs and steps into her clogs. She rakes her hair with her fingers, parts it down the middle, and ties it back in her two customary ponytails.

"I like the way that shows your tattoo," I say.

April rubs the back of her neck.

"What's your story today?"

She is almost ready to leave and begins searching the floor for her wallet and keys.

"Nothing special," I say. "It's just a regular Friday. You're leaving this afternoon?"

"Yeah. Three days in the suburbs. I hope I survive."

"I'm going to miss you," I say.

April stands in the open door of her bedroom. She leans against the doorframe. She stands as if she knows how lovely she looks.

"Don't get up yet. Stay where you are at least for a little bit."

"Okay," I say, but April doesn't leave.

"Hey, John. Listen, can I say something?"

"Sure," I say.

"First I have to make some rules," she says.

"Okay."

"Number one, you can't freak out. You're not allowed. Number two, I don't want you to answer me. I don't want you to say anything. Just let me say this thing and you can think about it and I'll see you when I get back into the city."

"Just those two rules?" I ask.

"Just the two."

"Okay," I say again.

April looks at the curtain of beads in front of her closet rather than at me.

"I'm falling for you," she says. Her eyes flicker over my face, but she doesn't hold my gaze. "Like love, John. I'm falling in love with you. For what that's worth."

I inhale and April puts a finger to her lips. She smiles, almost ruefully, blows me a kiss, and then she turns to leave. I turn over and bury my face in her pillow and breathe. I sink into a heavy, black sleep, and when I wake, it is too late to run home before meeting Eugene at the Fleetwood. I could skip it, or even call and cancel—I still have Eugene's card in my wallet—but then he'll just come lurking around Stew's. That's the last thing I need. The thought of Eugene and then Stew's and then John when I get home exhausts me, but what can I do? I drag myself out of April's bed, wash up at the sink in her bathroom, and face my day in the same clothes I've had on for more than twenty-four hours. Under my binder, my chest aches for one good, deep breath.

The Fleetwood looks like an old country store that has somehow found itself pinned between apartment blocks and a viaduct. The brick alley beneath the concrete arch stinks of urine. In spite of this, the outdoor seating is already full, ten or twelve tables corralled behind a wooden fence, its white paint blistered and peeling. A dilapidated roof of corrugated green plastic shades the sidewalk seating from the sun. The screen door to the restaurant squeaks on its hinges, and I wonder if they do something to make the hinges squeak, or if left in their natural state all screen doors squeak. The place smells of coffee and pancakes and sweet fruit syrups.

Sometimes, when I don't think I can do what I have to do, I convince myself I truly am dreaming. I can do anything. I can watch it happen. The real me is curled up somewhere, safe and protected from consequences. Maybe I am sixteen years old, a high school kid, asleep under my parents' roof, and John is off at college. Maybe everything that's happened since then has been nothing but a panicked morning dream. I am just about to watch myself tell the hostess that I'm expecting another when I see Eugene already seated at a tiny wooden table. He's reading a newspaper and already sipping a cup of coffee. He glances up, and his face lights with pleasure and what might be surprise. He smiles and stands, and the hostess abandons me to Eugene. I can't make my feet move. Eugene crosses the space between us and reaches out to shake my hand.

"Hi," he says. "I wasn't sure you'd come."

"Hi." I put my hand in Eugene's dry palm. He lays his left hand on my shoulder, and under his touch my feet come unglued. I am able to make it to the table. As we sit, I jostle the table. Eugene's coffee spills onto his newspaper.

"Sorry," I say.

"No problem," Eugene says.

A server comes over to ask if I'd like to start with coffee as well, and I say yes. He has a faint accent, something vaguely Slavic in the cadence of his speech. Eugene and I sit in silence until the server has returned with a heavy blue mug. All of the plates and saucers and cups are mismatched. It's part of the restaurant's charm. When we seem more safely alone at our table, Eugene takes his coffee cup in his hands and leans his weight on his forearms.

"Thank you for coming," he says. His voice is so low and soft I know no one else could possibly hear him. The café is noisy with conversation and children and flatware clanking. "Can I call you something?"

I stir clumpy brown sugar into my coffee, even though I usually drink it black. I meet Eugene's gaze.

"John calls me Johnny," I say.

"Okay," Eugene says.

Our server appears again. "Are you ready?" he asks.

"Maybe another minute," Eugene says, and then we both apply our attention to our menus. The Fleetwood is one of those breakfast-all-day sorts of places, and Eugene orders French toast. I decide on a complicated breakfast burrito with tofu.

"So," Eugene says, once our server has taken away our menus. "How are things?"

"Fine," I say. Eugene waits. I know him well enough to know that Eugene has the patience of a monk. "What do you want me to say?"

"I don't know," Eugene says. "I can't make you tell me anything, but I'd like to know that you're okay."

"Do I look okay?"

"You look a hell of a lot like John did back in high school."

"That's the point," I say.

"How is John?" Eugene asks. Perhaps he's changing tack.

"I take care of him," I say. "Listen, Eugene, how much do you know already? Who have you talked to? I doubt all this waltzing around is necessary."

Eugene sets down his coffee cup. "I heard, back when we were still in Saint Louis, that John had gotten sick. I've stayed in touch with people from my department, of course, and Frank Hartman filled me in on what your dad had told him. Not a lot of details, but enough to know he was pretty sick. When I heard you two had moved up here, I thought John must be back on his feet."

"Have you talked to our parents?"

Eugene's gaze falters. He looks past me for a moment, but doesn't speak again until our eyes meet. "No."

"Are you lying?"

"I don't have any reason to," Eugene says.

"Well don't," I say. "Don't lie to me and don't call my parents, okay?"

"Okay. Do you want to fill me in on what happened back then?"

"What happened back then is that John went off the fucking deep end, Eugene. He cracked like a walnut, and instead of finishing his sophomore year of college, our dad had to go pack him into the station wagon and bring him home like a raving lunatic. You were very busy having your own life at that point, I'm sure. He was so out of his head they put him in a hospital where the prevailing mores of modern medicine recommend confinement and torture for the mentally insane."

I know I sound more like John than I mean to, but it's all true. Eugene looks at me without blinking, and when our food arrives I want to crack my plate over his head. He's done nothing, of course. He hasn't done anything to me, but sitting across from him after all these years, I feel like he's betrayed me. Purposefully. I know that is a John thing to think. I hack into my burrito with my fork and knife. I eat two bites while Eugene sits in front of his French toast, the thin dusting of powdered sugar melting into a glaze.

"They put him on meds that turned him into a zombie, gave him nightmares, made him itch, and puffed him up like a marshmallow man. We all trouped through therapy. It was a riot, I'm telling you. He got better, and then he got worse, and then he got better, and then he got a shit-load worse." Eugene nods. He doesn't look like he's going to say anything. "I dropped out of the drum line before John's head exploded," I add.

"I heard," Eugene says.

"Yeah, well, that's great. I tried to stick it out without the two of you, but it wasn't any use. And then when John got sick, I dropped out of almost everything. It was pretty much all I could do to keep from going crazy, too. It was back and forth for a few years for John—on his meds, off his meds, on his meds, etcetera. About a year ago, we all thought for a minute that we'd figured out what life was going to look like, and then surprise, surprise, John went off his meds and nothing in heaven or on god's green earth could convince him to go through all that shit again. Who could blame him? Our parents were thinking about throwing him out, so John and I took matters into our own hands. That's what happened back then, Eugene, since you suddenly care." I take another stab at my burrito. "Your French toast is going to get cold."

Eugene lifts his silverware and examines his breakfast. He seems to choose where and how he'll cut a bite very carefully. I watch the muscles in his jaw work as he chews. When he swallows, he asks, "How sick is he now, Jane?"

My face is just as impervious as Eugene's. I don't even flinch when he says Jane.

"I'm standing between John and disaster," I say. "At first I hoped we could get him well, get him away from all those doctors and chemicals and bring him back to himself. He's no better or worse than he was before, but at least he's not strung out on meds. He might stay crazy forever, though. Who knows?"

"I'm sorry this has all happened to you," Eugene says.

"Me? Fuck me," I say. I've been watching to see if swearing will make Eugene's color rise, but it hasn't. "I'm the least of anybody's concerns."

"You're mine."

"A day late and a dollar short, my friend." I point my knife at Eugene's plate. "Keep eating. Let's pretend we're regular people having a regular breakfast."

Eugene complies and we both take a bite. I can't tell if he's frightened of me. Eugene takes another bite and then a swallow of coffee. A server who isn't our server comes by and fills our cups.

"Can you explain this whole Johnny thing to me?" Eugene asks.

"That's curious, hearing you say Johnny. Most people call me John, but John and I have to distinguish, you know? It could get awfully confusing. You're the only person in this whole city who knows that the two of us exist. As long as I have to take care of the both of us, I'm him. It's as simple as that."

"But why? Why be him? Why not be you?"

"Why not?"

"That's not an answer," Eugene says.

I plunge my knife into what's left of my breakfast and push the plate away from me. Eugene crosses his silverware carefully over his plate. I try to imagine Eugene doing something rash and reckless, something violent or destructive, but I can't. I wish he hadn't abandoned me. My life would have been different. Even if John had still gone off the deep end, my life would have been different had it contained Eugene.

"It helps keep John calm," I say. "At first we thought it could make him well. We thought I could kind of save a place for him. Give him something to remember, or something to look forward to, depending on how you look at it. He was really freaking out when we first got here. He didn't trust anything or anyone, not even Jane. I was scared shitless, Eugene. I couldn't find work. I couldn't keep John pacified. Every time I turned around he was accusing me of something. But this Johnny business? It just took care of so many things. I don't think John's going to suddenly come around and be the guy he used to be anymore, but this charade at least keeps a lid on things. Instead of freaking out all day wondering whether or not Jane's coming home to him, John gets to pretend. I can't walk away, right? I don't have my own life. I only have his. That's John's logic, at least."

"Don't you miss your own life?" Eugene asks. "Don't you miss being Jane?"

"There was never anything to that person. She was a shadow. She's hardly a memory. What did I give up? Hardly anything more than a name. If I were Jane out here in the big bad world, we'd be on a sinking ship. She was so stupid. Unbelievably naive."

"You weren't stupid," Eugene says. "You were bright and talented and wonderful."

"Oh, Eugene," I say. "Even you're using the past tense. You were bright. You were wonderful."

Eugene's face drains, but he recovers. I give him a sardonic grin.

"What are you trying to do?" I ask. "Are you trying to save me? Who from? John? Me?"

"I just want to talk to you," Eugene says. "I just want to make sure you're okay."

"Can I tell you something? Can I tell you something I can't even tell John?"

"Yes," Eugene says. "You can tell me anything."

"I've never been happier with my life. I know this doesn't look like an ideal situation, but it's true. If people really knew me, if they knew me the way you do, I know they'd think this was madness. Mom and Dad think John is brainwashing me. Or something. I don't quite know what they think. But things are better than okay. This whole world has come together for me."

"Tell me about it," Eugene says. "Tell me about you. I'm not trying to take anything away from you."

He leans in across the table, as if getting closer to me would help him understand. His face is no longer an inscrutable mask of no emotion. It's creased with worry and concern. I pick up my coffee cup.

"It's no special story. It's just life. I have a job I really like. I'm good at it. I like the guy I work for. You met Sean. He's a nutcase, but we have so much fun. I like the rhythm of the store. I've sat in with his band, and they dig me. I kind of click. I was just what they were looking for. You know how that feels."

"Yes," Eugene says. "I do."

I look past Eugene at all the couples and families having breakfast. There are a few people eating alone, reading newspapers and books. I can see into the kitchen through a pass-through window, dark heads bending over griddles. Servers pass in and out of the swinging doors with pitchers of water, carafes of coffee, plates of steaming food. I get a glimpse of our server downing a glass of orange juice in the kitchen. The world is full of wonders, ordinary people making their lives.

"There's a girl," I say, without looking back at Eugene. "You met her, too, actually. That night at the bar. You've gotten a glimpse of my whole life. April. I don't know what that's supposed to mean, but there you go. There's a girl. Who I like. Nobody ever looked at me the way she looks at me back when I was me."

Eugene taps his shoe against mine under the table.

"You are you," he says.

"You know what I mean."

"April only knows you as John?" Eugene asks.

"Yeah," I say.

"How long can that last?"

"I don't know. We made up a story to cover the bases for now. How long can anything last? Each time I thought I knew what my life looked like, the people I was clinging to vanished from me. I don't expect things to last forever anymore. I'm happy now. I can't even think about tomorrow."

"I'm glad you're happy," Eugene says. "You deserve to be."

"Are you afraid of me?" I ask.

"No."

"Are you afraid for me?"

Eugene looks at me for a long while before he says, "A little bit."

"What are you going to do about that?"

"I don't think there's anything I can do," Eugene says. "Sometimes we just have to feel what we feel, I think."

"Are you going to try to be around? Are you going to try to keep tabs on me?"

"I'm going to let you lead," Eugene says. He spreads his hands on the table. We both look at them, at his strong dark fingers and the smooth gold of his wedding ring. I like to think how long I've known those hands, how much they've taught me. He laces his fingers and we look at each other. I notice for the first time that his lips are dry and cracked. "You've got my number. You know how to find me. If you ever need anything, you can call me. Whatever it is. If you need something, say the word, and I'll do what I can do. No questions asked. I'd like to see you like this every now and again, just so I know you're okay, but I can't make you do anything."

"That's true, Eugene," I say. "You can't."

When our server stops by, Eugene asks for the check and then pays. We finish our coffee and collect ourselves to leave. Out on the sidewalk, Eugene offers me a ride to work, but I decline. I say I'd like to walk. Instead of offering me his hand, Eugene reaches out and takes me in his arms, wraps me in the kind of hug he used to give me when I was a kid. I hold back at first, but then I relax. I go slack, put my arms around him, and rest my cheek against his collarbone. I can smell lemon starch on his shirt. I wonder if Brenda irons his shirts for him, or if that's something Eugene does for himself. He puts a hand on the back of my head. When we breathe, he holds me closer. I don't even care what people passing on the street might think.

WORK IS WORK, EVEN THOUGH STEW'S IS DEAD FOR A Friday. Sean plays Al Green records, referring to the singer as "The Reverend," and we spend the afternoon shooting the shit and laughing. Sean asks about my lunch with Eugene, and I tell him it was good. I tell Sean stories from when John and I were kids taking drum lessons in the basement. I tell him about how Eugene taught us to read charts and music, how he taught us to march and play, to hit our marks without dropping a shot. I move between things that happened to me and things that happened to my brother seamlessly. And all afternoon I'm thinking about April, about the way she rested her weight against the door-jamb, about how she looked in the morning light, about how she said what she said. *I'm falling for you. Like love, John. I'm falling in love with you.* No one has ever fallen in love with me before. No one has ever come close. When Sean disappears into the office to smoke a cigarette, I call April's cell phone. I leave a message saying that I hope she has a good time with her family, that I miss her already, that I'd love to take her out on Monday night when she gets back to the city. When night falls around us, Sean tells me to count my drawer and run our numbers for the week. He says to take it easy as I'm leaving, and I promise to be at band practice on Sunday. By the time I step down from the bus a block from our apartment, I feel like I haven't been home for years.

I know, the instant I unlock our front door, that John is gone. The whole place feels different without him. Every light in the apartment is burning, and John has left a note taped to my bedroom door. It reads: *I have gone out to meet with some acquaintances. I write this since you find my absence so distressing. I'll return if and when I feel like it. JRF.* The whole apartment is a mess, but nothing seems to be deliberately destroyed. John has left no obvious messages to decode.

I can't tell by John's handwriting if he was angry when he wrote the note. It is just his regular scrawl. I turn out all of the lights and walk through the apartment in the dark, listening to the sounds of being alone. I shower in the dark. I massage my sore chest. My ribs ache with each breath. The taps squeak when I shut off the water. I step out of the tub but don't towel off. I cross the hall naked, my bare feet trailing puddles with each step. I toss my clothes in a heap, pull on a pair of boxer shorts and a sleeveless undershirt, and go to sleep.

The sound of John making coffee in the kitchen wakes me at dawn. At first I wonder if it's a dream, but when John begins singing, I know that it's not. He's got a nice tenor and a clear sense of pitch, and it takes me a moment to figure out that he's singing "Welcome to the Jungle." The song sounds like a ballad. Even at this painfully early hour of the morning, I laugh. I pull on clothes, eager to be with John in the kitchen. The apartment is full of his pungent, feral smell when I open my bedroom door. John's smell makes me think of hibernating animals. He almost smells good to me. I creep down the hall and stand quietly in the doorway until John's eyes fall on me. His whole face beams.

"Johnny, you're awake," he says. His eyes are bloodshot, his hair matted.

"Good morning," I say. "Have you slept?"

"Not in any traditional sense," John says. "I can do without it for days, I think. It's all nonsense, anyways. You fall asleep and immediately you're beset by dreams. They exhaust me, all those dreams. It's always better to be awake. Were you worried about me? When I wasn't home last night?"

"A little bit. I tried not to be, since you left me that note and everything. Maybe I wasn't worried so much as I was just thinking about you."

"That's good," John says. "I had a magnificent night."

"Do you want to tell me about it?" I ask.

John whirls from the coffee maker, the carafe in one hand and a cup in the other. Coffee sloshes onto the floor. "You know," John says, "I do. I forget that you don't have a trap door in my brain the way I have in yours. If I want to see what you're up to, I just creak,

creak, creak, lift the hatch and have a peek. There's hardly any difference between what you and I see. But you, poor thing, you're totally in the dark when it comes to me. Coffee?"

"Sure," I say.

John plunks his coffee down on the counter and pours me a cup. He hands me mine, loads his with sugar, and is just about to take a seat at the table when he seems to change his mind.

"Stay here," he says. "I have to get something."

John lumbers down the hall to his bedroom and returns with a portable alarm clock/radio. The machine is sleek and small, all green plastic. I've never seen the thing before.

"Where'd you get that?"

"Penny, of course," John says. "She gives me presents."

"Really?"

John ignores me. He clicks on the radio and tunes it to the local public radio station. The sound is scratchy with static, and the local host sounds like he's talking into a tin can.

"Just a second," John says. "What time is it?"

I glance at my watch. "Almost six."

"We have to wait until the top of the hour," John says. We both sit at the kitchen table watching his radio as if it might do a trick. The local host runs through a list of headlines and then tosses to the traffic announcer.

"Listen," John says. "Now you have to listen." As if I'd been doing something else.

A woman's voice crackles through the speakers. There are backups already on two freeways due to accidents, one involving a tanker truck. There's construction on a bridge, which has traffic narrowed down to two lanes. The woman rattles off travel times that are meaningless to me since I have only the vaguest notion about the web of expressways and toll roads around the city. When she sends the broadcast back to the local host, John clicks off the radio. His sharp eyes dance and snap.

"So?" he says.

"So, what?"

"You can't guess yet?"

"No," I say. "I've got no idea what this is all about."

"I met her yesterday," John says. He leans back in his chair and picks up his coffee cup. "The lady who does the traffic reports."

"Really?"

"Of course, really," John says. "Don't be ridiculous. What kind of question is that?"

"How?"

"That's a better question," John says. "That's a true interrogative. I met her at Starbucks. As soon as I stepped into the place, I knew it was her. She was sitting there at a table all by herself reading a book. She doesn't look like her voice—they never do, people in general, I mean—but she moved her lips as she was reading and I could tell how her voice would sound. It was simpler than you'd think. She has a very particular way with *o*'s. Did you notice?"

"No," I say. John's eyes dart from me to his coffee to the back door. He rakes his fingers through his short, dark curls. I don't know what I'm supposed to say. I'm not sure how far to push this fantasy. "Did you talk to her?"

"Of course," John says. "I learned a million things. She doesn't fly around in a helicopter. They haven't done that for years. There's a whole system of cameras and spies on the highways. People who call in when they see something. She asked me if I'd like to be a traffic spy, but you know I don't drive. Maybe I'll start, though. It'd be fun, I think."

"Is that where you were all night?" I ask. "Talking to the traffic lady?"

"I had a thousand questions as you might imagine, but it didn't take us all night. There were other things that kept me out, but she was the most interesting thing that happened to me. I'm going to try to see her again some time."

"How will you see her again?"

John fixes me with a perplexed look.

"The same way anybody sees anybody again. With my eyes, you idiot. I'd like her to meet Penny. They would be friends. Penny would be an excellent traffic spy. She sees everything. Speaking of, how's April? How's your little whore, Johnny?" I must bridle visibly, because John laughs and continues before I have the chance to say anything. "I'm kidding, I'm kidding. April is a very good girl. Even I know that. Give me the low-down. Tell me about your date night."

"I thought you could see everything through my eyes," I say.

"If I'm trying," John sighs, exasperated. "I wasn't trying last night."

"Should I start with work?"

"Start with April," John says. "Sean bores me to tears, if you want to know the truth."

"Okay." I try to remember Thursday night in a way that makes it less of a memory and more of a story for my brother. "So, when I got to April's apartment, the buzzer to unlock the security door wasn't working. I rang her bell, and the next thing I know she's raising the screen in the living room and she pokes her head out to talk to me."

"Me," John says. His eyes are closed, flickering with movement behind their lids.

"'The buzzer's broken,' she says, and she comes downstairs to let me in."

"Me," John says again. "Tell the story right, Johnny."

"What?"

"Tell it about me." John hasn't opened his eyes. He is totally relaxed, his head tipped back, lolling on his neck. Anger explodes in my chest. I wait for this wave of emotion to ebb, and then I begin again.

"So you're standing on the sidewalk in front of April's apartment waiting for her to buzz you in. You're kind of nervous and fluttery in your chest, which is how you feel every time you think of her, and then suddenly there she is. Her pink face suspended above you. Her smile wide and bright."

"That's better," John says. "Continue."

"'The buzzer's broken,' she says, and she comes downstairs to let you in."

"Does she think I'm gross and fat?" John asks. "I've been worried about that."

I sit at the table across the corner from my brother.

"No," I say. "She doesn't think you're fat."

"Does she like my hair? Does April like it now that I've cut it, or does she think it needs to be washed."

I swallow.

"She likes your hair," I say. "She likes everything about you."

"She doesn't think I stink?"

"No," I say.

"That's good," John says. "That's important, don't you think? You're doing a good job, Johnny. I like the April story better this way. Continue."

"April kisses you in the vestibule. She's been at the beach, and under her tank top and long skirt she's got on a pink bikini. The top is the kind that ties behind her neck. She's a little bit sunburned, even though she smells like sunscreen."

My voice sounds far away from me. Someone else is speaking. Someone else is saying these things. I get John and April upstairs. I get them through the kitchen and out onto the back porch. I describe the moon—an electric eyelash—and the alley and the brightly lit kitchens in the apartments across the way. Thankfully, John falls asleep before I get him and April back inside. He snores loudly. He'll have a stiff neck when he wakes, but I let him sleep.

The weekend passes as weekends do—the Laundromat, the grocery store, John banging away at the kit in the living room, band practice on Sunday—but Saturday and Sunday, and John and Sean and Leda and the rest of the band, everyone and everything feels like background noise, like shadow. What is real, what matters, is the way I feel about April. I feel feverish. People talk about being lovesick, but I never knew love felt like this. Delirium. Cold sweat. This gorgeous ache in my chest. John asked me once if I was going to fall in love with April and I said, how could I? I'm not me out there in the world; I'm you. But I'm falling like a cliff diver, my arms wide, the water blue beneath me. On Sunday night after band practice, John and Penny pass me on the stairs to our apartment, leaving as I return. Penny says hello, but John doesn't look at me. I run up the last flight, let myself in, and then watch them from the front windows. They walk so close to each other that their shoulders touch. John says something that makes Penny throw her head back and laugh. I hope to god that John feels like I do. Sick with love. I want him to have that, and I want to give him to Penny. That's the part I am only now, all these years later, coming to understand. I thought maybe, if he fell in love with Penny, he could transfer all his needs, all his hopes, and all his crazy dreams, to her. From me.

I loved—I love—my brother. But on that night in late July, I sit by the windows watching my brother walk away from me, and a dark corner of my heart hopes love will set me free.

April calls minutes after I get to Stew's on Monday to say yes, I should buy her dinner, I should pick her up at her place. So I do, and April and I have a wonderful night. She's wearing a thin black dress when I arrive at her apartment to pick her up. I've never seen her in a dress before. It wraps around in a complicated fashion and ties at the waist. There seem to be no other closures—no zippers or hooks or buttons or anything. In her heels, she is nearly as tall as me. She glows. Her eyes are incandescent. She suggests an Ethiopian restaurant and shows me how to eat spicy lentils with lemon-flavored bread. We eat with our hands. She tells me about the suburbs. I tell her about band practice. We stop at a smoky neighborhood bar on our way back to her place. We sit at the bar and drink martinis and then steer each other toward the door.

Much later, as April and I lie in her bed, both exhausted and sobering up, she picks up my hand. She props my elbow on her sternum and massages my palm and fingers.

"So about what you said on Friday," I say.

"How's this feel?" April asks. She presses her thumb into a pressure point and my whole hand tingles.

"Wow. Nice."

"I know," she says. "Feel this." She stretches my thumb away from the rest of my fingers, massaging the tight skin in between.

"That feels even better," I say. "Where'd you learn that?"

"John," April says. "Never ask a girl where she learned how to do what she does. She just invented it. Just for you."

We both laugh.

"So about Friday," I say.

"Switch first so I can do your other hand." We swap places, and April starts doing to my left hand what she's been doing to my right.

"Me, too," I say.

"You too, what?"

"I'm falling," I say. "I'm falling, too."

"Where?" April asks. "I want to hear you say it."

"I'm falling in love with you."

April laces her fingers through mine and holds my hand to her chest. I don't know how long we lie there together before I slip my hand out of hers.

"Can I tell you something?" I ask.

April props herself on an elbow and looks down at me. I lie beneath her on my back. I reach up and tuck her wayward hair behind her ear.

"Yes," she says.

"I have to be honest about something."

Even in the dark, I can see April's color change. She blinks. She struggles to be brave. April lies down again next to me, and though I can feel the halo of heat from her body all along my left side, we do not touch.

"I'm ready," April says. "You can tell me anything."

"You know how I told you about my brother?" I ask. "About James?"

"Yeah," April says.

"I didn't tell you everything that night."

"Okay."

"He lives with me," I say. "He's off his meds, and he's actively psychotic, and I'm trying to take care of him."

"Oh," April says. "My god, John."

I seek her hand under the sheet, and she lets me hold it.

"That's why you can't call me at home. That's why I've never asked you to come over. He's crazy, and I don't want you to have to get mixed up in all of that. I thought for a while that things were on an upswing. He seemed to be doing pretty well, at least staying stable and functioning. But I'm kind of worried about him now."

"Worried how? Worried like you might not be safe?"

"No," I say. "No, nothing like that. I'm just worried that I'm not going to be able to take care of him and hold down a job and keep everything else in my life going."

I turn toward April, and she turns toward me. Our faces are inches from each other. Her hair spills across the pillow. Her frightened eyes search my face.

"What are you saying?"

I fight tears. I put a hand on April's chest, and I can feel her heart beat.

"I'm just asking you to be patient with me," I say. "I'm afraid things are going to get even crazier before they get better. I'm asking you to hold tight, you know? Believe in me. If that's possible. I don't know if I can give you everything you deserve right away, but I'm going to figure something out. If you're willing to stick around."

"Stick around?" April asks. "My god, John. You scared the shit out of me." She touches my lips. A tear drips down my nose and wets her knuckles. "Oh, John," she whispers. "Nobody knows, do they? You're alone in this." I nod. "Where the fuck are your parents?"

"It's not their fault," I say. "This was my idea. I thought I could help him get well. I think I've made a spectacular mistake."

"Why didn't you tell me? You could have told me. You could tell Sean, even. We can help you figure this out."

"I didn't want to frighten you," I say. "I didn't want to freak everybody out. I've got this crazy fucking brother. I mean, I'm screwed up in all my own ways, and then there's James, one step away from his next psychotic meltdown. Who would want to be around that?"

"You are not your brother," April says.

"I know," I say.

She takes my head in her hands and draws my mouth down to hers. She kisses me tenderly, and then she kisses me harder. I collapse against her, my right leg between hers, her hipbone against my solar plexus, her breasts soft against my tightly bound chest. She runs her hands down my back. I shift my weight so that I am on top of her. She lifts me with each breath. I bury my face in the hollow between her shoulder the pillow and cry against her neck. April holds me. Her hands never cease soothing my back.

"It's okay," April says. "I know now. You can tell me anything. I'm not going anywhere. It's okay."

I wake in the morning before April. She is turned away from me, her body spread over more than half the mattress. She sleeps on her side, her mouth open, her arms curled protectively around her head.

I stroke her cheek and she doesn't so much as stir at my touch. I slip out of bed and search the clutter on the floor for something to write on and something to write with. I find an empty envelope from American Express and a pen from her work. *Dear April,* I write. *You are so beautiful when you sleep. I am a lucky guy to get to wake up next to you. Thank you. Thank you, thank you, thank you, for everything. JRF.* I leave the note on my pillow, turn the door handle slowly so it doesn't squeak. I find my shoes in the living room. I don't check my watch until I'm out of April's apartment, and I'm shocked to see it's not yet seven o'clock. The streets feel clean and empty this early in morning. When I get out to the main street, I decide to walk south along the bus route until one comes along rather than waiting at the stop. After two blocks, I pass a coin laundry with a payphone out front. I duck through the open doors—the place is already filled with the churning of washing machines—and get quarters for a five. It has been a couple of weeks since I called home. It's dangerously early for calling my parents. They're likely to be sitting at the kitchen table eating grapefruits with serrated spoons for all I know, but depending on the state I find John in, I might not have another chance to call them today. I feed quarters into the payphone, dial my parents' number, and listen to the telephone ring.

"Fields' residence," my father says when he picks up. "This is Richard speaking."

"Hi, Dad," I say.

"Jane. Oh, hello. Hi, Jane," my father says.

"Hi," I say again.

"My goodness, Jane. What a surprise. Oh, it's good to hear your voice," he says. "How are you?"

I wonder if my mother is in the same room with him, if they're exchanging hand signals and gestures with each other.

"I'm fine," I say. "Same old, same old. Nothing especially new around here. How about you? How are you?"

"We're good," he says. "We're fine. Your mother and I are just fine. We've been thinking about you."

"That's nice," I say.

"So, is everything okay? John's doing okay? Nothing has changed?"

"Yeah, no," I say. "Everything's the same. John's John. Why? What's going on?"

"Oh, nothing," our father says. "Nothing in particular. It just seems like a while since we've talked. That's all."

"I know. I'm sorry," I say. My bus rumbles past the bus stop at the end of the block. "Things are busy. I should call more than I do. I'm sorry if you worry."

"We're okay," my father says. "Your mother and I are fine."

We're both quiet for a moment, and I know my father is searching for something that will keep me on the line.

"Listen, Dad, I have to go," I say. "Just thought I'd give a quick ring to say hi. You know."

"Yeah, I know," he says. "Let me get your mother so she can say hello."

"That's okay," I say. "Just say hi for me. I have to go."

"It'll take a second, Jane."

"I know. But I have to go. I'm sorry. Tell Mom hi."

"I love you, Jane," my father says.

"I know, Dad," I say, and then I hang up the phone. I should have said goodbye. Hanging up without saying goodbye must be a bad habit I've picked up from John. I sit on the bench at the bus stop at the end of the block and wait for the next bus that will take me home.

When I reach the landing in front of our apartment door, I hear John thundering down the hall. He slams his bedroom door just as I unlock the front one.

"I'm home, John," I call, although he clearly knows that already. He ran from me when he heard me coming. The apartment is quiet.

The frosted glass globes have been removed from the fixtures in the hall and living room and are lined up on the windowsill. The light bulbs have been removed. The vacant sockets look strange and dangerous. I have no idea what any of this means. I hang my keys on the hook in the hall and knock on John's bedroom door. Something crashes. A one-person struggle ensues.

"John?" I ask.

"Yes?" John says, nonchalantly.

"What's up?" I ask. "What's going on?"

"What do you mean, Johnny?" my brother asks.

"Oh, I don't know. It seems like you've been up to something. You've removed our light bulbs, for one thing. And you're hiding."

"Who says I'm hiding?" John asks from behind the door. His voice is loud but oddly muffled. He might have his face pressed to the crack between the frame and the door. "You know where I am. Just because there's a door between us doesn't mean I've vanished or anything. You're the one who's often not where he's supposed to be."

"I told you I wasn't coming home last night."

"You talk and talk and talk about all sorts of things. It might serve you better if you practiced listening."

"Will you come out?" I ask.

"I will come out," John says, "but you'd better stand back."

I take two steps back, but the hall isn't wide enough for me to retreat further.

"Okay," I say.

John swings his door open. He's got a black eye and his right forearm is skinned wrist to elbow.

"Oh my god. Are you okay, John?"

"I'm fine," John says. "Everything is perfectly fine. Thanks for asking."

"What happened?"

I reach out for his injured arm but John snatches himself away from me. He considers the wound on his forearm and then gingerly touches the swollen purple flesh around his right eye.

"You couldn't possibly understand," he says. "You weren't here. You were doing other things while I got my ass kicked."

"Here?" I ask. "At home? What the fuck happened?"

"I wasn't home. I was somewhere else."

"My god," I say.

"It's not as bad as it looks. Penny took care of it for me."

"Let me see."

"Don't touch," John says, but he stretches his arm out to me. The deep abrasion has been cleaned and treated with ointment, so the raw skin glistens. "Gravel was stuck in there, but Penny got it out. She's very careful. And she felt like shit about the whole thing."

John has showered. It's not just the wound on his arm that's clean. His hair has been freshly washed. His skin smells like soap or lotion or something. His clothes are rumpled but not ripped or dirty.

"Are you going to tell me what happened? Who did this?"

"Johnny," John says, "how often do I have to tell you that what happens to me isn't any of your business?"

"I'm supposed to be taking care of you."

"You're supposed to be doing what I tell you to," John says.

We are standing in the apartment we've shared since early June. We're squared off. I know with a sudden sick feeling, as if my gut has dropped out of me, that we're in the middle of something I don't understand and can't control.

"What happened to the lights?" I ask.

John glances toward the living room. The frosted glass globes cup the morning light that streams through the windows. He glances at the empty sockets above us. He smiles, almost sweetly.

"You're stalling," he says.

"The lights?" I ask.

"What about them?"

"You've removed all the light bulbs."

"I know," John says. "Do you have other observations to make?"

"No."

"Good. We need to talk."

"I can tell you about last night," I say. "If that's what you mean, fine. I can tell you the story. You had a good time. You...April looked so pretty. Do you want to hear about it?"

"I don't think I'm interested in what you have to say," John says. "I'd like to tell you a few things." I have to put a hand out to steady myself against the wall. "I've got bad news, Johnny. I don't think I like April. I've had my questions and reservations since your first date. This girl seems to do something to you. Girls are unpredictable. They get in the way. We're only generating so much energy between the two of us and April seems to be sapping a great deal of it. You come in all ready to clap your jaws about girl stuff and you've been neglecting some of the more interesting aspects of our little experiment. You forget what I want when you're around her. You forget that the whole point is for you to come home and tell me."

"No I don't. I can tell you now, John. I said I would."

"Days late. Days late, my friend. Last night was more than twenty-four hours ago by my clock. I'm interested in where we could go with Sean's band. I've even told Penny a little bit about it, but I don't think you're giving it the serious consideration it deserves. Here's a little secret that's not just true to April. Girls fuck up bands. They do it left and right. There's something about them. I think it's in their biochemistry."

I can feel my pulse behind my eyes and in my wrists, thumping behind all of my pressure points.

"John," I say very quietly. "There's no reason why I have to choose between April and Sean's band."

"You?" John asks. He laughs. "You're not choosing. It's not your choice. It's my story, Johnny-Jane. You can't have what wasn't yours in the first place. I'm the crazy one and even I know that."

"I know what we're doing. Listen, I think you're just going to have to trust me on this. You're not in a position to be making these decisions."

"I don't think you have any idea who's steering this ship. You? Janie-Jane? You think you make this happen? I dream you up!"

The blinds in the living room rattle in a breeze. Bright music blasts from a car beneath our window, and then the car peels out and the music is gone. The world is full of people who don't know my brother exists, who couldn't care less about what he says they can and can't do.

"Fuck that," I say. "You don't dream me. Just because something's happening in your crazy fucked-up head doesn't mean it's true. If I weren't busting my ass to take care of you, you'd be raving in the streets. You're just another schizophrenic off your meds, John. You'd be lost without me."

John sweeps my legs out from under me with a swift kick. I had no idea my brother could move so fast. My head whacks the floor and light pops and sparkles in front of my eyes. John's face looms in my view as I struggle to grip consciousness. John's on top of me. He pins my shoulders to the floor. I can't breathe. My vision fades. The world threatens to go black.

"You've gotten too comfortable, little sister. You've forgotten who's the real John. I'm only letting you borrow me. I'm not yours or anything."

"I know you're John," I say, gasping. I am a fish on a boat deck. "I know who you are. You're hurting me. I can't breathe."

John leans his knees into my shoulders sockets, which takes his weight off my ribcage, but makes my arms go instantly numb. They don't even tingle. They just go cold and dead to me. John's eyes are wet and his nose runs.

"You aren't doing me any favors."

"I don't know what you're talking about."

"Are you afraid of me?" John asks. "Right now. Are you afraid of me?"

"How could I be afraid of you? I love you," I say.

"Oh, Jane," John says. "Don't be stupid. We all fear what we love best."

John rocks back on his haunches and hauls himself to his feet. Bolts of pain shoot down to my fingertips as blood rushes back into the arteries.

"Get up," he says, but I can't. He reaches down and pulls me up. I'm dizzy and staggered, woozy. My head throbs, but I know I have to concentrate. I have to follow John. There isn't any other choice.

"We've gotten way off base," John says. He steadies me. He takes my ringing head in his big, soft hands. "You have to let me put us back on course. I know you're not doing anything maliciously. I've checked up on that. You're just dangerously confused. You have to trust me."

"Tell me what you need me to do," I say. "I just want to help you."

He strokes my hair and my ears.

"You need to end this April foolishness. Let her down easy. Tell her whatever seems best, but tell her it's over. I'm sorry I sent you down that road. We've both made mistakes. I see that now. I see everything so much more clearly than you do. Let's walk away from this before it gets out of hand."

"John," I say. "Please."

"Hush," John says. "Keep what you can. I'm not asking you to give up Sean or Stew's or the band. Cut your losses and keep what you can. Talk to April this weekend. Today or tomorrow. I don't care when. Just so long as it's soon."

"I can't, John," I say.

"Sure you can. I know it hurts. I remember. Will you miss her?"

"Yes."

"More than that, will you miss the guy you got to be around her?"

"Yes," I whisper. My eyes burn. My throat aches.

"You're not the only one who's had to give that up," John says. "I remember. Giving that up isn't easy, but it's something you can do. I did it. I gave up everything. I'll help you," my brother says.

John takes me by the hand and guides me to the living room, which is filled with mid-morning light. Someone is selling ice cream out on the street. I sit on the edge of the couch. John hands me the telephone.

"Do you have her number in your brain, or do you need to look it up?"

"I know it by heart," I say.

John turns the receiver belly-up in my hand.

"Press the buttons, Johnny-Jane," he says.

I dial April's number and listen to her cell phone ring.

"John?" she asks when she picks up.

My eyes flash to my brother's. His are liquid. He gnaws at his bottom lip.

"Hi," I say.

"Why'd you take off this morning?" April asks. "I was lonely, waking up without you."

"Say, April, we need to talk," John whispers.

"April," I say, "we need to talk."

"Hey, John," April says. "Are you okay?"

"Say, When can I see you?" John says. "Tonight or tomorrow, maybe?"

"When can I see you?" I ask. "Tonight, or tomorrow, maybe?"

"What's going on?" she asks.

John and April both wait for me to say something. Sweat beads along John's hairline. On the other end of the line, I know that April is standing very still, the cell phone cupped in one hand, her eyes fixed but unfocused. She is picturing me rather than seeing what is in front of her.

"Tonight would be good," I say, as if she's suggested it. "I could come over."

"Is there something going on with James?" April asks.

"I'm okay," I say.

"That's not what I asked."

"I know," I say. "But I'm okay."

"I've got lessons in the afternoon," April says. "Do you want to come over after? Or do you need me to cancel? You can come right now."

"Yes," I say. "I'll come by your place this evening. Don't worry, okay?"

John nods.

"If you're in trouble," April says, "and you need me to do something, say no. But if you're okay and tonight is fine, and you're just being freaking weird for some reason that you'll explain when I see you, say yes."

"Yes," I say. "Yes."

"Okay," April says. "Okay. I'll see you tonight. I'll be home. Come as soon as you can, okay?"

"Okay," I say.

"Hey," April says.

"I know," I say. "I'll see you soon. Goodbye."

April is silent for a moment, but I wait for her to say, "Bye, John," and then I hang up.

"That was very good," my brother says. "I'm proud of you." He takes the phone away from me and places it in the cradle. He stands by the window, smiling to himself and fingering the tender flesh of his bruised eye. I've never learned what happened to him. He's never talked to me about that night. "You're such a good girl," John says.

I CAN'T STAY IN THE APARTMENT WITH JOHN. THERE'S not enough oxygen for the two of us to begin with. And then Penny shows up with her lit cigarettes and her smeared eye makeup, and I have to get the hell out of there. I spend the better part of the morning walking, just being out in the world. I feel dangerously free of a script. I don't have to do what my brother says just because he's told me to. Even as I think such wild thoughts, I do not know if they are true.

By noon I've found myself in a neighborhood I've never been in, and I stop in at a coffee shop. I have an hour still before I have to be at Stew's. The sign above the door identifies the place as A Traveler's Café. A line of clocks snakes its way around the walls, up near the tin ceiling, each set to a different hour with the name of a city fixed beneath. You can watch time tick by in Bangkok or Santiago or Berlin or Detroit. The bookshelves are stacked with travel guides and maps and memoirs set in exotic and hostile locations. There are scarves for sale, and hand-made crafts and sticks of incense. I order a cup of coffee and a sandwich at the counter.

A sign above the bookshelf reads *feel free to peruse,* so I pick up a Lonely Planet guide to Cambodia and sit at a tiny table. I'm not really reading, just thumbing through the book, sipping my coffee, eating a tuna sandwich on wheat, feeling anonymous and alive. The café is uncomfortably hot, but no one seems to mind.

"You ever been?" a girl asks.

I look up. I did not notice when she sat at a table opposite from mine. She is very lean, and she wears thick-rimmed, green glasses. Her hair is bleached dramatically, so blond it's almost white. When I look at her uncomprehendingly, she gestures toward my book with her bagel.

"Cambodia," she says. "Have you ever been?"

I turn the guidebook over in my hands. "No," I say. "You?"

"Yeah. Last summer. It was amazing. You think you know Southeast Asia, you know? I mean, Thailand—the beaches and everything. Hong Kong. Some of the islands. But nothing prepares you for Cambodia. It's stunning. Another world, really."

I blink at her. "Oh."

"You should go," the girl says. She takes a huge bite of her bagel and then moves her plate aside so she can open her newspaper in front of her. We don't say anything more until I get up to leave. "I'm serious," the girl says. "Go to Cambodia."

"I will," I say. I return the Lonely Planet to its shelf.

"See you around?" she asks.

"Yeah," I say. "Maybe."

If I were really John's brother, I could ask April to run away with me. If he were James and I were John, April and I could step out of his life forever. I swing open the door of the café. The sun is brilliant in a sky so blue it nearly sings. Light strikes the sidewalk and store windows. Traffic surges by me on the street.

The afternoon at Stew's is like any afternoon at Stew's, except that Clint stops by to chat about our first gig coming up this Saturday. They call Roger, and he agrees to add a practice Friday night, and I say I'm in. Absolutely. I'm up for anything. Just as he's leaving, Clint turns to me. He cocks his head to the side.

"You okay, Fields?" he asks.

"Yeah." I return his gaze. "Why?"

"Something's different," Clint says. "Your energy is off or something."

"Take that hippie shit with you when you go," Sean says. "John's energy is exactly how it's always been. So is his aura."

"I don't know anything about auras," Clint says. "That's just new age foolishness."

The three of us laugh.

"Later, dude," Sean says, saluting. "You're the mastermind."

"See you soon," Clint says. The bell above the door rings as the door closes behind him.

By the time I get to April's, she's waiting for me out on the sidewalk in a pool of orange streetlight. I cross over to her side of the street.

She holds her arms out to me, and I wrap her in mine. She settles in, her head nestled against my throat, as if we were going to stand on the sidewalk holding each other for a long time.

"What's going on?" she finally asks.

"Let's walk," I say.

April turns and takes my hand. She laces her fingers through mine, and we walk away from the main street and toward the darker interior of the neighborhood. A breeze rustles leaves above us. April is wearing leather-soled sandals that slap against the concrete. We pass from one pool of streetlamp light to another, dipping into shadow in between. We hit a block where the streetlights are out and step into surprising darkness.

"Tell me what's going on," April says.

"James has sent me to break up with you."

"Ah," April says. "That old line. It's not you—it's my crazy brother. I get so tired of that routine."

She says this so utterly deadpan that it takes us both a moment to laugh. My own laughter sounds closer to hysteria than I'd like it to. April keeps walking. She keeps holding my hand. She keeps on stroking my knuckles with her thumb. She doesn't look up at me.

"He was sitting there when I called this morning," I say. "He kind of made me."

"I figured as much."

"He's got this puppet-master thing. It's complicated. I've been playing into it. He's the crazy one, but I think I've been making things worse. Living in his reality, if that makes any sense."

"Sure," April says. "We can tell ourselves almost anything. We all do that."

"Not like this."

"Well, no," April says. "Probably not exactly like this, but not totally different from it either."

We walk in silence for a while. We turn up one street and down another, zigzagging our way away from her apartment.

"What are you going to do?" April finally asks.

"I don't know," I say. "I don't have the first fucking clue what I should do about my brother."

"I was kind of asking about me," April says. "What are you going to do about me?"

"Oh."

"You can't break up with me because James told you to. You can dump me for any number of reasons, but not that one. If he's the problem, let me help you figure out how to fix it. If I'm the problem, tell me. Break my heart and get it over with."

April turns us in a direction that will take us back toward her apartment.

"I love you," I say, after we've walked quietly for more than a block.

"I believe you," April says.

"You're the most amazing girl I've ever met."

"I'm nothing special," April says. "I just really like you."

"I don't want to break up with you."

"Will you lie to James? Are you going to tell him it's over?"

"Yes," I say. "For now. I think I have to."

April laughs, and by the sound of it, I can tell she's on the verge of tears. She rubs her eyes with her free hand and leans her head against my shoulder.

"Aw, shit," she says. "I've had guys lie to all sorts of people about me—their girlfriends, their frat brothers, their Percocet-country-club moms. But this is a new one. I don't know why it hurts my feelings."

"That's the last thing I want. It's not going to be forever. Just until I can figure out what to do about James."

April nods. She swings our hands and takes a deep breath. She smiles ruefully up at me. At the corner, we come upon a party spilling out of an apartment block. We duck our heads and step around people drinking beers on the sidewalk. We turn down the next street and the noise of the party subsides quickly.

Eventually, April asks, "So what are the options?"

"I don't know," I say. "There's this part of me, even now, that thinks if I could just figure out how to take care of him, James would get well. When we moved up here together, right before I started working at Stew's, I really thought he just needed a fresh start. He was so angry at our parents. He was so angry at the doctors and hospitals and drugs and I can't even tell you what all else. It felt like the problem was there, you know? The problem was located in this particular time and place and all he needed was room to breathe. I know it's stupid. It's delusional, probably."

"We believe what we need to believe."

"It doesn't do any good to believe something that's not true."

"Maybe," April says. "What about treatment? Like, the professional kind."

This time, I laugh. As if what John and I have been doing could be considered treatment, even of a nonprofessional kind.

"He'd never go willingly. I can't make him do anything."

"Could your parents?"

"No. He doesn't trust them for a minute. He'd never do anything at their suggestion."

"I mean legally. Can they make him get help? Could they have him committed? I feel like people do that. You see it on TV."

"He'd have to be hospitalized. He'd have to be a threat to himself or to someone else. And then he could only be held for a little while. Three days, maybe."

We fall silent as we pass a woman waiting for her dog to do its business, a plastic grocery bag ready in her hand.

"Is he?" April asks, once we're a few doors down. "A threat to himself or someone else?"

"No," I say. "He's not a fucking criminal. He's just psychotic. They're not the same thing."

"I'm sorry," April says. "I'm just asking. I don't know anything about it."

"Hey, no, I know," I say. "I'm just tired. I didn't mean to snap at you."

"You'll tell me, right?" April asks. "If there's anything I can do?"

"Absolutely."

We have looped back around to April's block. I glance at my watch in the glow of the security light above the door.

"You should go?"

"I think so," I say. "I told James I'd come home."

April takes both of my hands in hers. She presses our palms together and leans her weight against me.

"When can I see you again?" she asks. "Are we going to have to sneak around like teenagers?"

"For a little bit." I kiss her on the nose. I kiss her on the lips. "Hey! I almost forgot with all this James stuff. Our first gig. It's this Saturday."

"Really?"

"Yeah."

"Then that's where I'll see you," April says. "If not before. I'll come and be your groupie. I'll hang around by the stage door."

"You'll come?" I ask.

"Don't be an idiot," April says. "Of course I'll come. I'm your secret fucking girlfriend."

"I love you," I say. "I'm sorry this is all so complicated."

"Life is one complication after another. If things were suddenly easy, I'd get nervous."

I kiss her hard and say goodnight, and then watch through the glass door as she climbs the stairs to the second floor. When I return to our apartment, John greets me at the door. His eyes look like he hasn't slept in days.

"Is the deed done?" he asks. "Are you free?"

I look my brother straight in his crazy face and lie to him. "Yes," I say.

As I leave for work on Wednesday, John stands anxiously in the open door, fiddling with the deadbolts, watching without looking at me. When I get to Stew's, Sean is oddly dressed up. He wears a blue button-down instead of his customary ratty t-shirt, and though the shirt could use pressing, he looks nice. His jeans are clean and without holes. His wooly hair is damp, slicked back a little better than usual in its ponytail. He still smells like cigarettes. Somewhere in me, something jumps. I have almost forgotten how back in the early days, Sean used to make my pulse thump.

"Yo, John," Sean says. "How's it going?"

"Fine," I say. "What gives?"

"The threads? Stew's coming by. We're having a sit-down with someone who's interested in buying him out. I've got to be all presentable and go over the books."

"What?" I ask. "Stew's doing what?"

"Man, he's thinking about Florida. The guy's seventy. He's thinking about golf courses and condos and good-looking widows."

Sean examines his hair in the security mirror at the back of the store. The convex mirror sends back a distorted reflection.

"So what's that mean?" I ask. "Like, for us."

Sean turns to me and shrugs. "Probably nothing. I'm guessing if this guy wants to buy the place he'll need staff just the same. Unless he wants to liquidate and do something else. We'll know more after this meeting."

"How long has this been going on?"

"I don't know," Sean says. "A couple months. Why so hot and bothered?"

"Because it seems like something I should have known about," I say. I pull the drawer from the register. I lick my thumb and start counting twenties.

"John, you just work here, man. No offense, but really. Worst-case scenario, Stew sells the place, which takes a couple months, and we're out of jobs. We get other ones. There are a hundred jobs like this across the city."

"I know," I say. "I know. I'm just surprised, that's all. You're right. No big deal."

"So you can hold down the fort this afternoon?" Sean asks.

"Sure," I say. "You bet."

I can't even imagine what will happen to me if I'm out of a job at Stew's. I learned to be me here. I know exactly what to do. Sean and the store are such integral parts of my story that I'd have to reinvent everything with a new job. Returning to the chaos of those early days would be terrible. The vastness of the world makes life impossible. I can only manage what little I've got.

Stew arrives shortly. He is dapper and elderly, his gray suit well tailored over a purple paisley shirt. Sean introduces us, and we shake hands. The old man is in high spirits. He compliments my handshake, takes a cursory stroll around the store, briefly examines the spreadsheets Sean has prepared for him, and then nods toward the door. He slaps a hand on the counter and admonishes me to mind the till. Then he and Sean are gone. The Strokes album Sean had been playing comes to an end, and I can't think what to put on our sound system. I let the store descend into silence. I listen to the almost inaudible speaker hum. I try to quiet the riot in my heart.

Customers arrive and browse and ask questions. Some buy things. Others do not. Eventually, each one leaves. During a lull in the afternoon, I call April. I expect to get her voicemail, but she picks up.

"John?" she asks.

"Hey! Yeah, it's me," I say.

"What's up?"

"Aren't you at work?"

"Yeah, but I'm on break. Sort of. What do you need?"

"I was just calling. Sean's out and the store's empty. I wanted to hear your voice. I thought I'd get your voicemail."

"Are you okay, babe?" April asks.

"I'm just tired," I say.

In the background, I can hear some sort of commotion around April.

"Could you get away Friday?" April asks. "Could I see you?"

"Band practice. Clint wants to run through our set."

"Oh, okay," April says. Something happens that changes her attention. "Listen, I gotta go, John. But I'll see you Saturday. Tell James the band's going to have an after-party or something. Figure out a way to come home with me."

"I will. I promise. I can't wait."

"Bye," April says, and then her phone clicks off. I can picture her snapping it closed and slipping it into the pocket of her scrubs.

When Sean returns, he's got little information. He says the guy made Stew an offer and Stew countered and the two of them could be at this for weeks. He tells me not to fret my pretty little head. I tell him to fuck off.

Band practice on Friday night is more frenetic and driven than it has been before. We start late, after Sean and I close up the store. For the first hour we have to play beneath the thrashing of the metal band upstairs, but then they break down and pack up, and the whole neighborhood seems to get quiet, save for us. Clint keeps everyone on a short leash, limiting cigarette breaks, moving us from song to song, dropping out on the keyboards to listen to the rest of the band. He cuts everyone off in the middle of a song to snap, "John, dude, you're dragging. You're killing us. What the fuck?" I pick up the tempo. I drive the song on and Clint nods at me, satisfied. Even Leda receives his short-tempered direction. Leda adjusts her phrasing, but remains untroubled by Clint's tone. At twelve-thirty, Leda puts her foot down.

"Enough, Clint," she says. "We're good to go, love. It's a bar. It's a fifty-dollar gig. Now it's time to celebrate."

From behind the couch, Leda pulls out a cardboard box. She unwraps the waxed-paper contents, the Hungarian wedding bread she promised Sean. Roger hands over a pocketknife, and Leda cuts big hunks for everyone. The bread is flaky and sticky, glazed in honey and chopped nuts.

"A toast," Leda says, as if the bread were champagne. "To playing out. To having fun. To good music and good people and the good luck of landing John. Thanks for joining us," she says to me.

"Abso-fucking-lutely," Sean says. He raises his bread in my general direction, and we all say, "Cheers."

We all relax. We eat Leda's sweet bread and laugh. We wipe sticky hands on our jeans and Leda lets everyone drink from her water bottle. We pack up our instruments, including the drum kit, which we load into the back of Clint and Leda's van. There is a moment when Leda and I are alone in the alley, and she turns to me.

"Are you okay, John?" she asks.

I heft the bass drum into the back of the van and pack an old quilt around it. "Yeah," I say. "What do you mean?"

Her hair is an orange nimbus around her head in the sodium security lights. She tucks a lock behind her ear, but it doesn't do much to calm her curls. "You seem stressed out. I'm just checking in. That's all."

"Yeah, you and your husband," I say. "Clint says my energy's off. Maybe there's something up with the two of you." I unscrew the high-hat from its stand and slip the cymbals between free folds of the quilt.

Leda stands with a hand on the open hatch of the minivan.

When I finish with the kit, she closes the back and steps around to the driver's side.

"I'm a friend, John," she says, "if you need one. I'm not an enemy."

"Fields!" Sean says as he and Clint trot down the back steps. "A lift to April's?"

"No," I say. "I'm headed home."

"Where's the lady in your life?" Sean asks.

"Girls' night," I say. "Buckets of tequila. That's the last thing I need."

"Tomorrow, men," Clint says. He climbs into the passenger seat of the van and rolls his window down. "Go home and get some sleep. Don't be idiots tonight, and be there early tomorrow."

"Sure thing, Pops," Roger says. He, too, has loaded his gear into Clint and Leda's van. He mounts his bicycle and pedals off down the alley.

"So it's just me and you," Sean says. We both get into his car. "Want to grab a beer?" he asks.

"I'd better just head home," I say. "It's been a long week."

"Suit yourself," Sean says.

John is sitting on the floor in the hallway when I open the front door. He has installed two-hundred-watt bulbs in all of our light fixtures. The bright hall makes me wince when I come in from the dim stairwell. John sits with his legs spread wide in front of him, drawing on a pad of notebook paper on the floor. He hardly glances up when I come in. I step over him to hang my keys on the hook on the wall.

"Hey," I say, coming to sit next to him. I take my drumsticks and my wallet from my back pockets and drop them on the floor beside us.

"Hello, brother," John says.

He's working on a pencil drawing of Leda. The likeness is remarkable, especially since it's based entirely on my description. In John's rendering, Leda is astride a dragon. He is shading the individual feathers on the dragon's wings.

"It looks like her," I say.

"I know," John says. "Who else would it look like?"

"I'm just saying, it's impressive. You and Leda haven't actually met."

"We have a lot in common," John says. He looks up at me earnestly. "We have a connection, I think. Plus, I get a glimpse of her every time you look at her. She likes me, doesn't she?"

"Yes," I say. "A great deal. I don't think you'll ever be best friends or anything, but she probably likes you more than even Sean does."

"Girls are like that," John says. "Does Clint get jealous?"

"Clint's married to her. What does he have to be jealous of?"

"Marriage isn't everything."

"Marriage is almost everything," I say.

"I used to think about getting married," John says. He begins cross-hatching the underbelly of the dragon.

"Really?"

"Sure. Why not?"

"Like when?"

"Back when we were younger," John says. He cocks his head as he works. "Even when we were kids. When I started thinking about Mom and Dad as people and not just parents. Didn't you?"

"I don't know," I say, truly puzzled. I have no memory of such things. "Maybe not. Maybe I was different than you. Do you want to hear about work, or should I just start right in with band practice?"

"Did anything special happen at Stew's? Anything specifically noteworthy?"

I haven't told John about Stew's plans to sell the place. It's just one more thing he doesn't need to know.

"Nothing special," I say.

"Tell me about practice," John says.

"Clint is really starting to crack the whip," I say. "He's getting serious. He wasn't out front smoking with Roger when Sean and I got there. He was upstairs with Leda, working on the set list."

I close my eyes as I talk so I can work through the evening as methodically as possible. I describe the conversation Sean and Roger had about a bar-fight Roger claimed to have been in the previous night. Roger was trying to explain an abrasion under his right eye and his busted glasses, but Sean insisted he must have tried to ride his bike home drunk and taken a nosedive. I get us upstairs and through the first half of rehearsal. I describe Clint joining Sean and Roger for a cigarette in the middle of practice and the way Leda and I sat on the couch with our eyes closed. I describe the second half of rehearsal and then packing up our gear for tomorrow night, but I leave out the part where Leda asked if I was all right.

"Is Clint nervous?" John asks.

"Keyed up. Anxious for us to do well, but I wouldn't say nervous."

"Are you?" John asks. "Nervous, I mean?"

"Yeah," I say. "Not when we're playing, but when I think about it. Did you used to get nervous?"

"So nervous I'd puke."

"Really?"

"I swear to god. Every weekend of my drum line life."

"I never knew."

"You think I'd let you see me like that? You think I'd let Eugene?"

I look at my brother. I try to remember him, really see him from back then. Sometimes I'm shocked by how hard it is to do. He bites his pink tongue in concentration as he works his pencil over the notebook paper. Sweat wets the curls on his forehead. He adds leaping flames around Leda's head.

"Remember how I used to keep the drum line after the rest of the band went home? We'd have sectionals, and I'd want to keep on practicing even after Eugene got so tired he could hardly keep his eyes open? Do you remember that?"

"Yes," I say. "I do."

"Man, it makes me crazy to think about Eugene. Even after all these years. I think about him almost every day. Did you know that, Johnny-Jane?"

"No. How could I? You hardly ever talk about him."

"What could I say? What could I possibly say?"

John slaps the cover of his notebook shut and throws his pencil into the dark living room. He twists and tugs at the locks of hair above his ears.

"Can I come tomorrow?" he finally asks. "Do you think it'd be okay if I came to the bar to see you guys play? I'd be incognito, you know. No one would know anything. I could act like a normal person for a few hours. I could just sit at the bar and listen, and we wouldn't even have to acknowledge each other. Penny could come. She'd keep an eye on me."

John almost never asks me for permission to do anything. His dark eyes roam.

"What about Sean?" I ask.

"What about that wool-head?"

"He'd recognize you. From that night. He'd remember you, and he'd want to talk."

"I hadn't thought about that." John chews his lip. "I could talk to him. I could do that. I could be surprised to see him and everything. Don't you think I could pull that off?"

"Maybe for our second gig?" I ask. "It'd be best for me to see how things go the first time. You know, get a lay of the land. I'll scope everything out and let you know exactly what to expect the next time. We don't want to risk anything."

John nods. He looks at me sadly. "You're right. I think you're right. I'm very tired, Johnny. Do you think I should go to bed?"

"Yes," I say. "I think so."

"Move out of the way. I have to crawl there. I don't feel like standing up."

I scoot to the other side of the hall, and John crawls to his bedroom door. He butts the door open with his head.

"Goodnight, John," I say. I lean my head back against the wall and close my eyes. I can see the blood moving in the capillaries of my eyelids, the light above me is so bright.

"Johnny?" John asks eventually. A breeze rattles the blinds in the living room. I don't open my eyes.

"Yeah?"

"What are you hiding from me?"

My heart stops, and my blood tingles in my veins. It's not a chill so much as current that passes through me.

"What do you mean?"

"Something's going on," John says. "You're hiding something. I know you inside out. I knew you before you were formed. What are you keeping from me?"

John speaks to me from the dark cavern of his bedroom. He

doesn't come out into the hall where I can see him. I feel that strange sucking sensation of being dragged out of a dream.

"Stew might be selling the store," I hear myself say. My voice wavers, threatens to crack. "I didn't want to trouble you with it. We might be out of a job. If Stew sells and the guy wants to liquidate, we'll be back to square one."

"Are you crying, Johnny?" John asks.

Tears cut a hot path down my cheeks. I feel like I'm crying every time I turn around. I feel stretched so thin my skin might rip.

"Yes."

John emerges from his bedroom and kills the hall lights. We are plunged into a merciful dark.

"Johnny," he says, his voice smooth and soothing. "Hey, Johnny. Hush."

"I'm so tired," I say.

John sits beside me. I can feel him even though I've put my hands over my face.

"Johnny," he says. "See? You shouldn't hide things from me. It's not good for you. It makes both of us crazy. I'm over here imagining all sorts of things, and you're stretched like catgut. Isn't that how they make tennis rackets?"

I laugh and then choke. I rub my face hard with my hands.

"I think so," I say. "At least they used to."

"You have to tell me everything," John says. "It makes things better, not worse."

"I know," I say.

"You're probably all twisted up about tomorrow too, aren't you?"

"Yeah, you could say that," I say.

"And about April?" he asks.

Even in the dark, I can see that his eyes are screwed up with concern. I can see his eyelashes mesh and separate when he blinks. I can't answer my brother. I just nod.

"Do you miss her?"

"Yeah," I whisper.

"The thing about life, Johnny," John says, "is that once you know it one way, you can't possibly imagine it another. You know what I mean."

"Yeah," I say again.

"It's like me. I didn't think this was how everything would go. I thought I'd always be that guy you're trying to be. I couldn't imagine this version of myself, so my brain and the world and the whole universe had to imagine it for me. I'm trying to help, Janie-John. Are you listening to me?"

"I am," I say.

"Don't cry," John says. "I don't think it's good for us. April's just stardust. She's just made out of molecules."

"Okay."

"Get some sleep," John says. "You've told me now. I can help. We'll figure everything out."

"I know," I say.

John pats my head and then struggles to his feet. His knees pop. He shuts himself up in his room. I put my hands back over my face and breathe.

When morning sun streams through my window, I begin to wake intermittently, but cannot manage consciousness. I struggle to the surface just long enough to recognize daylight, to hear the sounds of John moving through the apartment, to suffer stabs of panic at my powerlessness, and then I am dragged back under into oblivion. This sleep is like sinking in a dark liquid. When I finally wake, it feels as if I've cut through a sticky membrane separating me from consciousness. I lie panting in my sheets, trying to clear my head. I fumble for my watch and find it is past nine o'clock. John never lets me sleep this long. I climb from bed and stretch. Every muscle aches. My joints are stiff. I can hear John in the living room, his voice rising and falling in a cadence and timbre he doesn't usually use when he's just talking to himself. He laughs loudly and then his voice drops to a rumble.

I wonder if Penny is in our apartment, but I don't hear her voice. All I hear is my brother in the living room, being himself. I dress for the day. My wallet is missing from its usual spot on my dresser, which puzzles me until I remember that I left it in the hall last night. When I finally crack open my bedroom door, I turn away from the sound of John cackling in the living room and opt for brushing my teeth instead of saying good-morning. I expect John to call out to me from the living room when he hears doors opening and closing, water running, all the usual signs of morning life, but he doesn't. I head for the living room but stop in the hall, arrested by John's words once I can distinguish them.

"Oh, I know," he is saying. "I know, I know, I know. The speed of light is hard to imagine, but multiply that by ten and you'll have some idea what I've been grappling with. Impossibility is what I'm talking about."

He falls silent. I can hear John breathe.

"But you're not listening to me," he starts in again. "That's the whole point. I'm talking about the beginning and the end of all things. From sun up to sun up, as they say. You only know half the story, so don't try your magic tricks on me. Johnny-John is bright—she's more imaginative than I'd first given her credit for—but that doesn't mean I can't catch on once I know the score. Sweetheart, honey, April," John says, "listen to me. I am John. Your boyfriend only exists in your dreams."

The world warps and reels. The air thins. Blood rushes in my ears, and for a surreal moment I am not thinking about John and April but my own circulatory system. I can picture the strong muscle of my heart, the hot liquid of my blood—a thing of wonder and beauty. I step into the living room. John looms and leers. His mouth is red and thick, his eyes very dark and very dangerous. My wallet lies open on the couch. John has rifled its contents. He holds the cordless phone to the side of his head and the base in his hand. John speaks into both the receiver and the cradle when he talks.

"Johnny," he says, delighted. His eyes flash when he says my name. "You told her you had a brother. I didn't know that. You've been very successful. April's sharp. She knew who I was in no time at all. There's the name thing, though. That part is confusing. James, the brother of John, right? Which one did Jesus love? I forget."

"What?" I ask.

"Never mind. We can talk about the New Testament later. April and I are in the middle of something."

The living room pitches. The world heaves and swells. I hold my hand out. "Give me the phone, John."

"Ah, did you hear that, April?" John shouts. "I am who I am. Even Janie-John has to call me John. I don't have another name."

"Give me the telephone," I say. "Please."

"It's easier this way, Janie," John says.

He's speaking to me and to the telephone.

"I'm only trying to help you," John says. "April thinks John loves her, which is sweet but impossible since I'm John and I think she and I would have a failure to communicate. I've tried to explain everything, but it's not easy since you've made such a mess of things. Lies, Janie-John. You've been lying to me. And to April, that poor thing. All this time. She and I have something in common, don't we sweetheart?" He looks at the telephone lovingly. "We'll both survive, April. We won't let Janie-John's lies get the best of us. You're a good girl. At least I think you are. Your voice sounds like the voice of a good girl."

John falls silent. April must be speaking. John's eyes are focused on something I can't see. I think about the different parts of the brain, about the electrical storms firing in different lobes and different hemispheres, one location for sight, another for speech. John's eyes clear and settle on me.

"You've had a very difficult morning, April. I think you're right. I think you do deserve some answers from Johnny. We'll see what he's capable of." John finally holds the telephone out. "Do your worst, little brother," he says.

My hand trembles. I can hear April sobbing before I even have the receiver to my ear. My throat is dry, my tongue thick. I cannot understand why I'm not hysterical. I am beset by calmness. I am separate from what's happening to April and me. I can see us both from a great distance. What a shame, I think.

"April." The word is a hoarse whisper, air forced over dry vocal cords.

"John?" she asks. "Are you there?"

"I'm here," I say. My eyes are locked on my brother's. He stands less than two feet from me. April gasps and struggles, trying to get a hold of herself. "April," I say.

"I think you should get out of there, John. Get the hell out of there. I don't think you're safe."

"I'm okay," I say.

"What the fuck is going on? Why did you call James John?"

"It would take me a lifetime to explain," I say. April is on a raft in a river. I am standing on the bank and she is calling to me, but reaching her is so impossible that I don't even move. The river carries her toward a waterfall, toward a void over which water tumbles and vanishes. I am transfixed by the horror of it. April calls to me. I must be suffering pain so intense that my brain has stepped in and cut its own circuits. Whatever emotion I'm about to suffer is confined in my skull. It's not happening to my body. Not yet.

"Then you better get your fucking ass over here and get started," April says. She is livid. I can hear that, but I don't feel it. Maybe that's because she's talking to John, and John, the one she knows, is about to be smashed to smithereens. Another lovely glass lamp.

"I'm so sorry, April," I say. "You deserve better than this."

"What are you saying?"

"I wish there were some way I could have told you the truth."

In the silence between us I can picture April, her round face mottled, her eyes puffy and swollen. I've seen her cry. She cried over the Mason jar of gasoline that exploded at my feet. That created me.

"Who are you?" April asks. "How much of the fucking crazy shit your brother just said to me is true?"

"I don't know," I say. "I didn't hear most of it."

"Oh my god," April says. "Oh my fucking god. Jane? Is that your name?"

I look at John. I think I feel terror. If I had to pick a word for what's happening to me, that might be it. John reaches out for me. He puts one hand on my shoulder and takes the phone in his other. I don't let go until he unpeels my fingers. The only sensation I register is the hot, sweaty point of contact between John's palm and my shoulder.

"Okay," John says. "There you go."

He places the telephone to his own ear. "April," he says, softly. "Listen to me. You weren't supposed to get so bound up in all of this. I told Johnny-Jane to set you free. Anything that's happened since then can't technically be my fault. What I want you to do is close your eyes and count to three, and when you hear the dial tone, you'll forget that we ever showed up in your life. One, two, three," John says, and then he disconnects the call with his thumb.

My ears ring. The air around us crackles and hums. Perhaps I am hearing the dial tone just as April must be. John lays the receiver in its base. He strokes the curved plastic. The phone rings. Without taking his eyes off of me, John bends down and removes the cord from the jack.

"There," John says. "It's as easy as that."

Whatever John has dreamed of doing to me has been done. I am a body now, nothing else. My heart beats. My lungs pump. Beyond that, nothing.

"Get out," John says.

"What?"

"You have to leave now. You've failed, Jane. There is no way I could ever trust you."

"John, please," I say.

John opens our front door.

"Leave. I don't care where you go, Janie-Judas. I don't care what you do. I don't care what happens to you."

THIS IS JOHN A MILLION YEARS AGO, BACK WHEN HE WAS him and I was me: He's sixteen, and it's winter. Just days away from our Christmas break. We are well into the deepest watches of the night, hours away from the first stirrings of life in our neighborhood and even more hours away from the first weak rays of sunlight. I am asleep as I ought to be, but John is not. I wake to the sound of the latch giving on my bedroom door. The hinges creak, and John walks in. The room seems strangely luminous, and for a confused moment I think John is generating his own light. He smiles his secret smile. His eyes are dark and quick with mischief. He is radiant and heartbreaking. Although, I wonder now if he was not heartbreaking to me then. Perhaps he was only radiant. Perhaps it is the memory that is heartbreaking now that I've seen the glass lamp of him shattered. In any case, there is too much light in the room for the middle of the night as John wakes me into wonder.

"Janie," John whispers, "it's snowed."

And then I understand the strange illumination of my bedroom. Large wet snowflakes batter my window. Now that I am awake, I can hear the wind worrying the storm window.

"It's still snowing, John."

"Let's go," my brother says, and, like a sleepwalker, I follow him. I pull on corduroys over my sweatpants. I find socks and a sweater. We sneak down the stairs. The steps complain, but for all we know, our parents are dead to the world. We take our coats and hats from hooks by the back door. We stuff our feet into boots. Once bundled, John leads me out into the cold, wet night. I am twelve. Almost thirteen.

This is not a winter wonderland. The neighborhood has not been transformed under a blanket of white fluff. The world is not new and virginal. This is a hard, cold, wet snow. A mid-December in the Midwest snow that's as much rain and ice as snowflake. The flakes are the size of nickels and sting when they plop against my face. The yard is covered in a skin of slush, but the scraggy brown and green of dead winter grass pokes through. If the sun manages to arrive in the morning, it will melt this snow with its touch. We send steaming clouds of breath out before us.

"It's perfect," John says.

"It sucks," I say.

"I know," John says, and we stifle laughter. Wild giggles threaten my chest and throat. John unlatches the side gate, and we make our way down the hill to the sidewalk, leaving great, sliding footprints as we go. Everything is slippery. The sidewalk and street have been shellacked with a bumpy glaze of ice. We run and slide, making a beeline for the park at the end of the block. We swing on the wet swings and break the crust of ice off the monkey bars. The snow falls heavy through the dark. We are intoxicated with ourselves, romping until my cheeks burn and my lungs ache with the damp and the cold. John has somehow become hatless and his hair is soaked to the scalp. He doesn't notice. The security lights in the park fracture the dark. They wear coronas of glittering orange light. We lie on our backs and watch the snow come down.

"The sky is falling," John says.

"They sky is falling, the sky is falling," I say.

By the time we get home, we couldn't care less about keeping quiet, about not waking our parents up. We are laughing and talking—nonsense, I'm sure, total gibberish—peeling out of wet things in the kitchen, when the light in the living room comes on.

"Oh, shit!" John says.

Our laughter melts us. We are helpless to it. I have a boot stuck. John is tangled in his sweater. When our parents appear in the kitchen door, baffled and blinking, still breathing out the dank scent of sleep, we collapse into each other. Our parents usher us into the house and order us to change into dry clothes. We are examined. John is accused of being on drugs. Our mother tips his face toward a lamp to get a good look at his eyes. I don't know what she sees in them. The pockets of his clothes and coat are searched. I am as wild and unknowable as my brother, but it is John's influence I'm assumed to be under. Nothing else. We compose ourselves into respectable children. We love our parents dearly for their worry, for how well they play their part. We are laughing together, at them, at us, at the world.

I could not have said this then, but I know now that my brother made me possible. Without him, I would have continued to sleep.

On an August Saturday in 2001, I stood, stunned on the sidewalk in front of our apartment building stripped of everything. John wasn't coming after me. There was no reason to run.

"I don't care where you go. I don't care what you do," John had said. "I don't care what happens to you. You don't matter to me. You're not my brother or my sister. You're not Johnny or Jane. I can't even see you in front of me. I dreamed you up. You're a terrible liar. When you vanish, I'll have another dream."

"John, you can't," I'd tried to say. John's eyes narrowed in a smile that shut me up.

"Don't tell me what I can and what I can't. You know nothing. You've never known anything. Get out."

On the sidewalk, in the sunlight, I don't know where to go. John watches me from our front window. A couple passing me, their elbows linked, their heads tipped toward each other, don't know what they're seeing. If they see a person in front of them, it's just some kid in loose jeans and a t-shirt, some guy paused in the continuum of his life, blocking the sidewalk, puzzling over something. They skirt around me and are gone. In their wake, I take one step and another. The Earth continues to hurtle around the sun. The sky spins above me, a flat disk of ermine. Trees rattle their leaves, the sound dry and papery. Summer will not last forever. In a few weeks those trees will be shot through with color. Eventually, they will scrape the air around them with naked, twiggy branches. My legs move of their own volition. Carrying me away from our apartment and into a future I can't account for. Where will I go? Who will I be? My body is a ship with no captain, loosed from its moorings. No one knows. No one could possibly imagine. I pass a café with an outdoor dining section that shunts me dangerously close to the street. A woman, sitting alone at a table, reading a paperback with a glass of wine and a plate of glistening salad in front of her, looks up at me. I grin at her and her eyes dart away. Blotches of color rise on her throat. I laugh. It sounds like John, and I whirl around looking for my brother. But of course the laughter is only coming from me.

I walk further until I come to a train station on a corner. There is a payphone at this station, just in front of the doors, just beneath the elevated tracks. I have used it before to call home to our parents, to tell them to stay where they are, to keep that other life at bay. I lift the sticky receiver and place it to my ear. I don't have my calling card. I don't have anything, actually. I am a girl dressed as a boy with nothing whatsoever in his pockets. A dial tone hums in my ear. I press zero and then dial Eugene's number from memory.

When the operator comes on, I tell her I am John. Eugene's cell phone rings, and then there is a click and Eugene's gentle voice saying, "This is Eugene." My brain floods my body with a chemical called relief.

"I have a collect call from John," the operator says. "Do you accept the charges?"

Eugene is silent for a long moment. Perhaps he's abandoning the kitchen where he and Brenda and the girls are making a late lunch for the privacy of some other room.

"Certainly," he says finally. "Put her through."

The line clicks. "Hi, Eugene," I say. I can hear there is something wrong with my voice.

"Johnny?" Eugene asks. My name is followed by a question mark. When I cannot answer, he tries again. "Jane?"

"I might be in trouble, Eugene," I say.

"Hey, okay. Where are you? What can I do?"

"I don't know," I say. Traffic comes to a halt behind me as the streetlights change. "About the doing part. I know where I am. I'm talking on a payphone. The doing is more complicated."

"Let me come get you. Where are you?"

"You can't come get me, Eugene, because I've vanished."

"You're scaring me, Jane," Eugene says. It is true. I can hear fear in his voice.

"Shhh," I say. I know I shouldn't let myself talk the way John does, especially not to Eugene, but I can't help it. I grip the phone so tightly that my hand tingles and goes numb. "Jane doesn't exist.

Something's happened to her and to Johnny and to John. If there were bodies, man, there'd be a body count. What do you think is going to happen to my brother?"

"Where are you? Where's John?"

"He was right," I say. "I think what's happened is that I am John now, which is not what was supposed to happen. I was just supposed to pretend. But you can't pretend without becoming, Eugene. That's the secret no one tells you. To do and to be are the same verb."

"And now you're in trouble with John, right?"

"Bingo. Ding, ding, ding."

"Have you talked to your parents recently? Are you in touch with them?"

"Not in a long time. Forever. Months and months," I say. "Or maybe just last week. I call them every now and again to prove I exist. They think John wants to eat me alive. At least Mom does. I know how she thinks."

People hurry in and out of the station behind my back. Trains make a great racket over my head, stopping at the platform, banging doors open and closed. Turnstiles beep and clank, and people pay fares. It's quite a commotion, but with the phone to my ear, what I hear most is the familiar sound of Eugene breathing. I listened to him breathe all through my childhood. I could curl up and sleep in that sound.

"What kind of help does John need? If I can help John, maybe I can help you."

Eugene's voice cracks the numbness I've been encased in. I gasp. I have a premonition of the pain I am about to suffer. I don't know if I'm going crazy, or if I just want to be. It's as if I am holding on to the tail end of a rope, dangling out over a black abyss. I could just let go. Falling into the void would be so much easier than hauling myself back up.

"Oh, god, Eugene," I say, "we've gone crazy. We've gone completely insane."

"What would happen to you if maybe John got some help so you didn't have to take care of him?"

"I can't take care of him. He's kicked me out."

"He can't stay in that apartment by himself."

"He and Penny probably have a plan."

"John's sick," Eugene says. "I don't know who the hell Penny is, but John needs help. What would happen if we all worked together to get him that help, and instead of being alone with John, you could go home and live with your folks?"

"John would never forgive me," I say. I lean my head against the damp, cool concrete wall.

"That's John," Eugene says. "I'm asking about you."

"I'd lose everything."

"Where are you? Let me come get you."

"I have to try to talk to April," I say. "I love her, Eugene."

"I know you do," Eugene says.

I lay the receiver in its cradle and start the long walk to April's.

If you'd seen us on that August afternoon, you would have thought we were any couple of kids having an embarrassingly public lovers' quarrel. The boy, disheveled, sweaty, wild-eyed, presses the buzzer to a girl's apartment. The girl doesn't let him in. She doesn't answer through the intercom. She opens her third-floor-apartment window, and leans her livid face out over the sidewalk.

"Go away," she says.

"Please," the boy says.

Two teenagers across the street stop to watch. One gives a low whistle. "Oh, shit," the other one says.

"Get the fuck out of here," the girl says.

"I just want to explain."

"You're going to explain?" the girl demands. She laughs. "You're going to explain this to me? Your fucking crazy-ass motherfucker of a brother calls to tell me you're not who you say you are and you come here to explain?"

"Dude's in trouble," one of the kids across the street sings.

"Fuck off, assholes," the girl yells at them. They laugh and whistle and say things. "Get your ass up here," the girl says to me.

April vanishes from the window, and moments later the security door buzzes. I step into this familiar hallway for what must be the last time. I climb April's familiar steps. She is waiting for me on the landing. She is furious. I've never seen her eyes look so fierce. She hurls a jade plant at me. It sails past my head and strikes the wall.

Pottery shards and dirt cascade down the steps. The pressure of my chest binder, a pressure I've become so accustomed to I usually can't even feel, cuts off my breath.

"I hate you," she says. She means it. Her voice is sharp-edged and glittering.

Language has left me. What could I possibly say? To be sorry I would have to exist. I am sorry she is angry. I am sorry April is hurt. But I'm not sorry I fell in love with her.

"Who are you?" April asks. "Who the fuck are you?"

I don't know how to answer. My mouth opens but nothing comes out.

"Jane? That's what your brother called you. Is that your name?"

"It used to be," I say.

April claps a hand over her mouth. "Oh my god," she says.

A door opens and closes above us. Some neighbor descends the stairs. He looks at April and at me. He has to pass between us. He steps over the jade plant and the dirt and the broken pottery. He doesn't say anything.

"Come in here," April says.

I follow her into her apartment. She closes the door behind me.

"I'm sorry," I say at last.

"You're what? Sorry? You're sor—" April stops. She runs her hands through her hair. "For what?"

"I didn't mean for you to get hurt."

April laughs. The sound is jagged. "That's great," she says. "You pretend to be someone you're not. And then you lie to me for six weeks. You make me feel fucking sorry for you, and I fall in love with you, and you didn't mean for me to get hurt? Really?"

"I wasn't lying," I say.

"Oh my god," April says. Her voice is so high she almost sings. "You're as crazy as your fucking brother. Who are you? Who do you think you are?"

"I don't know," I say. "I'm trying, April. I'm trying to explain."

Fear and pity and anger and sorrow war against each other on April's face. Her eyes cast about the room as if to look for exits. When they fall again on me, it seems pity and sorrow have won out.

"Fine," she says, "Explain."

We sit on opposite sides of the couch. April sits with her knees drawn up to her chest, her arms wrapped around her shins. I take a strangled breath. "I don't even know where to start. I was supposed to just pretend to be John. Things were bad, he was on and off his meds, and we had this idea. At first we were just going to live together like normal people, but somehow things weren't working out, and we got this idea that if I could just pretend to be him, it would make life easier."

"That's fucking crazy," April says.

"I know. But it's what we did. And at first, it seemed to work out. I really looked up to my brother, back before he got sick. He was... I don't know. I admired him. And there was something really nice about getting to be him for a minute. People see what you want them to see. It's so strange. First Sean saw me as John, and then Clint and Leda and everybody, and then you did. Even after we started...dating. John said people would see what we told them to see. You just need the right story and you tell it with a straight face. And it worked."

"I am such an idiot," April says. "Oh, my fucking god."

"It worked on me," I say. "I started to believe. By the time we went on our first date, I didn't feel like I was pretending. I felt like John. I felt like that guy you wanted to be around really was me. Nobody has ever looked at me the way you looked at me. I really wasn't lying to you."

"What about you?" April asks. "What about Jane. What happened to her?"

"I don't know," I say. It's as honest a thing as I have ever said.

"And now the game is up."

"Yeah."

"Who knows?"

"You," I say. "And Eugene."

"Not Sean or the band or anything?"

"Not yet. I don't know what to say to them. They've got a gig tonight. We do, I mean. I didn't know how much this could fuck up everybody else's life. I didn't think about anybody but me and John."

"Yeah," April says. "That's obvious."

I lean my head into April's couch and cry. I'm sick with grief. It's everywhere inside me. I'm choking on grief. It hurts, everywhere. I promised John I wouldn't let go of him, and I've lost us both. I've failed.

"Oh, god," April breathes. "Oh, shit."

I wish she would come to me, but she doesn't. She might as well be miles from me, across the expanse of the couch. I cry until I cannot cry anymore, and then we are both quiet for a long time, waiting for what will happen next.

"This is the most fucked up thing that's ever happened to me," April says.

I take a ragged breath. I wipe my nose and mouth with the hem of my shirt. I force myself to look at April. Her eyes are flinty and dry, her face a mask.

"The shittiest part is that I really loved you," she says.

"I loved you too. I mean, I still do."

"I don't know what that means," April says. She wraps her arms around her knees. She looks at the ceiling, and then at the window, and then back at me.

"Me neither."

"God, I should have known better," April says. She laughs again, that laugh that is not a laugh. "Guys like you don't exist. Guys who are sweet and shy and talented. And hot without really knowing it. And not trying to fuck me. Or fuck me over."

"I'm sorry," I say.

"How did you think this was going end, John?" April asks. I don't know what she means when she says that name.

"I didn't think about it ending. I can't explain it any better than that. I didn't think I could really fall in love with you, but then I did. And by that time it was too late to think about the end."

April looks at me for a long time. She tucks her hair behind her ears. She starts to speak and then stops. She crosses her legs. She laces her hands together and buries them in her lap.

"Take your shirt off," she says.

"You said you'd never—"

"Take your fucking shirt off. I said I wouldn't ask to see the kid who got his body burned up by a homemade bomb. You I want to see. I want to see who's been making love to me."

My hands quake so hard that I'd have trouble with buttons if my shirt had any, but it's just a t-shirt, so I grip it by the hem and pull it over my head. April studies my bare arms and the undershirt I wear over my chest binder.

"Take everything off," she says.

I can't look at her. I peel off my undershirt and pry off my chest binder and sit half naked on the couch looking at the wall above her head. I'm sure she can see my heart hammering beneath my naked flesh.

"Oh," April whispers. "Oh. Look at me."

Her eyes shine with fresh tears. She bites the thumbnail of her right hand.

"I didn't—" she starts, and then stops. "I kind of... I mean, I knew. But this tiny part of me thought you'd be all scarred up."

"I'm not," I say.

"Can I touch you?" she asks.

I nod. April reaches out one hand and touches my clavicle. Her fingers are cold. She touches my shoulder and my throat and my sternum. She scoots closer and places both palms on the muscle of my chest above the swell of my small breasts.

"I've never felt your skin like this," she says. "I never got to feel you breathe."

"This hurts," I say.

April wraps her arms around me and pulls me to her, my naked chest pressed to her clothed body, the inverse of how we've always been close to each other. I put my head in the crook of her neck. She runs her hands along my shoulder blades.

"Oh, god. It's over, isn't it?" she says. I wish she would kiss me, even if it was just the top of my head, but she doesn't.

"I keep thinking about tomorrow," I say. My lips move against the soft skin of her throat. "Now you know, and so this is over. And tomorrow I'll have to call my parents and explain how totally I've fucked up. We'll have to figure something out about John. I'll have missed the gig tonight. I'll have fucked up the band and probably lost my job. Even if by some miracle I've still got it, where do I go? What do I do?"

"God this sucks," April says.

She releases me. I sit up and wipe my nose and my eyes with the back of my hand. I don't have a shirt to wipe my nose on, which makes both of us laugh. April hands me a box of Kleenex that's been on the end table and we both blow our noses.

"We're seriously messed up," I say.

"Well, you are. I'm just a girl who got her heart broke."

I pull on my t-shirt without anything under it.

"What time were you guys supposed to play tonight?" April asks.

"Nine," I say. "Maybe they'll still play. I don't know."

"Why not go?" April asks. I look at her. "Why not have just one more night like this?"

"I don't," I say. "I'm not sure I even can. I don't know that I have that version of John still in me."

"I'll go with you," April says. She looks at me for a long moment, and then she touches my cheek. "Let's pretend. Let's be April and John. You're right about tomorrow, but tomorrow can go fuck itself."

April touches my cheeks, and I am John beneath her fingertips. I am as much John as I've ever been. April takes John by the ears and presses her forehead to his. She kisses him hard on the lips.

"Let's go out," she says. "Let me change, and then let's go out. I don't want to be cooped up in here. Let's have some fun. Let's pretend."

"Okay," John says.

April rises from the couch, but he catches her by the wrist. He presses her palm to his lips, and she lays her free hand on the back of his head.

An hour later, April is showered and in a summer dress with her hair pinned back in barrettes. John has found a gray button-down in her pile of clean laundry. He ironed it while April was in the shower. They look good, the way people always look good when they are young and in love. They hold hands as they walk down the sidewalk, their bodies at ease with each other. At a restaurant they've never been to, he holds the door open for her. He asks the hostess if they can sit on the patio, and at a little table out back, under the broken shadow of a lattice, she puts her hand in his lap as they read their menus. He's never had less to hide in his life. For one afternoon, for one evening, they can both be nothing but the versions of themselves they always wanted to be.

By the time they are on the way to the bar to meet up with the rest of the band, the sun's rays are being warped by the atmosphere. The sky is electric blue above them, everything lit in orange from the west. The sun will exhaust itself in setting. They take the train and a bus and then walk four blocks, John's arm dropped over April's shoulders, April's arm wrapped around his waist. They are in an industrial part of the city and have to turn down a narrow side street between two warehouses. Sidewalks come to gravely ends. April has been where they're going, and she assures John that around the next corner, back behind the Home Depot, there really is the bar they are looking for. He trusts her, and she is right. The bar must be a remnant of a time when this was some other kind of neighborhood. The entrance is strung with orange Christmas lights, and Sean and Clint sit smoking cigarettes at a picnic table by the door.

"John!" Sean says. "Just the man we've been looking for. *Hola,* April."

"*Hola,*" April says.

"The kit's in my van out back," Clint says. "We figured we'd let you do your own heavy lifting."

"No problem," John says.

He cuts through the bar, leaving April outside in the waning daylight. The bar is empty, just the bartender wiping down glasses and what must be his two kids sitting on bar stools, eating Happy Meals, swinging their feet. Leda and Roger are already setting up in the brightly lit back room. In an hour, the room will be dark save for the Klieg lights shining down on the stage and the tiny purple Christmas lights strung up along the ceiling. Now, Leda is testing microphones, conferring with the bar's sound guy about levels.

"John," she says with a smile. "John, John, John," she sings, instead of "testing," or "one, two, three." She's wearing a jean skirt that looks cut off and left un-hemmed, the denim fraying at mid-thigh, and what might be one of Clint's shirts, her breasts straining the buttons, the sleeves rolled up.

Roger tests his pedals. He loops one bass lick over another. He doesn't even look up as John heads out the propped-open fire exit. Clint's van sits behind a dumpster, hazards blinking. John hauls in the drum kit. Soon Sean and Clint join John and Leda and Roger, and the band works through a sound check. April sits at a high table by the back wall, sipping a rum and Coke.

That is the moment I remember like a film still. The room warm and growing warmer from the lights, my friends spread out around me, my sticks in my hands, my foot on the high-hat pedal. April's eyes on me, her gaze honest and open, and for now, unafraid. Leda's smoking voice rising over all of us. Clint's hands spread out on his keyboard, his graying dreadlocks pulled back in a rubber band. My sticks on the snare and the tom-toms and the cymbal. We are not figments or characters or puppets on John's string. Sometimes I feel I can hold that memory in my hands. Everyone in that memory is beautiful, April of course, and Leda with her untamable hair. Sean and Roger and Clint. The John version of me. I don't know if we'd be beautiful to anyone else, but we are beautiful to me because we are precious and fleeting, because none of us will last. We are already gone, in fact.

We have just finished warming up, Sean and Roger talking over a chord progression, Leda slipping her microphone into its stand, when the door between the bar and the back room swings open. Eugene. His eyes wide with concern. My heart falters.

"John," he says, and everyone looks toward him. April stands up. Her face oscillates between me and my old friend.

"Eugene," I say. There's a hitch in my voice. Leda looks at me. "What are you doing here?"

Eugene doesn't say anything. I leave my drumsticks on the snare and climb down from the stage. When I am close enough to touch Eugene, April comes to stand next to me.

"I need to talk to you," Eugene says. He is afraid. I've never seen fear on his face. He doesn't look at April. He only looks at me.

"Hey, guys," I say, turning back to the stage, "we've got a minute, right?"

Leda checks her watch. "A minute," she says.

"Shots on me," Sean says. "Eugene, right?" he asks, pointing at Eugene.

"Sean," Eugene says.

"Whiskey?" Sean asks.

"Not for me," Eugene says.

"Let's go boys," Leda says, and the band troops past us through the swinging door. The bar is beginning to fill up. The jukebox is playing. Soon all those people will spill into this room, and the show will begin.

Eugene looks at April, who hasn't gone anywhere.

"She knows," I say.

"How much?"

"Everything," April says.

Eugene looks at me. "You didn't tell John, did you?"

My blood is cold. "No."

"I gave you my card," Eugene says. "He must have found it. He called me."

"Oh god," I say. "What happened?"

"He was pretending to be you. He kept saying he was Jane. He said you were in trouble. I couldn't really get him to make sense. He was scaring me, Jane. I don't think you're safe. He knows where you are."

"Let's get out of here," April says. She slips her hand into mine. Her fingers are cold. "Let's go."

"I can't," I say. "We can't." I look between April and Eugene. They are both frightened. Maybe I'm afraid too. Of my brother? I've been afraid of John's ability to take my John-life away from me, but I've never been afraid of him, directly. Eugene and April know the truth. What more could John do?

Sean and Roger come swinging through the door.

"It's show time," Roger says. "You've missed your chance for a shot."

The lights dim. The rest of the band is around me. The door is propped open and everyone who wants to pay five bucks is let in. We should be taking the stage, but I am frozen at the sight of my brother handing the door guy a five-dollar bill. The door guy is slim with wire-rim glasses and a paperback in his back pocket. He doesn't know who he's looking at.

"Holy shit," Sean says. "I know this guy."

John advances toward us. His face is an unreadable mask, but behind it, his eyes are wild with rage. There is something about him that makes people step back. I look for Penny, but she's not with him. It is only my brother. It is only the guy I love more than my life. He advances like a dragon, his gaze unswerving and his gait unfaltering. April makes a stifled sound, a sound that would be a scream if she could breathe. She's never seen John before. Eugene hasn't seen my brother in years, but with his hair short and his beard shaved, there's no mistaking John and me as brothers.

"Who the hell?" Clint says.

"John," I say.

"You have done nothing but lie to me," John says. "You tell lies like most people breathe. Hello, Eugene." But John doesn't look at Eugene.

"What the fuck?" Sean asks.

The world falls away around us. The room is dark and hot. My vision swims. My heart melts. My heart is a river that flows out of me.

"I can explain," I say. John's face is menacing. April backs away, trying to drag me with her. Her hands are so small and so soft.

"I do not want to hear you speak," John says. Eugene steps between us, but John puts him aside with the sweep of an arm. Eugene is saying something, shouting maybe, but my hearing has gone haywire. I can't hear anything. John smiles, viciously, and grabs me by the throat. The room is spectacularly silent. I know there must be panic and chaos spreading out around us, I know Eugene grabs John, and maybe Sean and others try to separate us, but John's fingers close down hard, crushing my windpipe. I would be frightened, I would be choking, if I needed to breathe. But I am a phantom. I am a ghost. I am helpless in my brother's hands. I've forgotten how to struggle. The world fades. John's face is inches from my own, and he's screaming but I still can't hear anything. I can't hear even him.

Eugene wrestles to free me from John's grip. Sean grabs me, and I remember oxygen. I remember how to kick and twist. John swings at Eugene. He kicks Roger. I remember how to struggle, and suddenly sound comes rushing back to me, April screaming and screaming, all these men swearing, my brother saying, "You lied to me," over and over again. I am coughing and choking and gasping as John loses his grip on my throat. The door guy finally brings my brother down. He pins John's arms behind him and rams a knee into my brother's back. John's face is pressed to the filthy floor, and he's howling. He's crying. He's begging me for something, and I'm fighting again to be free, this time from Sean. Leda has April in her powerful grip. I don't know where April is trying to go, where she's trying to get to. I kick free from Sean and drop to the floor, my face again inches from John's. He's terrified now, too. His desperate eyes roam. He's sobbing, not struggling. People are shouting for the cops.

"John," I say. "Oh, John. Look at me. I'm here. It's me."

John's eyes find me. I put a hand on his cheek. I'd forgotten how frightened my brother can be. He's a scared, sick kid. He's my brother. He needs me.

"Janie," John says. "Oh my god. What are they going to do to me?"

I don't know what's happening above us. I hear the squawk of police radios and Eugene talking. I hear him asking for a psych unit.

"Janie," John says, "don't let them take me."

"Shhh," I say. "Shhh, John."

I know this drill. If Eugene can get John loaded into an ambulance instead of the back of a squad car, there will be a forced hospitalization. They'll be able to keep him for seventy-two hours. They'll medicate him against his will. There will be psychiatrists and social workers and hospital restraints. The next time I see John, he'll be so lost in a fog of drugs he won't recognize me. We'll start over with the anti-psychotics and the SRI uptake inhibitors and the mood stabilizers and anti-seizure medications. I stroke my brother's anguished face. I have failed him.

When the ambulance arrives, I stand, unsteadily. Eugene puts his arm around me, and I lean into him. John does not fight, but the medics restrain him to a gurney anyway. They tap a vein in his left hand. They'll pump in saline and tranquilizers for now. The doctors at the hospital will pour in the hard stuff. "Come with me, Janie?" John asks. "Please come with me."

"Okay," I say, but the EMTs don't let me. I follow them through the bar where everyone stands, aghast. I follow them out to the street where they load my brother into the back of an ambulance.

Then the ambulance pulls away, its red lights whirling. There are still two squad cars flashing their blue lights against the brick walls of warehouses. People have spilled out of the bar to watch my brother being driven away from me. Cops take statements. I could not stand if Eugene weren't helping me. Sean and Roger and Clint and Leda and April watch me.

"Who's Jane?" Sean asks.

"John," April says. "John's Jane."

"Who's John?" Sean asks.

"That guy," April says, pointing down the empty street where the ambulance has vanished.

"What the fuck?" he says.

"I'll explain," April says.

I turn to the people who have been John's friends. "I'm sorry, guys," I say.

"Are you going to take her?" April asks Eugene.

"Yes," he says.

"What happens next?" she asks me.

"I don't know," I say.

"Will you call me?" she asks. When I nod, she turns to Eugene. "Will you make sure he calls me?"

"I'll call," I say.

April hugs me. I let her take me in her soft, strong arms. I let her kiss me on the cheek. And then I let Eugene lead me to his car. It's parked illegally in a loading zone. The hazards blink. Light is reflected in its inky blue finish. Eugene opens the passenger door for me, and I climb in, sinking into the creamy leather seat. Eugene closes the door and crosses around to his side. Everyone who knew me as my brother stands in the gravel by the side of the street. April holds up a hand. Leda puts her arms around April. I am full of grief—a glacial lake of sorrow brims inside me—but I do not cry. Eugene starts the engine, checks his mirrors, and we pull away.

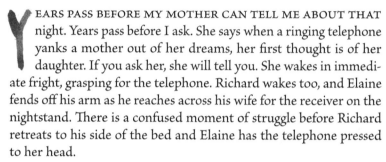

YEARS PASS BEFORE MY MOTHER CAN TELL ME ABOUT THAT night. Years pass before I ask. She says when a ringing telephone yanks a mother out of her dreams, her first thought is of her daughter. If you ask her, she will tell you. She wakes in immediate fright, grasping for the telephone. Richard wakes too, and Elaine fends off his arm as he reaches across his wife for the receiver on the nightstand. There is a confused moment of struggle before Richard retreats to his side of the bed and Elaine has the telephone pressed to her head.

"Janie?" Elaine says. "Hello? Hello?"

"Elaine?" the voice on the other end of the line asks.

Time collapses. Elaine would know Eugene's voice anywhere, though she hasn't heard it since Jane and John were both in high school.

"Yes," she says. "You know it's me. What's going on, Eugene?"

Richard snaps on the light. Elaine clutches the front of his pajama shirt. He squints, his irises screwing his pupils into pinpricks in the harsh nighttime light.

"I'm sorry to wake you," Eugene says.

"What is it?" Elaine demands.

Eugene breathes. Elaine waits.

"I have Jane with me," Eugene says. "I think it would be wise if you and Richard came to get her. There's been some trouble."

"Has John hurt her?" Elaine asks. Richard is beside himself, but his wife refuses to look at him. She needs to hear what has happened. She needs to focus on the sound of Eugene's voice.

"She's okay," Eugene says. "She's here. She's asleep. Elaine?" Eugene is still speaking softly. "John's been hospitalized. Jane's with me, but I think she might need some help."

Elaine holds the telephone out to Richard. She sinks down into the pillows and blankets and fluffy comforter of their bed. Her eyes are so wide and unblinking that they burn. She should stand up. She should pack a suitcase with her and Richard's things. She should do something, but her body refuses to cooperate.

Richard speaks competently into the telephone. He says, "My god," and, "Yes, certainly," and, "Thank you. Thank you, Eugene." Elaine is not listening. She's picturing Janie asleep in Eugene and Brenda's guest bedroom. They are the sort of lovely young couple who must have a lovely guest bedroom. A double bed with a white bedspread. A thick, shag throw rug on the hardwood floor. There are probably framed posters on the wall, matching prints of French theatre bills, a single stroke of color accenting the shade of the rug. Elaine pictures a vanity and a mirror, in which she can see her daughter's reflection. Jane is so pale, the color of her skin against the sheets like bone on bone. Jane's lips are parted, and she breathes through her mouth. Behind their lids, her eyes flicker with motion. She's dreaming. Sometimes over these long months of separation and fear, Elaine has pretended that she can send her spirit flying out to her daughter. She pretends that she can see her. That she can hover and protect. It is pagan, almost, some of the things Elaine wants to believe.

"Elaine," Richard says. He is standing. He has clicked off the telephone and tossed the receiver onto his rumpled side of the bed. Elaine tries to make sense of her husband.

"Come on, honey," he says. "Get up. Let's go."

"What time is it?" Elaine asks.

Richard's eyes dart to the clock radio on his bedside table.

"It's not even late. It's just past midnight."

"Did you get the whole story?" she asks.

"I don't know," her husband says. "There was an altercation, it seems. John accosted Jane and Eugene."

Elaine continues to lie in bed.

"Elaine?" Richard says. "John threatened Janie. We need to go see what we can do."

"For whom?"

"Our children," Richard says. He stands next to his side of the bed, his pajama shirt missing one button. "Please get up," he says.

Elaine does. She throws off the covers and stands and looks

about the room. She pulls a suitcase out from under the bed and unzips it. She begins finding things to put in it. They'll need a couple changes of clothes, something nice for meeting with doctors, a tie, at least, for Richard. She remembers feeling that their clothes mattered the last time. She didn't want the doctors thinking they'd let their son go mad through neglect or dereliction. She's not sure what they're going to try to do. Collect one damaged child and commit another? The last time they saw their son, John had sworn off treatment. Forever and ever a-fucking-men, he had said. Richard rummages in the bathroom. Elaine wouldn't put it past her husband to try to bring both of their children home. He appears in the doorway between the bedroom and the bathroom. He holds a toiletries bag half-filled with his own things—deodorant, shaving cream, a stiff-bristled brush.

"What do you want from in here?" Richard asks.

"My toothbrush," Elaine says.

"What else?"

"I don't know," Elaine says. "What's about to happen?"

Richard sets the toiletries bag on the bed. He takes Elaine's shoulders in his hands. He wraps his arms around her and draws his wife to his chest. She has pressed her face into his chest a million times in their married life. She knows every inch of this man. His sternum and ribs. His smell of skin and soap and cotton. His smell of books and faint, bitter sweat. Though he hasn't smoked in decades, Elaine remembers him smelling of pipe tobacco when they first met, a ridiculous affectation—a reaction to youth and graduate school. She presses her cheek to Richard's chest. She can feel the whorls of hair beneath his undershirt, now wiry and gone gray. Richard brings Elaine back to herself.

"We have to do this together," he says.

"I can't," she says.

"It doesn't matter. We have to."

"I'm too afraid," Elaine says.

"Don't think about that."

Such a husband's response. Such a perfectly Richard thing to say. Discipline the mind and the heart will follow—or at least it will cease to resist.

"Did Eugene give you any details about Jane?" Elaine asks. "He said she was going to need help. Maybe he said treatment. I don't know. Did he tell you any more than that?"

"No," Richard says.

"That's what I'm afraid of. I can manage whatever's happened to John. I remember from last time. But what if we've lost Jane?"

"We haven't lost anyone," Richard says sternly. "We're going to get Jane. We'll bring her home with us."

Her, he says. Elaine's heart thrills.

"I'll do the toiletries," she says. "You get John's records."

"Okay," Richard says with relief.

Then the two of them are all motion. They are efficient machines. They put on daytime clothes and stuff their still-warm pajamas in the open suitcase. Elaine makes sense of their necessaries. She gets a quart-sized Ziploc from the kitchen and collects the half-empty bottles of John's last regimen of psychotropic medications. Elaine is making the bed when Richard comes in for the suitcase.

"Are you ready?" he asks.

Elaine pats the pillows and runs both hands through her hair.

"I'll start the car, okay?" Richard says.

"Give me a minute," she says.

Once Richard is out the back door, Elaine runs upstairs. She opens the door to Janie's room, which she has left untouched all these months. She wishes now that it were clean. She wishes the room were dusted and vacuumed, and the sheets were freshly laundered. Janie left in such a whirlwind, such a desperate escape. Elaine steps into the bedroom and closes a dresser drawer. She picks up a sweatshirt from the floor and hangs it on the bedpost. There is no time for anything else. Elaine crosses the hall and peeks into John's room. John's room is empty, even the bed has been stripped. He sometimes slept in that bedroom after Richard brought him home from college, but John more or less lived in the basement after he got sick. Elaine sees her son before her again, that bright, charming, devilish boy. Sometimes he ran from his mother when it was time for bed. She would chase him, pretending to be stern, but it was a game they both played. Elaine would eventually catch John and lift his lean little body in her arms. Such boy strength. She would wrestle him into bed, both of them laughing, and then he would go soft and compliant, a child wanting the covers tucked. Elaine would kneel beside his bed, her arms across him, feeling the hummingbird flight of her son's heart in his chest. She would lay her cheek on his pillow to say goodnight, inhaling his breath. The thing Elaine could have never known about being a mother is how her children have stayed with her. Their child ghosts haunt her house. In the darkest days of John's illness—and here Elaine steels herself against the fact that the darkest days may be yet to come—there was always the shadow of his former self. A child, bright and serious. A small, quick fire of love. Elaine closes the door to John's bedroom. She heads downstairs and steps out into the damp night.

Richard has the car running and the garage door up. Elaine slips into the front passenger seat. The car door seals them in together, seals out the thrill and terror of the night.

"All set?" Richard's face is lit by the dashboard.

"Yes."

It is almost one o'clock. Richard pilots the station wagon down the alley. The engine hums in the very heart of the machine. They creep through the sleeping neighborhood, past familiar porches and front yards and lampposts. Windows loom dark and empty like eye sockets, but here and there, a lamp burns behind curtains. We are mysteries to each other, Elaine thinks.

Richard takes the on-ramp to the interstate, and they are cloaked in anonymity. There is nothing about which to speculate on an interstate. There is only the ribbon of cement and the trees or fields or aluminum-sided subdivisions that stream past. They are rocketing toward their children in a Swedish-engineered machine. Richard and Elaine travel in silence. Elaine can't fathom what her husband might be thinking. He grips the steering wheel at ten and two as if he were in an instructional video about how to drive responsibly. Elaine would have assumed that she would be able to read her husband's mind completely after twenty-eight years of marriage. She thought that marriage meant they would both be known and understood, at least by each other. It took her years to understand the folly of that. She was so young, really, when she married Richard. They were such kids. And yet, she is glad to have bound her life to his. Richard was such a serious graduate student. Elaine laughed to herself at the time about how most graduate students in history looked like Russian revolutionaries. On her first three dates with Richard, she had to keep from giggling at his proletariat hat and his silly moustache. It took her some months to discover that she loved him. He loved her instantly. But perhaps that was only how Richard made Elaine feel. Perhaps he too had to wait and question and wonder. Perhaps Richard weighed Elaine in the balance of a number of dreams, just as she weighed him. However their love first came to be, she is glad that it did. She could not face what they are speeding toward without Richard. She puts a hand on her husband's leg. He glances sideways at her, smiles, takes one hand from the steering wheel to rub her knuckles with his thumb. His palm is sweaty. They are both wonderstruck and afraid.

Dawn is a hint of pale gray on the horizon when Richard and Elaine arrive at Eugene's door. They have negotiated a deserted toll-way and a labyrinth of unfamiliar streets. They have taken two wrong turns and found a parking space and scrutinized numbers above doors and now they are standing on the steps to Eugene's home. It is a new-construction townhouse in a bleak part of the city. Eugene's block, with its natural gas streetlamps and brick façades, is trying bravely to turn things around. The leaded glass window in the oak door speaks of respectability and security. Elaine is glad her daughter is behind that door. Eugene is a good man. He will have taken care of Jane. The porch light has been left on for them. Richard takes Elaine's hand as they mount the cement steps. Through the wobbly glass, Elaine can see Eugene's front hall bathed in amber light. Richard rings the doorbell, and they wait.

Eugene throws a deadbolt and opens the door, and he is as beautiful and young to Elaine as he was that first wintry night fourteen years ago when he showed up to teach her son. He is clean and pressed and close shaven, but he has the look of a man who has not slept. They all stand, staring at each other across Eugene's threshold. Richard chokes on his greeting. He tries to extend a hand to Eugene, but the younger man takes the older man in an embrace.

"Richard," Eugene says finally. The two men separate and Eugene opens his arms to Elaine. "Elaine."

"Hello, Eugene," Elaine says. She steps into Eugene's home and permits herself to be drawn gently into Eugene's arms. Brenda joins the trio in the foyer.

"Oh, Elaine," Brenda says, and there is more hugging and more repeating of names.

They speak in hushed voices. Then Brenda shepherds everyone out of the vestibule and away from the foot of the stairs where all of their sounds float up to the second floor. Elaine knows Brenda and Eugene's daughters must be sleeping up there, just as Janie is. Brenda leads them through the living room and the dining room, and then through a swinging door and short hall into the spacious kitchen. Stainless steel appliances glow dully in the bright light. A butcher's block island takes up the center of the room, and the four adults draw up stools around it. Glass doors at the back of the kitchen must lead out onto a patio, but for now they reveal nothing more than a mirror image of the kitchen. Brenda sets out coffee and a sugar bowl and a little pewter pitcher of cream.

"Please tell us what's happened," Richard says. "We're ready."

Eugene glances up at Richard and then at Elaine, and then he returns his gaze to his coffee cup. "I don't know how much to tell you. Jane will want to tell you much of it herself, I'm sure, but I can tell you what I've seen. Okay?"

Elaine and Richard nod. They wait.

"A while back, I ran into Jane at a bar. I was playing with a new band, and Jane was there with a friend. Except at first I didn't know it was Jane. I thought at first that Jane was John."

Something catches in her throat when Elaine tries to breathe.

"It wasn't just that they've come to look so similar," Eugene says. "Jane's been using John's identity."

"What's this?" Richard asks. "How do you mean?"

Eugene turns his coffee cup in his hands.

"It's an idea the two of them came up with. I don't know why, exactly. Jane has a hard time explaining it. Jane says John has been more or less housebound for a while now, and Jane has been living out in the world as him."

"She said he had a job," Richard says. "She said he was getting out and maybe even playing music again. Jane said he had a girlfriend."

Elaine feels as if this is a conversation only these men have to have. She doesn't know more than her husband, but she understands everything. She doesn't need to be here in this kitchen. She would prefer to be upstairs watching her daughter sleep.

"That's Jane," Eugene says carefully. "That's her version of John. I don't know what kind of life John has had."

Why hasn't Brenda suggested they go look at her, Elaine wonders. Why are they down here when Jane is upstairs?

"What happened yesterday?" Richard asks.

"I got a phone call from each of them," Eugene says. "Jane sounded—strained. I think the whole scheme was beginning to unravel. John didn't trust Jane anymore. Jane seemed afraid, but she wouldn't let me come get her. I told her I was going to call you two, but before I could, John called. I haven't seen him or spoken to him this whole time. I've only been in touch with Jane. John acted as if he were Jane trying to convince me she was John. I couldn't follow much of what he said, but he told me where Jane was, and he said she was in trouble. I went to find her. I showed up at the bar where her band was supposed to play just minutes before John."

"And he threatened her?" Richard asked. "That's when John threatened Jane?"

The two men look at each other. "Yes," Eugene says. "It was all pretty chaotic. John was beside himself. He lashed out."

"He struck her?"

"He grabbed her by the throat. It was terrifying, Richard."

They sit in silence. Richard's expression is hard, his mouth set, his eyes wet.

"How did John look?" he finally asks.

"He was very, very angry, and I think, very afraid."

"Were you afraid of him?"

"Yes."

"Was Jane?" Richard asks.

"I don't know. Jane seemed beyond fear. Or maybe she was more afraid for him than for herself. She didn't want to see him hospitalized. She didn't want him to be alone."

"And he's been admitted?" Richard asks.

"Yes," Eugene says.

Richard considers the refrigerator door. His eyes are fixed and staring. Elaine knows her husband doesn't see anything in this kitchen.

"How is Janie?" he finally asks.

"She's going to need to talk to someone."

"Does she know we're here?" Elaine asks.

"I told her I'd call," Eugene says. "She seemed to understand that I had to."

"What does she go by?" Elaine asks. "What name does she use?"

"At work and with people she's met since they've moved here, she's John. John calls her Johnny."

"What do you call her," Elaine asks.

"Johnny, sometimes," Eugene says, as if he's admitting something. "But sometimes I call her Jane."

"I thought I heard the voices of the dead," Jane says from the hall.

All four heads in the kitchen snap toward the sound of Jane's voice. Jane stands half in the shadow of the hall and half in kitchen light. She leans her narrow frame against the doorjamb. Elaine is struck by the sight of her daughter in pajamas—they must be Brenda's. Jane has never in her life owned a pair of satin pajamas. The wide-lapelled shirt reveals Jane's clavicle and bruises purpling at her throat. Elaine feels as if her daughter has changed shape. Her eyes flash. She steps into the kitchen, her movements so completely those of her brother that Elaine loses her breath. Jane moves with John's adolescent swagger, that aggressive way some teenage boys learn to wield their bodies. If Elaine were standing, her knees would buckle.

Elaine looks for Jane's breasts. She has a quick memory of Jane running through the back door when she was twelve, maybe just turned thirteen. Jane had been out on the patio doing god-knows-what, and when she dashed headlong through the kitchen on her way to god-knows-where, Elaine saw for the first time how Jane's t-shirt clung to new breasts. They were just little fists of firm flesh.

"Hi, Janie," Richard says.

My husband, Elaine thinks. The father of my children. The man who can look at our daughter disappeared and say with utter love the simple fact of her name. Elaine's heart splits. Elaine has come to think of married love like a volcano. It can lie so quietly, so calmly dormant in her for years that she thinks to herself, well, that part's over. That dangerous, stunning, unpredictable love that rains fire and makes the soil of your marriage black and rich. You build the village of yourself beneath its peak, Elaine thinks. And then, with no warning, the mountain of your heart fissures. Love cracks the crust and leaps skyward, all fire and light, the red-hot glow of liquid rock.

Jane looks at her father, a current of emotion passing so swiftly beneath her expression that her mother can't even imagine what Jane feels. She looks ready to grab a rolling pin and defend herself. Her eyes are sunk into shadows, but Elaine can see that her daughter's ears are still the same shape. Perfect little curls. Elaine remembers studying them when Jane was a newborn, one tiny, perfect ear at a time as her daughter fed at her breast.

"Hi, Dad," Jane says. She has taken a position in the corner of the kitchen by the sink. No one else has moved.

"How are you?" Richard asks.

"I'm fine," Jane says. "Why? Don't I look fine? Do I frighten you?"

"Not even a little bit," Richard says.

"Has Eugene told you the whole, sad story?"

"I don't know," Richard says. "He's told us some, at least. You'll have to tell us the rest."

"You'll be shocked and amazed," Jane says. Her gaze flickers to her mother. At first Elaine doesn't think she'll be strong enough to return it, but then, remarkably, she is. "Have you come to claim me?" Jane asks. "Are you here to make me behave?"

"We're just here because we love you," Elaine says.

"Hi, Mom," Jane says.

"Hi, honey," Elaine says. Her voice breaks.

"I lost John," Jane says. She looks past her parents. Both Richard and Elaine follow their daughter's gaze. The patio doors have begun to lighten. The yard and garage and the rooftops beyond the alley have all begun to take shape. "You're going to be furious when you see him," Jane says. "I didn't take care of him like I was supposed to, and now he's lost. Maybe more lost than he was before." Something shudders in her. Something threatens to collapse.

"No one's furious," Elaine says. "No one's angry with you."

"Oh, John is," Jane says. "John has achieved new ecstasies of rage."

Jane turns and opens cabinets until she finds the coffee cups. Her sleeve falls to the elbow as she reaches into the cabinet, revealing the hard muscle and sinew of her forearm. She pours herself a cup of coffee from the carafe. Elaine, Richard, Brenda, and Eugene all sit as if they are in the wilderness and their camp is being foraged by a grizzly bear.

"We are going to get John the help that he needs," Richard says.

She laughs, a sound like broken glass. "You have a brilliant track record, Professor Fields."

"We'll do better," Richard says.

"Sometimes there is no doing better," Jane says. She speaks only to her father.

"He's my son, Jane," Richard says.

"He's my brother, Dad," Jane says. She turns her mercury eyes on Brenda and Eugene. "Can you guys get out? I know it's your place and everything, but can you get out of here? And you too, Dad? I need to talk to Mom."

Everyone looks at each other.

"Let's sit in the living room," Brenda says, as if this were a dinner party.

"May I hug you, Jane?" Richard asks before he goes.

"No," Jane says. "Not yet."

"Okay," Richard says, and follows Eugene and Brenda out of the room. On their first date, Richard asked Elaine if he could kiss her. They were standing on the sidewalk in front of the apartment building where Elaine shared a one-bedroom with another pianist in the conservatory. "May I kiss you, Elaine?" he had asked, and Elaine had offered him her cheek.

Jane looks at her mother over the rim of her coffee cup. "I have to tell you a secret," she says.

"Tell me, honey," Elaine says.

"John is right." Jane's voice has dropped to a whisper. "I liked being John better than I ever liked being Jane. I tried to take for good what I was just supposed to be watching for a little bit. That's why John flew off the handle. That's why I let them lock him up. I think I planned everything without thinking about it."

"You didn't take anything from your brother. He got sick. He's been sick. That has nothing to do with you."

The river of emotion churns behind Jane's eyes. For a moment it is whitewater, all jagged, killer rocks.

"You haven't been here, Mom. You can't imagine what I've done."

"What have you done?" Elaine asks.

"Do you hate John?" Jane asks. "Are you going to blame him for what's happened to me?"

Jane leans against the counter, her dark, glittering eyes on her mother's face. Elaine touches her empty coffee cup. She can feel the tiny muscles in her fingers quake.

"When John got sick, your dad and I did the best that we could, but it wasn't very good. I don't blame John for anything, but I think your dad and I failed you back then. We failed to look after you. We all lost something when John got sick, and I think, maybe, you lost the most. No one was paying attention to you. Your dad and I failed to protect you."

"John says you've been waiting all these years to lock him up and swallow the key. He said stuff like that even back when we were kids."

"Me?" Elaine asks. "Or me and your dad?"

"You, mostly," Jane says. "He's got other grudges against Dad."

So we have reached a new plateau of honesty, Elaine thinks. We're thousands of miles up and in such thin air. Elaine does not know what kind of land she and her daughter are in. She does not know how much good or harm she can do.

"I love John," Elaine says. "I love your brother, Jane." She has to avoid saying *but.* "From the time you were very little, I had this secret fear that he'd overpower you. I worried that you couldn't truly bloom under his influence. So maybe I tried to love you just a little bit more. John had such magnetism. Such gravitational pull. He was a powerful influence."

"Is," Jane says.

"What?"

"John. He's not living in the past tense, Mom."

"Oh, god. Jane. I know," Elaine says.

Jane crosses to the sliding glass doors. The garden is filling up with predawn light. The sky glows neon, with pink and red creeping up over garage roofs. Elaine watches Jane's back. The girl is all straight lines and sharp angles. Her head looks solid with her hair cropped close to the scalp. When she shifts, Elaine can see half of Jane's face reflected in the glass.

"When the sun comes up, will it be Sunday?" Jane asks.

"Yes."

"Can I tell you something else?"

"Yes," Elaine says.

"John's in love." Jane presses her fingertips to the glass. Her mother can imagine how cool it must be. Elaine can feel the smooth, cold glass against her own fingertips.

"I've gathered as much," Elaine says.

"Me-John," Jane says. She meets her mother's eyes in the reflection. "Not John-John."

"I know, Jane."

"You keep calling me Jane, but I don't think that person exists. John is in love. No one has ever been in love with Jane."

My daughter is so young, Elaine thinks. Jane is at the beginning of almost everything, so this could be true. Elaine cannot fathom what she should say or do.

"Do you think I'm crazy, now?" Jane asks.

Elaine watches her reflection in the glass.

"I think you've tried to do something no one could really do."

"I'm so sad," Jane says. "I'm so sad for John and me."

"I'm sorry," Elaine says.

Jane isn't looking at her mother any more. She is gazing out into the morning. Elaine goes to her. She risks standing beside Jane. She risks letting their shoulders touch. When Jane doesn't flinch, Elaine risks putting an arm around Jane's waist.

"I don't know how to do this," Jane says. "You're going to take me to doctors and counselors and everything, but I don't know how to be a girl called Jane. I'll have to make her up. April loved John. She still does. April's her name. She loves John, and I don't get to be him anymore. Now that's over. It feels good when you or Dad or Eugene says Jane, but it feels good like thinking of someone I used to know a long time ago and no longer see. It doesn't feel like me."

"Oh, honey," Elaine says. She wraps her free arm around Jane, one arm around her daughter's waist, one arm around her shoulder. "What can I do?"

"Do you know about supernovas?" Jane asks.

"Supernovas?"

"Exploded stars," Jane says.

"Well, not a whole lot, I suppose."

"I think John is like a supernova," Jane says. "I like to think about the cosmos. I think he's so beautiful and brilliant and far away that we can't quite understand him. I think it hurts my eyes to look at him."

"What are you?" Elaine asks.

"Stardust," Jane says. "April and me, we're stardust. John told me April was stardust. He said it as if that meant April wasn't made out of anything. But that's not true. We're all stardust. We're all made out of the same stuff."

"That's true," Elaine says. She rests her head on Jane's shoulder. Jane tips her head away from her mother's. She lays her cheek on the back of Elaine's hand.

"I'm sad, Mom," Jane says.

"I know," Elaine says.

Here is my daughter, Elaine thinks. This is my child. This soft flesh and these strong bones.

Here is something I wouldn't have known. Two people can make anything real. I thought I only existed as my John-self as long as John made me possible. When one person says you are who you say you are, you leap into vivid relief. It is amazing. It is like magic. And then for one afternoon April made my John-self real. In all the years between then and now, this has continued to be true. Now, when the telephone rings in my small apartment and I lay the book I've been reading face down on the windowsill and rise from the couch, when I pick up the receiver and my mother's voice says, "Hi, Jane," a whole universe is manifest. When I say, "Hi, Mom," I am secretly saying, yes, I am who you say I am, you are who I say you are. I agree. I believe.

Acknowledgements

I WOULD NOT BE THE WRITER I AM WITHOUT THE EARLY intervention of the creative writing program at the University of Michigan. A debt is owed to my cohorts and colleagues and to all my teachers, but especially to my advisors Peter Ho Davies and Eileen Pollack.

This novel would not have come to be without the community that is the Program for Writers at the University of Illinois at Chicago. Much appreciation is owed, particularly to Cris Mazza and the novel workshop.

My appreciation is especially extended to fellow writers and friends who, over the years, have gone above and beyond the call of duty by reading early drafts of this and helping me believe: Michelle Mounts and Melodie Edwards, Cheryl Beredo, Zeeshan Shah again and again, Maggie Andersen, Sara Tracey, and Glenda Garelli. Finally, I would like to thank Dana Kaye for her vision, and everyone at Scarletta, especially Desiree Bussiere, Nora Evans, and Josh Plattner, for their dedication and wisdom.

L AURA KRUGHOFF IS A FICTION WRITER WHOSE WORK has been appearing in literary magazines and journals over the past decade. Her stories have been published in prestigious American venues such as *Threepenny Review*, *The Seattle Review*, *Washington Square Review*, and *Chicago Tribune's Printers Row Journal*, and internationally in the feminist Canadian magazine *Room of One's Own* (now known as *Room Magazine*). She is a recipient of the Washington Square Prize for Fiction for her story "This Is One Way," a Pushcart Prize for her story "Halley's Comet," and a rur⋯⋯une for her⋯r the Uni⋯Short Fict⋯tory-telli⋯riter, sch⋯

FICTION KRUGHOFF

**Krughoff, Laura.
My brother's name**